Dedalus Original Fiction in Paperback

DIRTY OLD TRICKS

Pat Gray was born in Belfast.

He is the author of three previous novels: *Mr Narrator*, and *The Political Map of the Heart* – an account of growing up in Belfast which won the World One Day Novel Cup and was published in an extended form in 2001. His satirical novel *The Cat* was re-issued in 2015 and has been translated into several languages.

He has worked extensively in Eastern Europe, but now lives in London. He is currently working on a sequel to *Dirty Old Tricks*.

Pat Gray

DIRTY OLD TRICKS

Dedalus

Supported using public funding by
**ARTS COUNCIL
ENGLAND**

Published in the UK by Dedalus Limited
24-26, St Judith's Lane, Sawtry, Cambs, PE28 5XE
email: info@dedalusbooks.com
www.dedalusbooks.com

ISBN printed book 978 1 912868 26 1
ISBN ebook 978 1 912868 43 8

Dedalus is distributed in the USA & Canada by SCB Distributors
15608 South New Century Drive, Gardena, CA 90248
email: info@scbdistributors.com   web: www.scbdistributors.com

Dedalus is distributed in Australia by Peribo Pty Ltd
58, Beaumont Road, Mount Kuring-gai, N.S.W. 2080
email: info@peribo.com.au

First published by Dedalus in 2020

Printed and bound in the UK by Clays Elcograf S.p.A
Typeset by Marie Lane

A C.I.P. listing for this book is available on request.

Acknowledgements

Blackstaff Press for their permission to use an extract from 'The Coasters' by John Hewitt, from *The Selected Poems of John Hewitt*, ed. Michael Longley and Frank Ormsby (Blackstaff Press, 2007) on behalf of the estate of John Hewitt.

An extract from 'The Ballad of Gerry Kelly: Newsagent' by James Simmons, from *Poems 1956-1986* (1986) is reproduced by kind permission of the estate of James Simmons and the Gallery Press, Loughcrew, Oldcastle, County Meath, Ireland.

Cover photograph by Frankie Quinn www.frankiequinn.com

I would also like to thank all of those who have read and commented on the manuscript of the book and helped so much in seeing it completed: my wife Jane Klauber, Juri Gabriel, Mark Caulfield, Eric Lane at Dedalus, and all the members of the ex-Morley writers group. Particular thanks to my brother John Gray, who helped point out where my failing memory had things wrong. Though a work of fiction, any errors in the book are mine alone.

The cloud of infection hangs over the city,
A quick change of wind and it
Might spill over the leafy suburbs.

John Hewitt,   *The Coasters*

Down the hill of lies and horror
Belfast city slipped.

James Simmons,   *The Ballad of Gerry Kelly: Newsagent*

Chapter One

Belfast, 1975

McCann lay awake in the bedroom. Occasionally a car would pass on the road outside. Its headlights would send the shadowy branches of trees careering starkly across the ceiling, then briefly illuminating the open cupboard doors and his cast-off uniform on the floor beside the ashtray, like the chalked line around a dead man. Then everything descended again into darkness. The noise of the car tyres swished away on the wet road outside and McCann's breathing eased. The slight arching of tension in his spine relaxed as he realised that the car was not slowing and that no one was coming to call for him.

He shook one leg out sideways, feeling the cool, wide space in the bed beside him. He hoped that somehow sleep would creep upon him if he were to change his position, but knew that whatever he did, the sense of numbness and disbelief would still be there. At first the cool, unrumpled sheets beside him had been a novelty, almost exciting in their potential. He turned on his back and placed his hands under his head, trying to imagine the room back to how it had been, with her things on the back of the chair, her photo on the bedside table, her boots carelessly discarded and her mysterious sleeping breath beside him. That had been so fine when, on nights like these, he had not been able to sleep and had put his face in the back of her neck and smelt the scent in her hair.

He hadn't closed the curtains. He wouldn't close them now. They could come for him. He wouldn't mind. They would come and take him out but he wouldn't do it for them. That was not McCann's way. Better to lie like this and suffer the night. He lit a cigarette and drew on it in the dark, the glow a little comforting, the smoke lifting him up. He looked at his watch and saw it was four fifteen. He'd make a cup of tea and sit in the kitchen watching the first faint light come up. It would be cold. He could hear the rain, drip-dripping from the gutters. It'd keep them off him, a wet night. He smiled as he flipped the kettle on. Crazy that the rain could keep them off the murdering, how inconsequential it made him.

'Better leave off killing that peeler because it's so fucking wet. We'll do him another night, shall we?' He winced at the sudden surge of hatred of them, like an outbreak of acid juices in his stomach. Did having a woman with him make him safer, he wondered? They weren't squeamish, but it didn't look so good to blow away a man's wife, still less a child. Ah well, to hell with that, he thought. He peered out into the garden, the light silhouetting him. Let them come for him, he didn't care if they did.

'Come on then,' he breathed, 'You'll think you're hurting us, but me, you'll be setting me free.'

And then by the old inevitable logic his gloom began to lift and the night to merge into dawn and his shoulders sagged and he lay forward on the formica tabletop in the kitchen and he slept for half an hour or so with strange, jumbled dreams. He awoke with his mouth dry and dribble down the front of his pyjamas but rested, as if a curse had been lifted from him. He went back to bed and turned the radio on low, dozing through the news of shootings and events in God knows where, till he heard the sound of a police Land Rover on the gravel and the toot of the horn and leapt up to get the uniform on, to clean his teeth and shave and start the day.

He shouted down the hall, inarticulately, pulled on the trousers, the woollen vest, the pale green shirt, the braces, then into the bathroom. At the mirror his own face looked out at him round-eyed, frowning at the bags doubling under his eyes, the jowls around the mouth as he reached for his soap and razor.

'A minute. Just a minute.' He could hear the engine of the Land Rover running outside on the drive and the chatter of the police radio. A quick slap of cold water then the jacket, socks and shoes and he was out of the door. A constable was waiting on the step, with his submachine gun idly slung round up his back. McCann knew he should have told him off on account of it, but had never liked the men having weapons anyway so he just said: 'What's up? Can you not let a fellow sleep in peace?'

'We were told to pick you up, sir.'

'Aye well you've got me now,' said McCann and shrugged his collar up against the soft rain that was drifting across the street, smelling for a moment the sea off the lough and the green fields. Then he was up and into the fug of the front seat. The heater was blowing and the wipers were going back and forth. The driver was smoking with the window half open to take away the smoke. McCann nodded to the driver and he slammed the motor into gear and swung the armoured vehicle round in a handbrake turn across the gravel and out through the gates accelerating for a moment onto the wrong side of the road, the vehicle rolling. McCann felt sick. He always felt sick, with or without breakfast. He yawned and looked out at the traffic bunched back off the motorway in the rain.

The driver started to swear, hating being caught in traffic, being a stationary target.

'What's the hurry anyway pal?' said McCann. 'How'd Linfield do?' he asked.

'Three-one.'

'Three-one! That's great.'

'Aye, McKinley came on late and gave them a good belting.'

'So, where are we going?'

'I'm afraid it's up the mountain again, Inspector.' There was a pause in the conversation then as the Land Rover stopped and started, edging forward up the line of cars in the rain. The radio burbled police small talk in the lull of the day when the bad men slept and the honest folk tried to begin their daily business.

Then they were on the Shore Road, neat rows of modern houses with their darkened windows giving way to repair yards and low-rise offices. At the bottom of Duncairn Gardens two army Saracen armoured cars had pulled over under a mural of a hooded man looking down from a gable end with his gun, declaring 'UVF[1] for God and Ulster.' They passed along York Street, then right before they reached the security barriers, passing the cathedral on the left and away up onto the ring road, accelerating fast through the lights outside the Divis Flats. McCann could see the sun turning the clouds red and

---

1 UVF – Ulster Volunteer Force

ochre above the hills, as if suffused with blood, the moorland of the Black Mountain turning sludge green as colour began to fill the day.

When they pulled off the motorway and began to climb up out of Belfast towards the mountain, he heard the constable at the rear doors checking the magazine on his gun.

'Here we go,' said the driver, dropping a gear for the climb, racing the engine to keep the speed up along the exposed estate road. Halfway up there was another Saracen blocking the way and a couple of squaddies sheltering against it, turning the traffic back. The driver pulled up alongside and wound the window down. The officer in charge of the roadblock was very young and nervously self-confident with it.

'Good morning Inspector! You'll find them two hundred yards up on the left,' he said. 'It's well covered. Forensics up there already. I'd keep your head down though. Paddy's got a good line of fire on the right.' McCann smiled and wound the window back up in the man's face.

'Paddy's got a good line of fire,' he imitated the officer's English accent and the driver smiled wanly too as the Land Rover eased through the roadblock onto the empty wet road, on one side the mountain, then on the right away across some scrubby fields the line of the city, the drab grey estate, the walls daubed with 'IRA', the occasional green white and gold flag fluttering. Further up the road another armoured patrol had stopped the cars coming the other way. A thin rain was still falling, making the road black and slick.

McCann climbed down from the Land Rover. In the ditch below on the left he could see the white suits of the forensic team working. He slid down the embankment through the brambles, relieved to be away from the exposed roadway. The body was twisted, as if she had been thrown from a passing car and had tumbled lifeless, her limbs knotting as she fell, face down into the bottom of the ditch, discarded amongst the other litter. The faces of the men were pinched and white and silence hung there, punctuated only by their breathing as they searched in the long grass.

McCann stumbled up to where the body lay. They were still taking photographs, the flash going off irregularly, cutting the gloom for a moment, freezing the image of the girl.

'Oh God,' said McCann involuntarily. 'How old is she?'

It was not what you expected at a time like this. Who'd do something like that to someone that age? That was too much. It was a shock. He'd expected some tattooed lout with his hands tied behind his back, a beating gone wrong maybe, but not a teenage girl in school uniform.

'This is wrong,' he said suddenly. 'This is quite wrong.'

The forensic officer straightened up with a small groan of pain.

'My back,' he said. 'My back's killing me. You'd think they'd show a bit of consideration to a fellow my age.'

'Oh dear God,' said McCann again. Her face was pale, with smooth, alabaster skin, one eye open and staring lifelessly at the sky. It was as if she had fallen there from heaven unannounced.

The forensic officer wiped his hands and peeled off his rubber gloves, looked at his watch.

'You'll be McCann,' he said. 'Are you the only one they've got?'

'Me and him,' said McCann, gesturing at the constable who

was halfway down the bank behind him.

When they had photographed her from every angle McCann bent over her. He was not sure if the smell was just the smell of the ditch; of rotting, winter undergrowth or if her body had started to rot or perhaps it was something they had done to her, that faint faecal smell that assailed him. He nodded to the forensic officer and gently he rolled her body over so McCann could reach inside her blazer pocket. He knew children and hadn't he had one of his own and though he didn't know this one he knew where they'd find the name, sewn in the back of the jacket (but that would mean moving her more) or in the homework diary. Sure enough in her inside pocket he found the sodden blue booklet and the name written on the front cover. He peeled on rubber gloves and held the diary to the light but needed his glasses and put the book back down, laying it on her corpse, then picked it up again, as the name 'Elizabeth McCabe 4C' swam into view along with the name of the school printed there.

The forensic officer leant over his shoulder, peering too.

'Is that an Academy girl?' he said, disbelievingly.

'Aye,' said McCann, flicking through the pages, prizing them apart.

'Algebra,' he said, looking at the homework entry, a wee smiley face beside it and a love heart and the name of some pop star doodled there and decorated.

'This is a weird one,' said the forensic officer. 'Almost normal. Almost like the old days.'

'What d'you mean normal?' said McCann, suddenly disgusted and turning away he climbed back up the bank, slipping as he went, right up onto the deserted roadway, drawing in the air up there, looking over at the grey estate walls and the tricolour flags flying. He put his police hat on and glared at the blank windows opposite, took out a cigarette and lit it up, drawing down the smoke, his hands shaking. Then he walked back to the Land Rover, taking his time.

On the drive back to the station he asked the driver to stop to pick up a couple of packs of cigarettes, choosing one of the big outlets on the Lisburn Road that was anonymous, with armoured glass in the windows. Once he'd got the cigarettes he used the radio to call in, recognising the desk sergeant's voice.

'Morning Amanda.'

'Peter?' she said.

'Michael.'

'Oh sorry. I thought you were Peter.'

'You're taking the piss.'

She laughed.

'You boys are all the same to me,' she said. 'What can I do for you?'

'I need more fellows on this,' he said.

'Don't we all,' she said.

'I've got a girl been murdered. Can you ask the boss to give us a minute this morning? He'll be wanting the branch on it too,' he added as an afterthought, biting his thumbnail, regretting the mess that would involve. But he knew it was unavoidable; bringing in Castlereagh[2] with its fancy special branch men. Better to ask first and start on the right foot than

2 Castlereagh was where the special branch was located. The branch concentrated on intelligence work.

have the branch feel they'd to impose themselves later.

But when he checked the missing persons' reports back at Division, there was nothing that resembled the missing girl. He sucked his lower lip, leaning over the desk sergeant as her finger ran down the reports.

'From the Royal Academy, you say?'

'Aye.'

The desk sergeant raised her eyebrows. She looked very tired, traces of make-up around her eyes, faint lines. McCann had always liked her – she had a certain weariness, a kind of vulnerability that appealed, but that was where he had gone wrong with Irene. There was something oddly humorous about the turn of her mouth too.

'People don't top girls from the Academy.'

'They have this time.'

'Did they, you know…' And the desk sergeant lowered her eyes. 'Interfere with her?'

'Not that I could see. Forensic's dealing with it now,' he said.

Odd the way the girl had become a forensic case, from being Elizabeth McCabe, overnight into the nameless shadows. So, who was she? Not yet missed, maybe she had actually been dropped from heaven. Or already reported somewhere else and in the developing chaos the report had slipped by unnoticed or been ignored.

McCann felt the muscles in his cheek twitching. He hadn't had a cup of tea since coming down off the mountain. Felt like he needed a bath, someone to ask how he was. Why had the desk sergeant said 'they' when it was obvious this would be some single sad, loner, loser who would be easy to find, he wondered? The City would spew him up, spit him out in a matter of hours or days. It was not a place where that kind of crime went unnoticed, particularly not on an Academy girl, a Protestant girl, nor on any girl of any religion. Despite what was becoming of the place, they were decent folk and no one would condone that.

Upstairs he found the corridor to his room full of builders, planks of wood, sheets of fibreboard and he heard the sound of a staple gun. The pace of work was furious and they'd rigged additional lights so they could work on into the evening. Someone had knocked a hole through one of the old barrack walls and the grit and dust of demolition still lingered, fragments of brick scrunching underfoot as he tried to get through to his room, bags of plaster stacked across the corridor.

'Bringing in some more fellows,' explained one of the builders.

'What for?'

'Fuck knows. They've told us to make room for another fifteen fellows.'

'Keeps you in work anyhow,' said McCann, unlocking his room, putting on the electric kettle, closing the door behind him trying to drown out the sound of a jack hammer, but then it stopped and someone else started banging in nails and singing 'The sash my father wore.'

'For fuck's sake,' said McCann and stepped out into the corridor, where a figure in a black leather jacket blocked his way, a duffle bag over his shoulder, heavy fisted, with a red face and a shock of glistening grey hair curling over the back of his open collar. For a moment the two men looked at each other, until the man stood back on his heels, his eyebrows raised with a look of humorous disbelief.

'Well, well Michael McCann. You here too?'

The snarling face of Deevery, looming up to him, righteous at the loss of the ball, and McCann just straight into his face with his fist as hard as he could. Whack! Onto Deevery's nose, the blood spurting like out of a geyser, Deevery falling back, the whistle shrieking and the referee up there separating them, putting a lint pad on Deevery's nose, the fellows milling about, peering in.

'Hey pal,' said the referee. 'You'd better control that temper.'

'He was winding me up,' said McCann.

And afterwards in the changing rooms the air had been densely humid, the walls dripping with condensation from the showers, the floor splattered with mud, pale bodies steaming in the hot showers, Deevery laid out on the wooden slatted bench with the pad held to his nose by the coach, red blood filling it. There was a space around McCann; a sense of repressed congratulation. In the shower he soaped himself, feeling the hot water take away the pain of the match, the pain of all of it. Deevery laid out flat with a nose bleed! How good had that been?

'Deevery,' said McCann. 'William Deevery. How are you son?'

And he reached out his hand and Deevery gripped it hard, leant in to him, clapped him on the shoulder and held him.

'What're you doing here? Not keeping you busy enough in Londonderry?'

'Need to show you boys how the job's done,' said Deevery.

'How's that?'

'I'm up for the DCI's job. You're not on the shortlist then?'
'Shortlist?'
'You'll have applied then?'

McCann felt a moment's panic. He had been told to apply, but he'd heard nothing, not expected to hear anything yet and here was Deevery with his interview uniform still in its dry cleaner's cellophane poking out of the bag over his shoulder.

The Superintendent's office was up a flight of uncarpeted stairs at the back of the building, and from the window the Superintendent could look down into the car park below to see who was coming and going.

'I'll just see if he's in,' said his secretary, the door half open into the spacious interior, where McCann could see Superintendent Ray Jones behind his desk with the table lamp on casting a soft yellow glow, an early morning cup of tea steaming on its green baize surface, which was spread with papers arranged for signing. He was a large man, with fine grey hair, glossy in the light from the lamp and a slightly red complexion. Behind him on the wall an almost life-size photograph of the Queen and Prince Phillip looked down approvingly. He was known by the men as the Poet for his loquacious fondness for a literary turn of phrase. While the secretary pushed buttons and knobs on her phone, trying to ring through to him, McCann stuck his head round the door and he looked up.

'Ah McCann,' he said. And then in the same moment he glanced conspicuously at the clock on the wall just as the phone rang on his desk and his secretary announced McCann's arrival.

'Yes, he's here already standing in front of me as bold as brass, Deirdre,' he said.

'You know it'd be a lot easier if she'd stop people coming in and used the new system effectively. She's a new girl you know,' he explained, stepping away from the desk and walking over to close the door behind McCann. 'Very nice girl too. She's a McGready you know, daughter of Bill McGready that has the rose business at Balmoral. Was up there just the other day with Maureen to get some new White Goddess, lovely blooms, McCann. You're not a gardener, are you? No, I suppose not. It can be very helpful though, lifts the spirits. What is it they say: "A scent is heaven sent to lift the suffering soul"?'

McCann found himself guided across the floor to what the men referred to as the Poet's 'romper room', where he'd arranged three soft leather armchairs in a U shape, with a slightly larger armchair at its centre upon which the Poet enthroned himself, inviting McCann to settle himself in one of the smaller armchairs next to it.

'So, McCann. Bad news I expect.'

'We've a girl been killed,' said McCann. 'She's a young girl out of the Academy.'

The Poet leant forward.

'That's bad,' he said. 'That's very bad indeed. I don't like to hear that McCann. I don't like to hear that at all. Lisburn will not be pleased.' It was as if it was his fault, thought McCann, or he had done it himself. Rather than thinking how he could resource the investigation, the Poet was already wondering how he'd explain it to the high ups in their regular briefing at Lisburn, where the Army, the Police, the Intelligence agencies briefed the Minister. When would it be? Monday. It gave him five days at most before they were onto him.

'So, I'll need a couple of constables, a decent sergeant or two and we'll need the branch on it too sir,' he said, asking for the maximum, hoping for whatever he could get.

'I've a Detective Inspector Deevery, just attached here from Londonderry,' said the Poet. 'You'll like him. He's a tough man, hard as the granite rock of our native hills as they say. I'll ask him to lend you a hand.'

'I know him already,' said McCann.

'All the better then,' said the Poet. 'And we've a new sergeant, sergeant Thompson, who's volunteered to come here. She asked to be posted. Must be an ambitious girl McCann, so I'd watch out. Bit of an unknown quantity but you'd need a lady on a case like that, for the family liaison. There'll be tears involved no doubt McCann and a female officer can be helpful with that.'

'Yes sir,' said McCann. It was better than expected, or at least the bad of Deevery was maybe cancelled by the good of having a newly-posted sergeant, a clean pair of hands to balance Deevery's dirty ones.

'And the branch will need to be involved of course. Could be political, could be more tit for tat McCann. I'm worried by that. Lisburn will be worried by that. I'll give Castlereagh a bell.'

'I'd thought of that sir. Yes of course.'

Now that one was another wild card, thought McCann. He'd never trusted the branch, the same way the branch never trusted the uniformed service, never shared what they knew, just took what they needed and went about things their own way. He hoped the branch would send him someone sensible who would play by the rules.

It was raining, a soft, insistent rain that left tiny droplets of silver moisture across the windscreen of sergeant Emily Thompson's car. Her daughter sat beside her, belted up in the passenger seat, her school bag at her feet. Thompson had picked her up at eight that morning from her grandmother's house, where she had stayed overnight and now the girl was tired and listless, responding to Thompson's questions with 'yes' and 'no' answers, interspersed with the occasional 'alright' as she fiddled with the controls on the radio, ranging through the channels until she found some jangling pop with crackling reception. Thompson was still overcome with affection for her; her knees in their regulation laddered tights, the skirt she'd turned up to the limit of the rules, her neat hands like Thompson's own, almost a copy of herself, except that she had her father's brown eyes. She'd had the girl young, married young and now the marriage part was over the girl was all she had left.

'We're here,' she said, patting the girl's knee as they turned at the school gates. 'Best get on.'

'OK. Bye.' And then she was gone, with a scramble from the car, Thompson passing her schoolbag out to her, the door slamming, disappearing into the crowd bustling with their umbrellas in front of the school gates as Thompson watched in the rear-view mirror. She adjusted the mirror, checked the last trace of eye shadow was removed, frowning at the first faint lines at the corner of the eyes and around the mouth. She tied her hair back tightly with a hairband, then fiddled with the radio to get the news as she pulled away, one eye watching the cars behind.

She drove down along the motorway, grey mud merging with the water of Belfast Lough away on the left, the familiar gantries of Harland and Wolff shipyard growing larger beneath a lowering sky. Further on, she passed the courthouse and the prison and then up to Carlisle Circus, a no-man's-land owned by neither party, sandwiched between the Republican New Lodge and Loyalist Shankill. On instinct, she adjusted the rear-view mirror to make sure she'd not picked up anyone along the way and was pleased to see an army foot patrol fanning out from a side street, moving from doorway to doorway. They'd given her a new number plate just the previous week, but a pale blue Morris Minor with a scrape down the offside door would still be recognised and it'd only be matter of time before they'd have it marked.

Along the Crumlin Road a few shops were open, Union flags flying, the kerbstones painted on the Shankill side in red, white and blue. Higher up on the right in the Ardoyne, everything would be in green, white and gold instead. As she approached the police station she wondered where the watcher or watchers would be. Maybe they'd a whole rota for them; the milkman, the paperboy, the fellows working on the roads could be noticing that blue Morris Minor turning into the barracks. She'd get herself a new car now she'd had the promotion, something like a Cortina that everyone had, two years old, get the numbers changed straight away. If only Brian would pay the alimony money that was due. Then she was there, hard left by the church, then hard right through the chicane of steel doors and up into the car pound with its high walls and wire netting overhead, like she was a fish in a tank in some smart restaurant.

'I'm looking for Inspector McCann,' she said, showing her ID at the desk and was given directions to his room; along a corridor with green linoleum, through battered swing doors, up two floors in a lift that smelt of sweat and creaked and swayed, left along another corridor full of builders, past an open door where she knocked and entered.

McCann stood up, pre-occupied, awkward.

'Hello sir. I'm sergeant Thompson. I've come to C Division and they tell me you've some work for me to do?'

'Aye, yes that's right. Just in the nick of time sergeant. You've got your coat? Good. You can come with me right now.' And McCann turned her round by the elbow, like he was arresting her for some minor misdemeanour and marched her back down in the lift to the car pound.

Out on the road he explained the situation. Thompson sat silent for a while as they drove, watching the traffic as they turned towards the girl's school.

'Children of your own then?' asked McCann, almost in passing, as he pulled out into a gap in the slow-moving traffic.

'Girl of fifteen.'

'I'm sorry about that.'

'What do you mean, sorry?' said Thompson.

'Might be hard for you, that's all,' he said.

Detective Sergeant Clarke caught a glimpse of himself in the full-length mirror, sideways on, checked that there was no sign of a belly yet, his stomach still tanned and flat, the legs muscular. He shaved using his new electric razor, running it up and down the smooth jawbone, keeping an eye on himself in the mirror as he did so, then dabbing aftershave and giving his hair a careful brush. Back in the bedroom he opened the cupboard, the smell of fresh woodwork and clean, laundered shirts came from inside. He selected a light blue shirt, brand new, with a crisp collar and heavy fabric and slipped it on, leaving the top two buttons undone, then a pair of cords from Austin Reed, the new season's cut, with a heavy drape at the knee. Anonymous, but smart too, so you could get closer to the people that mattered.

He buckled his heavy leather belt and walked into the kitchen. The coffee machine burbled gently on the white Formica worktop. He poured and sipped the coffee, looking down at the City from his fourth-floor window. He wondered about the new attachment; he'd to make contact with an Inspector McCann. Something about a Protestant girl killed and dumped in a Republican area. He frowned at that dangerous new development. He could see over to the hills where a column of black smoke was beginning to rise from near the Springfield Road, like a curled fist at first, slowly unfurling, opening out and widening as it rose into the air. Overhead an army helicopter buzzed like an angry wasp in and out of the column of smoke, tilting and turning to get a view of what was happening down below. He knocked back his coffee, picked up his Walther in its holster from the bedside table, buckled it on, then slung a loose-fitting blue cashmere-wool jacket on top, so the comforting bulge wouldn't show. He went down in the lift to the car park, bending to check for booby traps underneath the car, running his hand along the floor pan either side, before unlocking and using a tissue from a fresh packet beneath the dashboard to clean the filth away, putting the soiled paper neatly in the bin by the exit.

Before going on to C Division Clarke dropped over to headquarters to get a bit of background on McCann. It was not a name he'd heard before. He thanked the girl in Personnel who brought him the file and sat himself down in the waiting area to flick over it. McCann had been born in Achnakerrig, County Armagh, educated locally, passed out in 1953. He was a decorated officer, received the Commander's medal in 1974. He had been posted to Londonderry, then Belfast, eight years an Inspector at C Division. That was a long stretch for any man, thought Clarke, to be in one of the worst posts. That would break the toughest fellow, he thought. That would make you wonder if McCann was really the man for the job.

Chapter Two

The Academy was a large school, set back from the road behind high railings, the main buildings in a granite gothic style darkened by coal smoke. A pair of silver birches, stripped bare and stark, overlooked the school office. The pupils were all in class and the place seemed deserted as McCann parked his car in the visitor's parking bay next to the space reserved for the head teacher. He glanced into the car that was parked there as he climbed out, noticing it was new, the slew of papers on the floor in the front, automatically checking the licence disk like some weird inappropriate reflex. He chucked his keys in one hand and hummed a nameless tune as he hunched into the rain, Thompson following behind.

'Like the grim reaper,' he thought to himself, involuntarily, his coat tails flapping in the wind, the rain seeping through.

'We've come to see the head teacher,' he said and put his ID down on the high desk at reception.

'Have you an appointment?'

'I don't need one,' said McCann, adding unnecessarily, 'I'm a police officer.' The secretary rang through to the head-mistress from the inside office, behind glass so McCann couldn't hear what their introduction would be.

Soon enough though she took up her bunch of keys and led

them through a series of locked doors down into the school, walking in silence across a wet quadrangle.

'Been here long?' he asked.

'Long enough,' she said.

The headmistress greeted McCann and Thompson like old friends.

'Inspector McCann!' she cried. 'And sergeant Thompson!' coming out from behind her desk and shaking hands warmly.

'I'm Annie Brown. Can I get you anything? A cup of coffee or tea or anything at all? It's such a grim old day, isn't it?'

Her hair was cut in a bob, her face very pale, with a poor complexion disguised with powder, but she had a pleasing figure and was smartly dressed in a dark suit with a short jacket in a modern style.

'So, you'll be here for the security,' she said. 'I can't remember the man that did it last year. Morrison maybe, Morton?' She squinted in a perplexed kind of way and then waved her hand. 'No matter,' she said, as if names associated with tedious form-filling were not worth remembering. She had the slightly intense movements of a smoker. McCann shifted in his seat.

'Eh no,' he said. 'Actually it's a wee bit more serious other-wise we wouldn't bother you like this.'

Her eyes opened wider and she fixed him with a still gaze.

'D'you have a girl called Elizabeth McCabe?' he asked.

'Oh Lizzie!' she said. 'Oh, dear God what's she done now?'

He ignored the question.

'Can we see if she's in school today?'

'Oh yes, certainly.' She picked up the phone, checking the morning register with the form master. As she listened to the answer somewhere a bell tolled and McCann heard the noise of shouts, of chairs being pushed back, of doors banging and living feet clattering along the corridors as if his question had raised the dead.

'She's not. The form master was just ringing her parents. She's not been home,' she said. And McCann saw her warmth towards him evaporate and she took one slight, imperceptible step back from him, awkwardly, as if there was some kind of smell now coming from him that she was too polite to mention.

'She's been found dead,' said McCann.

'Oh!' said the head teacher. 'Oh, dear God!' and she put her hand to her mouth and turned her back to them for a moment while she looked out at the mountain, composing herself.

'Murdered, and we've to consider anyone who might have been in contact with her or know anything about it.'

'You'll be wanting to talk to the staff, her friends, I suppose.'

'We'll do the parents first,' said McCann.

'You've not told them! No of course not, that's stupid of me. Yes, yes, you'll need to do that of course. Dear God I'll have to tell the school too.' Then she looked at her watch, suddenly efficient, calculating the best time to break the news.

They found the house easily. It was well set back from the road, with a long drive that curved back from the gates, rhododendrons pressing in on either side, the leaves deep green and streaming with the recent rain. He left the car outside in the road, opened the gate and began to walk up to the house, the path newly laid in fine red gravel, the stones scattered a little in the borders of the lawn by the passage of cars. In front of the house a new Mini was parked, with space for another car alongside. A fellow was out spreading mulch in the flowerbeds and paused in his work to stare at them both. He rang the bell and waited for a moment, a faint hope stirring that he could postpone it all until he saw a face at the door and heard the bolts being drawn back.

'Good morning. Mrs McCabe is it?' he said. The woman was dressed as if for an aerobics class, or one of those new-fangled step classes that his own wife had tried and then given up. She was rich enough to be able to look ten years younger than maybe she was, too young looking even to be the mother of the dead girl.

'Mrs McCabe? I'm DI McCann from Castle Street. And this is sergeant Thompson. Do you mind if we come in?'

The house was modern, with a wide-open hall with a parquet floor of freshly polished beech wood that was flooded with light from the open front door. He could hear a radio playing.

'It'll be about Lizzie won't it? I've had a call from the school asking if we'd seen her. She was due a sleepover and she never arrived,' she said, alarm rising in her voice.

'Is your husband at home?' McCann asked.

'What's happened? What do you need him for?'

'It'd be best if the two of you were here.'

'He's at work. I'll give him a call. I was just doing that,' half moving towards the phone, then back towards McCann.

'I wonder is there somewhere we can sit down?' suggested Thompson, looking through towards the living room.

'Maybe it's best you take a seat,' said McCann. 'The sergeant here can make us some tea. I've some bad news to share I'm afraid.' And very gently he touched her elbow, and led her to the sofa in the living room.

'Do you have any idea at all how she could've been taken?' McCann asked. The coffee table between them was strewn with tissues, her tea untouched, her face wet with tears. The living room alone was almost the same size as McCann's house, with a ceiling to floor picture window running the length of one wall. Outside the lawn fell away to the lough, around freshly laid beds of roses, edged with stone.

'She was due to stay at her friend Minnie's,' her mother repeated. Her make-up had run. From time to time she sobbed, awful wrenching sobs that made her shoulders shake.

'We'll need the address, the name, details of the girl,' said Thompson. Although the room was large and light and designed to give an airy sense of space, it was still claustrophobic and hard to breathe, as if the double glazing had restricted the oxygen supply.

'Yes, yes, of course,' she said, brought out her diary, fumbling with it on the table while Thompson took down the details.

'I don't know what to do,' she said. 'I just don't know what we're going to do.'

Just then there was the noise of a car turning on the gravel outside, a key in the lock and rapid footsteps in the hall. McCann stood up as a tall man, dressed in a dark business suit entered the room, glanced around, introduced himself.

'Peter McCabe. What's all this about Inspector?'

The suit hung loosely on him and he was older than his wife, with a slight stoop and a shock of sandy hair that fell to one side over his high forehead. McCann repeated what he knew, just the bare detail of location, time, a factual death, emptying out of it anything that could bring the scene to mind, or fire the imagination. Even with that care he saw Mr McCabe's mouth drop open and his face drain of colour, his hands clenching into fists.

'Any idea yet who done it Inspector?' he growled, but before he could answer Mrs McCabe blurted out: 'It's all gone wrong Inspector, hasn't it? I mean everything is falling to pieces. I mean you're not going to find them, are you?' She looked up at him, her eyes round with some sudden undermining realisation of his weakness, of the situation they were in. 'I mean how can you Inspector. I mean the police can't do anything in this.' She stopped, with her husband's restraining hand on her arm and said in a quieter tone: 'We're all going to the devil aren't we Inspector?' McCann found that he wanted to stand, to pace around, to smoke, to do anything to deflect her misery and the blame in her eyes.

'We're still solving crimes,' said Thompson, holding her hand to try to comfort her, but Mrs McCabe pulled it away.

'So, she'd arranged to stay at this friend's house?' McCann persisted.

'Aye. That's where I thought she was. We'd packed her stuff. She took it to school so she could go off straight after.'

'What kind of stuff?'

'Nightdress, toothbrush, usual girl's stuff.'

'We'll need a list. We'll need a recent photo too. Can you let me have anything you've got?'

'Aye, certainly Inspector.'

'Did she have any boyfriends?'

'At fifteen? God no, Inspector.'

'Anyone she would have trusted enough to go off with?'

'Not without telling us. She'd never have done that.'

'Maybe she thought she'd a right. Nearly sixteen and all that.'

'Everyone thinks they've rights now and look where it's got us.'

McCann explained briefly what they would be doing; interviews at the school, house to house inquiries opposite the murder site, retracing Lizzie's steps.

'Often youngsters will go off with someone they know and trust,' he said, not adding the possibility she'd been forcibly seized. 'Who could that be? Who do you know that Lizzie would trust enough to go off with on impulse, maybe someone you don't quite approve of, so she'd need a cover story like a sleepover.'

He watched their faces carefully, for the slight, involuntary give-aways, for too-patness and nervousness, foot tapping and fidgeting and then for those little inconsistencies with the prehistoric map of the country and its tribes that he carried in his head. She bit her lip, weighing something up. Mr McCabe seemed on the point of speaking and a look passed between them.

'There's no one we'd see as a threat,' said Peter McCabe. 'No one that'd do this disgusting thing, if that's what you're suggesting Inspector, that we'd let someone like that near our daughter.' And his face suddenly reddened with anger.

'I'm not suggesting that but maybe someone who might – with the best intentions, or by bad judgement or bad luck – inadvertently place her in harm's way.'

'There's no one like that we'd trust her with,' said Peter McCabe.

There was a silence before Mrs McCabe said, as if remembering a duty of politeness: 'You'll be wanting a smoke I imagine, Inspector.'

'No, no. Bad habit,' he said. 'I can do without.'

'Have a smoke,' instructed Mr McCabe. 'You can have a smoke outside.' He stood up and walked over to the picture windows, unlocked and slid the glass doors apart. A gust of wind off the lough had blown in, stirring the lampshade from side to side.

'Go on,' said Mrs McCabe. 'I know you fellows smoke like chimneys.'

Gratefully McCann got up and patted his pockets for cigarette and lighter and stepped out onto the patio, with its panoramic view out over the lough. Mrs McCabe stepped out with him, rubbing her arms against the cold and leant on the rail looking out.

'We thought this was a nice place you know. Ideal in fact,' she said. He offered her a cigarette, but she refused.

'Ideal?' he prompted.

'Ideal for Peter's work. Ideal for children. Sure, didn't everyone want to live here?'

McCann remembered. It was true; he and Irene had wanted to have a house out by the lough, but it had been way out of their reach and now, well who would want the isolation and the night drives in winter, in and out of the city? Irene certainly wouldn't. Maybe even then she had sensed how dangerous things were becoming.

McCann slid in sideways on the fixed Formica seat, slopping the tea on the tray carrying his lunch, not even bothering to look at Clarke as he sat down, picking the napkins from the dispenser and mopping the tea. Clarke sat down opposite him. He looked like a twenty-year-old, thought McCann; fresh faced, slightly built, dressed in the conventionally smart way that the branch men had; a light blue shirt well pressed and open at the collar, his hair neatly trimmed, an expensive tan. He had an expensive watch too, a big heavy silver item like the ones McCann would look at in the jeweller's window but which were always beyond the money he had.

'I've been thinking of you boys,' said Clarke. 'This new case you're on.'

'That's nice,' said McCann, reaching for his knife and fork, cutting into his pie determinedly, still not looking at Clarke, cutting out a big chunk and stuffing it into his mouth, chewing, dabbing at his lips with another napkin and grunting as he ate, waiting for Clarke to continue.

'The Superintendent says you asked for the branch to get involved.' Clarke had an open face, maybe capable of listening and taking in information, maybe unsullied if that were possible, thought McCann. Clarke should have access to informers in the paramilitaries, a knowledge of security operations that might be shared with him. Clarke might be able to pull strings or stop the wrong ones being pulled at the wrong time.

'I thought it'd be useful, that maybe you'd have some information not available to the likes of us,' he said, swallowing, dabbing his mouth again, noting Clarke's salad untouched before him on the plastic tray.

'Well I'm sure you fellows know as much as any of us, with your experience Inspector,' said Clarke, fluently deferential, picking at his salad with a plastic fork. 'It's a big case.'

'In what way?'

'It's got implications.'

'And what kind of implications would those be?'

'Ah well now Inspector you'd be the best judge of that I'm sure. Jesus would you look at this lettuce for fuck's sake.' Clarke turned the lettuce leaf over with his plastic fork. In the fluorescent underground light of the canteen it appeared grey and colourless, as if the vital juices had been sucked from it.

'Here,' he said, swivelling on the seat to catch the eye of one of the canteen staff. 'Here. Call this a lettuce? It's been dead a week. For fuck's sake how can you not get decent lettuce in this country?'

'You a vegetarian then?'

'I'm not'

'Then why're eating that rabbit food?' McCann gestured at Clarke's plate with his plastic fork.

'It'll kill you. All those beans and fries,' retorted Clarke. 'The cholesterol will get you, block the arteries. One day your heart will just explode, I'm telling you.' And he pointed at McCann's plate with his fork. It was good humoured, but a sharp jest nonetheless. McCann grinned and pulled out a pack of Weights, methodically sliding out the cigarette, tapping it on the table top, lighting it, watching the girl clearing away and thinking what a fine pair of legs she had, enjoying the way she moved in her tight blue nylon pinafore, lighting and drawing the smoke in, letting it out, funnelling it across the table at Clarke. For all his smooth talk and enthusiasm Clarke seemed jumpy and distracted, maybe scared of death the way they all were. He realised he'd been silent too long, that he might have missed something Clarke had said.

'Eh, what was that?' he said, just in case.

'Nothing. I said nothing,' said Clarke, looking at him curiously, like he'd seen McCann was beginning to lose it. So McCann ran through the little he knew as competently as he could. Not being alone on the case meant he had to raise his game, make it look as if he knew what he was doing. Clarke nodded while he spoke, pulled out his notebook and entered the key points, leaving the salad unfinished.

Chapter Three

He'd not told anyone that Irene had left him of course, though everyone knew. It had been such a shock, he had taken a week just to believe it had happened at all, that she wasn't coming back and to consider why, to have some explanations ready, were anyone to ask. He'd gone around like an automaton, feet, legs arms working away as before, but inside there was just surprise and hurt as he realised what it would be like in the house by himself. He'd tried everything – he'd rung her, tried to get at her through her mutual friends, written, but her mind it seemed had been made up, so much so that he began to think there had been other men, before the one she'd eventually gone with. The obsessive brooding had started up then, running back over the year before her departure, seeing innocent actions in a new, starker light; the evenings working late at the school, the curriculum study days. But that was not her style at all. Sometimes he would think of her as they had been together, cast in a romantic light, perhaps making love together and then this had tormented him, aroused his desire and for a few weeks he had become obsessed with replacing her with anyone as revenge, yet found he now lacked the skills, the attractiveness and the confidence that was required to do so. In the church, they preached forgiveness, but what was that? How could you forgive her? That was plain ridiculous. But he knew he had to forgive her, if she were ever to show him love again. But of course, as the churchmen would say, self-interested forgiveness was not true forgiveness but calculation and usury and the opposite of love.

He came in through the hall door with the shopping bursting from the plastic carrier bags, dropping tins of meat and beans on the floor amongst the mail and the circulars that had come through the letterbox. He went into the kitchen and put the kettle on, lit a cigarette and went to the phone, head held on one side, cradling it while he riffled in the address book for her new number. Not so many people he could call now. He'd maybe cross out all the people that had belonged to her and not to him, or that had left Ireland altogether and existed now only on Christmas cards or tombstones. He dialled and frowned when he heard a man's voice.

'Hello, John,' he said. 'It's McCann. McCann. Yes, Michael McCann. Irene's husband.' He felt a sudden surge of anger that the man on the other end of the line seemed to pretend not to know him, a sudden urge to add a 'you prick' to the end of the sentence.

'Is Irene there?'

'Hold on Mike. I'll see if she's free.' Mike? No one ever called him Mike. The fellow must have known that. He could hear his footsteps going away down the hall, imagined her lounging there on the sofa maybe with a magazine spread out, her shoes kicked off, in his house. He imagined their conversation and the way she would frown at the awkward mention of his name. But then she came on the line and he heard her familiar voice.

'Hello Michael, how are you?'

'I'm very well.'

There was a pause.

'And yourself?'

'I'm fine too, thanks,' she said.

There was another pause and he ran his finger across the polished surface of the table in the hall, cradling the receiver, his mind suddenly freezing; an old mental trick he had, that made him seem an idiot, when he couldn't cope, couldn't process painful information.

'Michael?'

'I was just wondering if maybe we could meet up for a wee chat about Elaine.'

'Elaine!' her voice sounded alarmed. 'There's nothing wrong is there?'

'No, no. Just thought I'd catch up that's all.'

'She's not due back from University till March, Michael. We could meet up then.'

'Have you had any news?'

'She's doing fine Michael, you know that.'

'I was just wondering had you heard anything that's all,' he said. He could hear her new man in the background now, asking what he was after.

'Nothing you don't know,' she said.

'Well we could meet up anyway, to keep in touch,' he suggested, but his voice had become high pitched, almost desperate, like he was on the verge of another argument.

Afterwards he fried himself up three big pork sausages and emptied a warmed tin of beans out on a plate and ate them up with brown sauce, wiping the plate clean with a slab of soda bread and then when he was feeling better he got a couple of sheets of paper out and propped Elizabeth McCabe's picture in front of him on the table. She smiled back at him in her school uniform. It was not a particularly good photograph and made her look like almost any schoolgirl. The curly dark hair, like his own daughter's that must have been hard to manage, tied back with something to comply with the rules and the eyes, wide open as if slightly surprised to find herself stepping out so boldly upon the planet with so many limitless years ahead. He held the photograph out at arm's length in different lights, as if somehow lighting would turn up some hidden facet, but her face remained as it had been, uncomplicated, optimistic, almost bland, except for the lips perhaps which seemed somehow full for a girl of her age and the confident almost truculent look in her eye. He stood up and stretched, groaning, then rootled in the desk drawer, pulling out a magnifying glass. He held the glass over the photograph and explored it carefully for any clues. Her eyes, distorted, jumped out at him and swerved away for a moment as if she were alive and seeking to escape his gaze. Feeling uneasy, he went back out to the kitchen and poured himself a small whiskey, put her photo back in its envelope, his feet on the desk and blew smoke rings in the air until the evening darkened and the room was thick with his smoke.

Either, he reasoned, she was the victim of some crazed paedophile abduction, or of some sectarian tit-for-tat, or of some dark family business. It would be unusual for sex to figure in the kind of warfare that was breaking out – sex was frowned upon and never talked of, the violence was more often driven by an absence of it, of people without release, wound up by their self-imposed frustrations. But it was a strange case with none of the usual, normal methods; no drills or guns, no Black and Decker surgery, no braggart sloganeering or warning messages by the corpse. But despite the absence of those things the murder was somehow far more disgusting than anything he'd seen before. He felt an awful wave of nauseous revulsion sweep over him, his limbs ached and felt heavy, he almost retched, feeling dyspepsia mounting in his stomach again. He went into the kitchen and drank a full glass of cold water from the tap, soft clear rainwater from the Mourne mountains. Then he went to the window. The wind was blowing up outside and he could see it shaking the trees, creeping round the gaps in the window frames, making the curtains twitch as if some ghost were there in the room with him. He could hear the gusts roaring down off the mountain, throwing themselves against the house, making the cheap PVC windows boom and buckle.

Later, he could feel the draughts from under the door against his cheek even as he lay in bed in the darkness and hear the occasional splatter of raindrops on the pane like fingers drumming the warm up for some Irish traditional dance. In the distance was the sound of a sheet of corrugated iron loosened from its fastenings banging intermittently. The air in the room was close and heavy with his smoke. He lay awake propped up with both hands behind his head, resisting the temptation to light another cigarette because if he smoked any more he knew that sooner or later he'd need tea from the kitchen and if he started with that he'd be in there listening to the late-night phone ins and then the shipping and then the morning farmers' programme and that would be that. So, he lay there listening to the wind and wondering if the weather was bad enough to keep the man that'd done it indoors for one night more.

Chapter Four

The army turned over the estate at seven in the morning of the next day, securing the mountain road top and bottom with Saracens and two platoons of paratroopers, one in the ditch where the body had been found, another platoon coming up through the back of the estate and a helicopter overhead to keep the rooftops clear. McCann's team worked methodically up along the road overlooking the murder scene. It was a warm morning for February and McCann sweated in his heavy bullet proof vest. Almost immediately the racket started up, of bin lids clattering and banging, warning the residents that a raid was on. As the light came up the streets began to fill with youths.

McCann knocked on doors, one by one.

'Hello missus. We're inquiring after the recent death of Elizabeth McCabe,' he said. 'I'm sorry to disturb you, but did you see anything unusual on the road the night before last?'

The houses were narrow corporation maisonettes with thin partition walls, thrown together. When the shooting started they said bullets would go through two or three houses, clean through the bedroom and the kitchen walls.

'Hey missus, I'm sorry but did you see anything unusual?' The place seemed full of kids; no sooner had he knocked than

45

gangs of them would flood down the stairs in pants and shorts, wee nightdresses, clutching babies, clustering around his feet. There'd be folk asleep on sofas, folk on the toilet. It was some kind of bedlam. The army Major in charge of the operation had told him he'd at best thirty minutes before the situation would get unmanageable, that he needed to be out by then. Clarke was with him too, like some kind of crazed ferret, straight past him once a door was opened, up the stairs into the bedrooms. If there was any sign of argument the Major would send in the troops, big lads, up the stairs with the guns shouting out: 'Down on the floor. Down on the floor. Everyone down on the floor.' Ripping out drawers, cupboards, where they met resistance, McCann standing there, trying to ask questions as the drawers were emptied, the bins overturned in the kitchens, the children crying, the women shouting, out in the street the sound of the bin lids banging and the throb of the helicopter overhead. Through the window he saw the troops grab a lad and bundle him out of his house and into the back of a Saracen.

'That's a terrible business with that wee girlie,' said the woman. She had a sad, lined face, wore a tired mauve nightgown. McCann hesitated. He could hear feet running up the stairs in the house next door and the sounds of shouting, furniture crashing. He stepped into the still curtained living room. A large crucifix, garish and distorted, hung from the wall, the legs knotted and nailed, the blood dripping from the crown of thorns. There was a smell of frying, of unwashed clothes, cigarette smoke. Another Jesus, alabaster this time, looked down from the opposite wall, with a look of infinite sadness.

'There was a van,' she said.

'What kind of a van.'

'I didn't see. It was white or grey. I'll tell you if you leave us alone,' she hissed at him. 'If you leave my boys alone.'

'What time?' he asked.

'Five. Just after the news was on. I thought it was odd, him stopping like that. Thought he'd a flat or something.' Then he heard the sound of a shot in the street outside and the woman hissed at him.

'Get away mister. It's starting up.'

And then his radio began to shout urgent instructions and, as she pushed him towards the hall, she whispered: 'Big fellow in a parka.'

When he ducked out into the street it had emptied. There were troops in the gardens, crouched behind walls, behind cars in the road. He heard the shrill whine of a Saracen reversing back up to them and the sudden whang of a ricocheting bullet. A minute later they were in the dark armoured interior, speeding away.

'If it was the IRA done it that woman would never have told us about the van,' said McCann.

'Could have been a spoiler,' said Clarke. 'Put you off the scent.'

The two men were in McCann's office. The blinds were down and the bare yellow lightbulb cast the room in a kind of sepia gloom. Clarke was dressed in new jeans, trainers, a half-open zip-up bomber jacket.

'What scent? A white van, maybe grey, fellow in a parka. Welcome to Ulster, Clarke; it's us, it's who we are. That could have been anyone.'

'I'd bring her in,' said Clarke. 'See if we can get more detail.' He looked around, distracted, almost bored, his fingers flicking absently through the file on his desk as if searching for some inspiration.

'Too dangerous, for her. She'd be a target then. Up there they'd think she was informing and she might end up dead or tarred[3] for it.'

'But that would mean it's the Republicans that done it, once and for all,' said Clarke smugly. '*Prima facie* if they do that to her, they're covering something up. And we'd get the fellows that organised it then.'

'Or just that they're vicious bastards, and we'd be giving them an excuse to be more vicious,' said McCann.

Clarke looked thoughtful, swung down off his swivel chair.

'Jesus, whichever side gets the blame for this murder is going to lose a lot of support. No one's going to want the death of a young girl on their tally. Who knows, the fellow that done it could even be dead by now and we wouldn't know it.'

'He's not dead yet. He's still out there somewhere,' said McCann. He pulled back the blinds from the windows and peered out into the inner courtyard. In the distance he heard the faint thump of an explosion, the sound of sirens, the clatter of feet as a small platoon burst from the police station doors into the courtyard and into the back of a Land Rover, the headlights on full beam, engine revving.

'We just need to wait till the body floats then,' said Clarke.

'It's a lovely wee country right enough,' said McCann.

3 Tarring and feathering was a traditional punishment for those suspected of being informers who would be doused in tar, tied to a lamppost and feathers scattered over them.

'Warm, friendly people.'

'When you come and stay you'll never leave.'

'You're sure she said there was just the one?' asked Thompson, who until then had been silent, sitting in the corner, listening to the two men.

'She said "he", in the singular.'

'Could have been more of them,' said Clarke. 'Maybe just meant she saw only one, doesn't mean he wasn't part of a group. You didn't ask her?'

'We couldn't because the army pulled us out when the shooting started.'

Just then the phone rang, a sharp jangling note and Thompson reached for it but Clarke got there first.

'C Division, murder squad,' he said. A bit of a smile crept over McCann's face at that and he caught Thompson's eye and thought she could see the funny side of it too, because her face had two dimples, either side of her mouth.

'Yes,' said Clarke, listening to the voice on the phone, looking for a pencil and paper on McCann's desk, then snapping his fingers at Thompson to get a pen for him.

'Aye, got that. A van you say? What colour? They're up there now are they? Tell them to wait, touch nothing d'you hear till we get there. Aye, I've got the location.'

It was drizzling again and much colder up the mountain amidst a network of narrow roads, old quarries, isolated farms, just ten miles outside the city but it could have been another country. The van lay on its side. All around the heather had been burned back by the force of the blaze, just bare blackened branches for twenty feet away from the track. The smell of petrol was still strong in the air. A low mist obscured the view, closing it in. The scene of crime officers had already taped off the area, set bollards up in the road and were waving traffic past. The van had fared worse than the heather, such had been the heat of the blaze that the door posts had buckled, the roof caved in, the bonnet crumpled, just the springs of the upholstered seats visible, already rusting in the damp atmosphere. The back doors hung open, the tyres gone, wheel hubs resting on the melted tarmac.

'They took the plates,' said the officer.

'Aye I can see that,' said McCann

'Inspector!' the mechanic greeted McCann cheerfully, wiping his hands on a rag before shaking his hand. A short man in overalls, with the harassed look of the self-employed, Tom Biggar did a fine line in forensic recovery of vehicles: burned out, smashed up, blood and petrol soaked, the mechanical equivalent of a pathologist.

'These fellows work for the Ford motor company, I'm sure,' he said and led McCann to the wreck, picked up an inspection lamp and shone it on the cylinder block. McCann leant in.

'They took the engine number off,' said Biggar, showing him the fine lines of file strokes and the area of burnished metal.

'Chassis number?'

'Same thing,' said Biggar, shining the light.

'Popped right off – drilled out the rivets and took the chassis plate off too.'

McCann swore. What kind of person took that kind of trouble? Someone able to do that was organised, had to have had help maybe.

'She's a '73 Ford. E300 Econoline, I can tell you that at least – had a new engine though, quite recently. Unusual colour, in fact she's not white at all, looks like she's been resprayed. Originally she'd have been Pearl White. Fuck knows where they get these colours from: Aubergine, Granita, Barley Mow, it's just ridiculous.'

'Any idea who might have sold it?'

'Main dealer originally.'

'It would be knocked off though?'

'Aye, certainly. You could check that but I doubt it'd get you anywhere if you've not the chassis or engine number.'

'You got anything else for me?'

'Aye,' said the mechanic. 'You had best have a look at this.'

He pulled out a Tupperware box that seemed at first glance to be full of nothing but old screws, pieces of carpet, indeterminate parts of the interior fixings of a transit van, heavily damaged by fire. McCann borrowed a pair of pliers to move the debris around carefully, peering in.

'Ah,' he said, and pulled out some twisted pink plastic, half melted, half burned, a few bristles still attached. McCann held it under the light of the inspection lamp for a second.

He turned the pliers through the debris again, catching a glimpse of a flash of metal, extracting another object. Though twisted by the heat of the fire the bronze still glistened. There was something familiar about the pin, the kind of thing McCann had seen around but he couldn't yet place.

'Any idea on this?' he asked. The two men bent their heads together in the glare of the light.

'Looks like the temperance league,' said the mechanic.

'Where'd you find it?'

'In the floor pan, driver's side. Slipped right down into the handbrake mounting like it'd fallen out as the fellow was bending down.'

'Or struggling with something maybe?'

'Maybe Inspector. Sure, you're the expert on these things.'

He could see in his mind's eye what had happened now, but the who of it eluded him, who had done it to Elizabeth McCabe, maybe in the back of that van, now burned and torched as if by the fires of hell. He stood up, feeling suddenly dizzy with the smell of petrol and burned upholstery, walked away to the edge of the moor and watched as the forensic team set about photographing, labelling, cataloguing like archaeologists in some primeval bone yard. He could see the orange flashing lights of the towing truck coming up the road, haloed in the mist and stood and watched until what was left of the van was winched up onto the trailer to be towed away back down into the city.

The pathologist washed her hands in the sink and peeled off her rubber gloves, tossing them in the pedal bin marked 'for incineration' and turned towards McCann. An unpleasant dark brown stain ran down her white coat over her right breast and her blue eyes were unnaturally large behind her severe, black framed spectacles.

'I'm just done Inspector. You've missed the best bit,' she said. 'Blow to the back of the head. Right good heavy belting, a goodly whack that'd take your head off except he must have missed,' she said. 'Hit her on the upper back and broke her neck low down. Would've been quick, poor wee dear,' she said, sniffing, then reaching for her handkerchief in the pocket of her white coat and blowing her nose loudly.

'Dreadful cold.' she said. 'Can't seem to shake it off, stuck down here all day.'

'He? You sure it was a he?'

'Oh aye. A belt like that couldn't have been a lady.'

'Weapon?'

'Something heavy.'

'Lead piping,' he suggested.

'Mr Mustard with the lead piping? God no, you're out of touch, Inspector.' There was a mournful air in the autopsy room, with the cold refrigerated air flowing out of the vents over the stainless steel tables and the frosted glass of the windows. He tried not to look at the table in the middle, thankfully covered with a green cloth.

'So, what was it then?'

'Something rusty, maybe one or two inches diameter, some engineering component or bit of old scrap. You've not found anything yourself?'

'We've not looked properly yet. It's too dangerous to be up there for long, poking in the ditches in bandit country.' He paused.

'Anything else?' he asked. 'Anything at all?'

'Aye,' she said. 'She'd had intercourse, maybe a couple of hours before, hard to tell when exactly.' She paused.

'Intercourse?'

'But not in the usual way.'

'What d'ye mean?'

She gestured, embarrassed, to show him what she meant.

'Willingly?' he asked.

'Something like that would never be willing now would it Inspector?'

53

'You'll keep samples?'

'Aye the usual routine, Inspector, till you get us a suspect or two to work on.'

Chapter Five

'I need a woman with me at the school for the interviews,' said McCann, reaching for his coat. Thompson stood up, collected her things from the desk, while he stood there waiting for her. Then Deevery's head appeared round the door, a big grin on his face, his eyes taking in McCann, Clarke at his desk by the window, lingering for a moment too long on Thompson, like he had a special interest in her.

'Ah Inspector McCann,' he said. 'I've something for you.' And he stepped into the office, deposited a beige folder on McCann's desk with an air of finality, like he was pleased to be rid of it.

'What's that?' said McCann.

'Sex offenders,' said Deevery. 'In case you're not following up on that.'

'Its early days,' said McCann.

'Is it now?' said Deevery.

There was a vicious curl to his upper lip, that brought it back to McCann. The presence of him always brought him back to Achnakerrig; Deevery climbing up into the school bus out of the rain, pushing his way up towards the back, the sudden rabbit punch to McCann's arm, so quick you could hardly see it, then away past with that weird smile on his face.

'Are you in a different time zone, McCann? You've to wake up and smell the coffee, pal.'

McCann looked down at the file on his desk. There was a silence, Thompson and Clarke watching to see what he would do.

'I'm a tea drinker myself, but thank you all the same,' said McCann. Leaving the file untouched on his desk, he nodded Thompson towards the door, pushing past Deevery and out into the corridor.

He drove out of the car park, the guard waving him through as the red and white barrier lifted ahead of him. Thompson sat beside him in the passenger seat, her hands clasped in her lap as he wrenched the gears, leaning forwards to check the road.

'That Deevery,' said Thompson. 'You worked with him before?' The car lodged in the traffic, moving slowly forwards, but McCann barely noticed.

'Me and Deevery go way back.'

'Enniskillen? You train together?'

'He was a year below me. We were in the same class at school.'

'How come he was behind you then at training?'

'He had a car accident,' said McCann. 'A girl was killed.' He didn't tell her that Mary Channon had been his first girlfriend. McCann could remember her laugh, the neat bob of her blonde hair, the way she'd stand close and her calm eyes would smile at him mysteriously. There was something about Thompson that reminded him of Mary, though he tried to put that away in the back of his mind. He swung the car out into the traffic, flicked on the radio, took a cigarette out of the packet in the door with one hand, lit up with the lighter, pulling the smoke down. Inconsequential conversation twittered on the radio, punctuated by laughter. Thompson tapped her fingers on the armrest, drumming a little tune in time to the music, wishing she'd never asked.

When they turned into the Academy McCann climbed out.

'Let's get on sergeant. We've a few hours yet to get these interviews done,' slammed the car door, hitched up his trousers and walked away to the school reception, leaving Thompson to follow behind.

The mother of the schoolgirl was rather overweight and untidy, bulging from a buttoned red winter coat, the daughter shy, perched in a well-worn uniform on the edge of her seat. McCann noticed her shoes which were badly scuffed.

'So,' he asked gently. 'Lizzie had a sleepover arranged?' The girl looked at him, her eyes very round and watery. She sniffed and her mother gave her a handkerchief.

'Sleepover!' said the mother. 'You'd arranged a sleepover!'

'Aye but she changed her mind,' said the girl, but her voice was so indistinct that at first McCann could not hear it.

'Changed her mind?' he prompted. 'Did she say why?'

'First I've heard of this,' said the mother. 'Minnie ? what's all this about?'

'Girls do arrange things sometimes,' said Thompson gently, leaning forwards. 'Minnie'd be no different to any other.'

'But not telling, not telling when she didn't show up for Christ's sake, Minnie. What kind of an idiotic thing is that to do at all? Sure, if you'd have told me we could have…'

'Ah now missus,' McCann raised his hand to intervene. 'Let's not think that way.'

'Wasn't definite,' said the girl. 'Wasn't definite she would come.'

'She told her mother she was coming,' said McCann. 'Packed her stuff for the night.'

'Well she didn't come,' said the girl.

'Did she have any other special friends?'

'Lots,' said the girl. 'She was lovely,' she whispered so it was barely audible.

'Any boys? Any men? Did she ever mention anyone?' McCann asked, but the girl seemed to have shrunk back into her seat. Her mother put her arm round her protectively.

'Ach Inspector she'd be too young for that kind of caper.'

The girl shifted uneasily in her seat. Thompson leant forwards slightly and placed her hand softly on the girl's own hand.

'Any fellows, maybe waiting at the gate, after school?'

'Big fellow. Used to meet her after school,' she whispered.

'Are you sure?'

'What age? What did he look like?'

'I don't know, maybe forty. Long hair, big coat on him. Some kind of a toggle thing on the back of his hair.'

'A pigtail? A pony tail?'

The girl nodded.

'And what would you say their attitude was to each other? Was it friendly?'

The girl frowned, trying to think.

'Did they touch each other?'

'Just said hullo,' said the girl.

'No kiss?'

'What sort of a question is that?' intervened the mother.

'On the lips, or like…' Thompson struggled to explain.

'Like a bird pecking,' she suggested, leaning forward, as if to peck.

The girl nodded, looked away from Thompson, her eyes baffled, bewildered, on the verge of tears.

Afterwards McCann and Thompson strolled to the school gates. McCann lit a cigarette and sucked in his cheeks. It was the end of the school day and pupils streamed out around them, running for buses, or making for the nearest sweet shop for snacks, an energetic kind of chaos. Further up the road he recognised two special constables he'd set to work, ducking in and out of the shops with their clipboards and photos of the girl, asking had anyone seen her. Lizzie would have walked out this way on her last day after school and maybe the fellow had met her and spirited her away from the very spot where they were standing. The thoughts crowded in… a fellow she would trust enough, close enough for a kiss, a family member maybe, sent to collect her? But why had Peter McCabe or his wife not mentioned that? Or maybe the fellow wasn't important, except that he'd not turned up thinking she was on a sleepover and someone else had seized his opportunity? Looked at like that anyone in the city crowds could have been responsible for her death. But that was a warped view. How come most of the people he met were the same kind, warm folk they'd always been? Not all killers, no, but ready to look the other way, to pretend not to have seen because it was safer to do that. That's what was becoming of the lovely folk of his lovely country, thought McCann. Not all actual killers no, but maybe indirectly getting that way.

'Inspector! Inspector!' are you away with the fairies or what?' Thompson was speaking to him, concerned. 'I've been talking to you and you were far away. D'you want a cup of tea or something? We could go to the cafe, eh?'

'Oh aye, why not?' said McCann.

There was a big queue at the self-service, the cafe being popular at that time of day.

'I see they've an offer for the steak and kidney pie, with pudding and custard.'

'Ach I couldn't. I'd be asleep at my desk,' she said. 'Put on a stone by Friday.'

They squeezed into a space at the end of a four person table, their legs almost touching underneath.

'So who do you reckon this fellow is?' he asked her, lighting her cigarette then another for himself.

'Relative maybe? If it was a relationship he'd not have been open about it. Wouldn't have let himself be seen,' said Thompson, blowing the smoke out in a funnel over McCann's head.

'Peter McCabe didn't mention it when we saw him. But it sounds like it was a regular pick-up.'

'Person of interest all the same,' said Thompson, frowning, as if trying to clear an annoying pain in her head.

'I mean everyone knew her and liked her and couldn't think how or why she could have ended up where she did,' he said.

'Left footer,'[4] Thompson said stolidly. 'I'd have said she

---

4 Catholics were sometimes referred to as 'left footers' on account of a belief that the spades they used for cutting turf were different to those used by Protestants. 'To dig with the left foot' – to be a Catholic, untrustworthy, disloyal.

was doing a sleepover with a Fenian[5] and someone didn't like it.'

'With a Fenian? For God's sake!' McCann reeled back through the interview and suddenly it seemed plausible, angry for not picking up on the family name of the girl they had interviewed. The Academy was proud of its three Catholic pupils, the head teacher had said, no doubt paraded them around like guttering candles of hope in the gathering sectarian darkness. But not everyone liked the idea of that kind of mixing.

'Though it could've been the Fenians,' she suggested. 'Retaliation.'

'For what?' he said dismissively. It was not a possibility he wished to consider.

'Sure, there's always grounds now,' she said. 'The UVF have been killing Catholics since the Miami Showband massacre[6] last year.'

'And the Provos[7] have been doing the same the other way since way before that.'

'But not teenage girls.'

'That'd be a new low,' agreed McCann.

'But why her?'

'Why not?' It was true, recognised McCann; once killers

5 Fenian a term used to describe Catholics. The Fenians were early fighters for Irish independence.

6 The Miami Showband killing was an infamous sectarian attack by the Ulster Volunteer Force, a leading Protestant paramilitary group, and rogue members of the security forces. A minibus carrying a popular Irish band was halted at a fake roadblock and three members of the band were killed.

7 'Provos' were the Provisional IRA, themselves responsible for many civilian deaths during the troubles.

decided on the mathematics of tit for tat, of one side for another, it didn't matter who the specific victim was, all motives and emotions became general, unhitched from relationships of any kind. Anyone could kill anyone else, provided they were the wrong religion. It made police work so much harder, the pool of suspects and victims almost without limit, the motives generalised, all specifics lost in a sudden blur of hatred. That was the reason there were nearly a hundred unsolved murders on the city's books, the reason he'd a tiny, mostly inexperienced team to work with. He sighed heavily.

'Never mind Inspector,' said Thompson, taking a small bite of her sandwich. 'It's what we're here for and you'll get him in the end, I'm sure of it.' He looked at her, surprised by the way she'd read his thoughts, amused by her optimism. But she was only young and maybe entitled to that kind of delusion.

Chapter Six

McCann's ageing Morris Marina undulated through the rolling countryside, slowing on the upturns, then accelerating on the down swoops. The landscape was one of near androgynous human forms – ancient clay ground beneath ice glaciers – armpits and buttocks of land, felted with meadow grass, punctuated by small lakes dotted with birds. At normal times he would have enjoyed this escape from the city. He and Irene had done it dozens of times in the summer when Elaine was young. How strange it was that he had never appreciated it at the time, sweeping along with the windows wound down and her hair blowing beside him, his daughter in the back on the way down to the beach at Newcastle.

He pulled over at a petrol station for fuel. After waiting a while, he tooted the horn and the fellow came out scratching his arse and filled the tank, giving him a cold, hard stare. McCann stared back and dropped the money when he paid him, scattering the coins across the forecourt.

'Sorry, pal,' he said. 'Could never hold onto the money,' taking satisfaction in watching the fellow – so fat his buttocks burst from his trousers – as he scrabbled for the loose coppers on the tarmac. Small humiliation he thought, for a man with no respect for the law.

Dirty Old Tricks

The church was at the end of the long main street, set on top of a rise by the ruined castle, with a view out over the Mourne mountains and the sea. Cars clogged the road up to the gates and out on one of the flat fields that'd been opened up specially. McCann was already late and he double parked and walked up the hill, through the lychgate and the churchyard. It was a bright day with sudden early spring sunshine and the birds warbling and tweeting. There were fresh spring flowers around the gravestones: primroses and snowdrops. Halfway up he paused for breath and turned, looking back. The tide was in and the entire bay on the far side of town was filled with blue water, with Slieve Donard rising behind, dusted with snow. He waited for a moment, sucking in the pure, clean air as the organ struck up. Through the open doors of the church he heard the first strains of:

'My God accept my heart this day' and saw at the bottom of the hill the slow turn of the hearse at the corner, carrying the body of Elizabeth McCabe towards the church.

McCann slipped in unobtrusively, finding a seat on a pew along the side wall, looking across the church so he could have a clear view of proceedings without craning his neck or drawing attention to himself. He could see Mr and Mrs McCabe at the front, standing rigid, protected by phalanxes of relatives on either side. He could see the head teacher four or five rows back, with a scattering of youngsters and their parents, friends of Lizzie and the family no doubt. The organ wheezed to a final halt and a terrible empty hush descended on the church, the pastor standing at the unadorned pulpit, his hands resting on the edge, watching for the bearers and the coffin at the door. The church with its plain, high windows and its grey granite walls seemed to concentrate the mind on the hard futility of this death, as with a shuffle of the bearers' steps, the coffin appeared and made its unsteady, awful progress down the aisle, then was gently lowered before the pulpit for all to reflect upon. Some sobs of anguish broke out, sniffles, here and there. McCann found his throat was twisted with grief, but for what? He had never known the girl and he was, God knows, no stranger to funerals of the innocent and the guilty alike. Many times he had stood in this position, mingling with the mourners, caught up in the moment, while the other half of him watched with a cold, professional eye. The people to watch would be at the front, the closest family. Not easy to detect clues in a hard country where men never cried. Even jocularity, levity did not indicate guilt as often the joking started at the door of the church after the service, or coming away from the grave at the parked cars, with the release after the dreadful job had been done. It was not easy, but McCann's eye – though stinging with a tear – was good, his observations as sharp as a pathologist's scalpel or a dentist's probe. Not always accurate, but fruitful in its generation of hypotheses.

The pastor was winding down to the end of the first psalm in the order of service:

'Surely goodness and mercy shall follow me
All the days of my life
And I shall dwell in the house of the Lord forever.'

A sigh seemed to fill the church and despite himself McCann felt soothed by the words. The pastor was a plump man, with a round, red, country face and a mellifluous voice. There followed a reading from Luke, on the resurrection of the daughter of Jairus, but McCann found the soothing moment had passed, as it always did for him when resurrection or eternal life was suggested. Death was what it was and there was no escaping that.

When the pastor had finished the reading, he began his address. McCann's eye ranged intently on the front row, picking out an unfamiliar figure next to Peter McCabe. A thick-set man, with a heavy black leather jacket draped over his shoulders against the cold. As the pastor described Elizabeth's childhood, her friends, her school, her pleasures in life, the man's head scanned slowly to left and right, as if he were seeking someone in the crowd. The pastor's voice rose.

'Friends I say to you it is written in Romans 12:19: "Do not take revenge, my friends, but leave room for God's wrath, for it is written: It is mine to avenge; I will repay," says the Lord. And God tells us in Deuteronomy 32:35: "In due time their foot will slip; their day of disaster is near and their doom rushes upon them." ' The pastor's words boomed loudly in the high space of the nave, the tall man nodding slightly with agreement. And suddenly McCann was impatient for the service to end, to push back through the crowd and out into the fresh air outside.

At the graveside he was able to study the man standing by Mr and Mrs McCabe; black gloves, black shoes, black tie, black eyes, everything seemed to be black except for his white shirt and his face, bloodless and blue-white in the cold air.

'For the trumpet will sound and the dead will be raised imperishable and we shall be changed.'

'A likely story,' he found himself thinking, suddenly impatient with the pious blether of the pastor, angry with his obfuscation of the facts of death. Then the coffin was lowered into the grave as the congregation recited, *'The Lord is my shepherd.'* But the pastor's words were carried away on the cold wind off the mountains.

When the last prayer was finished and the first sods thrown down on the wooden coffin, the crowd began to break up, stepping over to greet the bereaved parents, or making off to their cars.

McCann thrust himself forwards.

'Mrs McCabe, Mr McCabe,' he said, 'Let me offer sympathy on behalf of the Royal Ulster Constabulary.' He shook hands formally. Mr McCabe nodded. Mrs McCabe looked down. Her face was puffed and swollen, her eyes red.

'It's kind of you to come, Inspector,' she said. Mr McCabe nodded, his eyes seeming to follow the scrape of the shovel by the graveside. The second man hovered awkwardly, a step behind Mr and Mrs McCabe, until McCann offered his hand, which the man shook in a perfunctory way as if he had not expected to be included.

'Inspector, this is Wilbur,' said Mrs McCabe.

'OK pal,' said the man and nodded, his eyes not making contact but seeming to survey the mourners behind McCann with an alert cautiousness, restlessly balanced on the balls of his feet as if prepared for action. McCann noticed the tattoo, just under the cuff of the glove, and then the pigtail, tied off with a brass toggle.

McCabe's electrical business was housed in a newly built warehouse, with daffodils nodding in the breeze outside the reception. McCann shook Peter McCabe's hand, quietly solicitous, apologising gently for the intrusion.

'I'd to get away from the house,' explained McCabe gruffly. 'I'd to get back to work or I'd go crazy. Amanda's still in bits after the funeral, but her mother has come over to keep her company.'

'Aye it must be a very sad time for you all,' said McCann, as they walked through the reception with its chrome and mahogany desk with the logo of the company on the front.

'Smart place,' he said.

'We were relocated when the old place at Duncrue Street was torched. We done well out of that with the insurance, the compensation. We got a big grant from the Development Agency.'

McCabe led him through the door into the workshops and almost immediately the noise of machinery took over, McCabe shouting to make himself heard.

'We're using computer controlled lathes so we don't need so many men.' And then they were back out the other side of the workshop, into the drawing offices and up the stairs to McCabe's own office. Through the window, McCann could hear the faint rhythmic thrumming of the traffic on the nearby motorway, punctuated from time to time by the sharp whine of metal being cut down below. The office was comfortable, with a solid wood parquet floor, rather than the industrial lino he'd seen elsewhere in the plant. McCabe had decorated the walls with photos and McCann took in the images of awards and celebrations that seemed to be part of McCabe's life.

'We had the Queen's award for exports last year,' explained McCabe, seeing his interest. There was a picture of him shaking hands with the Secretary of State for Northern Ireland, smiling men in suits on the steps of Stormont.[8]

'Take a seat, Inspector. Can I get you a coffee or anything?'

'Tea would be fine,' said McCann, still standing looking at the framed photographs, several of McCabe with laughing gangs of schoolchildren on the steps of some large mansion, presenting prizes to girls in uniform.

'I'm a governor of the Peace Foundation,' he explained. 'We started it after Bill McBride was killed. Bill was our chief draftsman and he was caught in the bomb at Lisnaskea. So we figured we had to do something to stop all this madness. Started in a small way, just with sport, though it's difficult enough to find sports in common now isn't it? Then we hit on outdoor activities; that's the centre you see there, the Black Lodge at Cushendun. We did all sorts: orienteering, night walks, environmental works with the children of all denominations.'

'You think that could have made you victims?'

'Maybe.'

'Or was it that you didn't pay protection? I saw that fellow with you at the funeral. Hear tell he was at the school, picking up Lizzie too. What was all that about Mr McCabe? Why'd you not mention it?'

And at that McCabe seemed to stiffen, like he was trying to guard himself from the pain of an old wound or injury.

'I should have said, Inspector, but it's not so simple as all that. Everyone in business has the same story these days. There's every kind of hoodlum out there trying to make a quick buck.'

'There'd been threats?'

'There had. Everyone's had the same thing so I didn't give

---

8 Stormont is the Parliament building of Northern Ireland.

it much attention. Let's see, it would have been two years ago at least they first asked. It wasn't obvious; I mean no 'give us money or we'll do this or that.' No, it was subtler than that, insidious in fact. We had a few incidents of stuff being pilfered from the plant, tyres on the wagons slashed, that kind of thing. The police were just useless, I'm sorry Inspector but that's just a bare fact you can't ignore. Advised us to put up security fences, floodlights, bring in dogs. They couldn't catch the fellows that done it, they made no effort in fact, till it got so that there was hardly a week when something wasn't going wrong, like someone was at war with us.'

McCann nodded.

'And then I had a visit. Late one Friday my secretary let this fellow up to see me. He said he was a rep for some outfit that could do us a deal on armature wire. He was most insistent, said it was an offer we'd be foolish to turn down. So I let him up here and he sat just where you are now, in that exact same spot.'

They were interrupted by a discreet tap at the door and the receptionist came in with a tray loaded with tea and biscuits, cups and saucers. When she had gone and the tea had been poured, McCabe turned to McCann.

'You know I think I even gave him tea as well, come to think of it. He said he could do us a deal on security too and that he'd heard I'd been having problems. I said we were all right, that we could cope. And then he said would we be able to cope with something worse, something far worse and wasn't it better to be assured now than repent at leisure? I didn't like his tone at all, so I asked him what he meant and he said sometimes it wasn't just the firms that these people went for but the families. He asked me how many children I had. Said the conversation was a confidential one, between friends, trying to be helpful, because in the current security situation everyone had to be careful, hadn't they? I was curious, asked him how much it would cost and he mentioned a figure that was just ridiculous, that the firm could no way afford and anyway I wasn't going to pay that kind of gangster. He stood up then, like he was sad, genuinely sorry, suggested I should think about it, that he'd give me a call later in the week. I told him he'd better not bother, because my mind was made up, but I was scared of him then, the way he was so calm, like it was a sales pitch he'd given hundreds of times before. Like he was genuinely selling a service. *It's disappointing Mr McCabe*, he said, *that you can't support the people of Ulster in their hour of need, when they've supported you in your factory every week.*' McCabe's voice rose, distressed at the memory of the conversation.

'Maybe it was the worst decision I've ever made.'

'So, what did he look like,' asked McCann.

'He was like any of the fellows you'd see any day. He'd a suit on, not an expensive one, flared, bit of a stripe on it, black loafers, tassels too I think, kind of kipper tie with a flowery pattern. Kept his coat on though, a new parka.'

'His face?' asked McCann. 'What age? Anything distin-guishing?'

'Thirty something, maybe nearer forty, black hair in a kind of a quiff, brylcreemed, pocked like he'd had a bit of acne as a lad.'

'Overweight? Thin?'

'Average, I'd say,' said McCabe. 'About five ten in height,

bit of a gut on him. Jesus he was just like any salesman you'd have in here any day of the week, except for what it was he was selling.'

'Did he leave you a number? Anything you could use to contact him'

'He didn't. He just said he'd be in touch with me. But he never was.'

'Car number? Did you get his number, so you could have contacted the police, on the confidential hotline maybe?'

'I didn't think of it Inspector, I was in shock. To have the fellow there in front of you in your own office as bold as brass. And anyhow even if I'd had the foresight I wouldn't have done it Inspector on account of what he said as he was going out.'

'What was that?'

'Said it was important no one heard about our wee chat, on account of the consequences that might follow.'

'What kind of consequences?'

'He said it was hard to predict how his colleagues would react to having their quite reasonable offer of help not merely turned down, but turned against them, as if it were some kind of crime. That they might take it personally.'

'And that fellow at the funeral with you?'

'That was Wilbur. My brother.'

'Your brother!' McCann had not expected that.

'Why'd you not mention him the first time we spoke? What were you hiding there, Mr McCabe?'

'Ach Wilbur was in enough trouble already Inspector,' said McCabe almost in disgust and ran his hand through his hair distractedly. 'My brother Wilbur. That was another fine choice we made, trying to help Wilbur, trying to do things on the cheap.' McCann nodded, asked him to explain.

'Aye, Wilbur was the reason I had to take on the firm after my father died, because no one would trust Wilbur with it.'

'Why not?'

'Wilbur was always the bad boy. He wasn't really, I mean he's a good lad, but he had no sense. I was always the sensible one, the one the firm was intended for.

'Why'd you ask him for help then? I seen him at the funeral, watching out.'

'Maybe I felt guilty. Guilty about how things had turned out for Wilbur. We always tried to help Wilbur, no matter what Wilbur did.'

'What did Wilbur do?'

'Wilbur was determined to foul the nest.'

'What kind of things?'

'Oh God what didn't Wilbur do? By the time I met my wife, Wilbur had already done a three month stretch in prison. He was already getting notorious. There were photos of him in the Belfast Newsletter, that's what the old fellow couldn't take, when that happened. We were hardly like brothers at all. Wilbur was in the band, doing drugs every night, out of control and then he seemed to get in even deeper, so I nearly despaired of him altogether, until he found God, started to clean up his act. When the threats started I felt Wilbur's prison contacts could help deal with it,' he said heavily. 'You've got to understand Inspector, I was very preoccupied. That was when I put Wilbur on the case. And he wanted to help. I said it would give him something to do, make him feel important. And Lizzie got on with Wilbur. Wilbur liked kids. He was like a big bear to her when she was still young. I told him to be discreet about it, not to make himself a target. Told him to try and find out what was going on.'

'Did you tell Lizzie there'd been threats?'

'Not in so many words, just obliquely, mentioning all the trouble in the city.' McCabe stood up, paced to the window, his hand clenched behind his back.

'I could have paid them and I didn't, so you see where sticking on principle got me.'

McCann sat silently for a moment, unable to relieve McCabe's guilt.

'I can't abide these troubles. Just can't abide them,' McCabe continued angrily. 'You know I even set up the Peace Foundation with some of my own money. I got the employer's federation to contribute too. Even took Lizzie up to help at the Black Lodge. I thought it would be something on her CV, said she'd to think ahead. I thought I was doing some good.' His eyes seemed to water for a moment and he took a sip of tea.

'Aye, well, anyhow,' he said, placing the cup back on its saucer on the table so it wouldn't spill, looking away through the window at the mountain looming up behind, so McCann wouldn't see his tears.

Later that same day, McCann went down Donegall Place and into the Washington Bar, by the back entrance. Even at three in the afternoon it was more or less full. The racing was on the television, a low satisfying routine of runners and odds, repeating as if on an endless loop that would absorb the time until nightfall. He went to the bar and leant on it, hoisting himself up onto a stool, examining himself in the bar mirror as he did so. It was true he was a mess. He was letting himself go. But then that wasn't his fault, that was hers; she'd left him. If he had a decent woman, he'd smarten up a bit, but maybe he was past getting any decent women, past smartening. The barman came up, discreetly solicitous. Just right, as you wouldn't be needing a superciliously friendly little git serving you at a time like this, thought McCann.

'I'll have a pint of double,' he said. Halfway through his pint, a man in a long heavy coat slid up on the stool beside him, placed his cap on the bar and said in a not particularly friendly way: 'Well, if it isn't Mr Inspector himself. How are you anyway, you big fat cunt?'

'Not so bad Sammy, and you?'

'I've been keeping well Inspector, actually.' The big man leant across the bar and clicked his fingers at the barman, behind his head as he passed, so that he spun round in his white jacket.

'I'll be right with you Mr McGuigan. What'll it be?'

'Give us a pint of double and the same for the Inspector here.'

'Not for me,' said McCann and placed his hand over his glass.

'Gi 'im one anyway,' said McGuigan.

'I won't.'

'That's not like you.'

'I'm fine Sammy,' he said again, but the drinks came anyway, another tall glass of Guinness with the moisture standing on its long sides and a large whiskey, both resting there on the bar as they talked.

'So,' said Mr McGuigan. 'What's up Inspector? What's going on?'

His face was hard, a great white knobbly lump with a bent nose, the chin marked with shaving injuries, a wisp of grey hair splayed vainly across his forehead. A silver earring and a tattoo on his neck with the letters UVF from time to time popping up above the white collar like some depraved Adam's apple. McCann checked in the long bar mirror that McGuigan's men had not insinuated themselves into the early evening crowd, checked the two possible exits were clear. McGuigan leant forward and slid his pint across the bar, leaving a trail of moisture on the mahogany, like some sort of snail that lived down the back of drains and U bends.

'I've a wee question,' said McCann.

'A question is it?' said McGuigan, raising one hairless eyebrow, his mouth a round 'O' of satirical surprise.

'And what'll I get in return?'

McCann could see he was in good humour and knew he was a betting man.

'Look on it as a lucky dip, Sammy,' he said. 'You could get nothing or on the other hand you might get something, but you've to pay for your ticket all the same.'

'That's a good one. A lucky dip is it?' McGuigan laughed and pointed at McCann's untouched drink.

'For God's sake knock that one back McCann, then we'll see.' McCann, who'd been wanting the drink, reached for it and lashed it down his throat in one smooth gesture, feeling the alcohol hit almost immediately; that slight, dangerous slackness and lightness of mood. And McGuigan, seeing this, took a deep draw of his own drink and licked the foam from his lips and there was a moment's satisfied silence between them both.

'D'you know a fellow called Wilbur McCabe?' asked McCann.

'Wilbur?' said McGuigan, as if riffling through a large filing cabinet stuffed with McCabes of every kind.

'Big fellow, six-one, long greasy black hair, black eyes, tattoo here,' McCann touched his cuffs, showing where Wilbur had his tattoos. McGuigan seemed to search through the imaginary files, hesitating before extracting the file McCann wanted.

'What's he supposed to have done?'

'Nothing,' said McCann, then after a pause said: 'Would have been in Crumlin Road jail with some of the boys after the Rose and Crown.'[9] Since the talk with Peter McCabe he'd done a quick bit of homework on Wilbur's criminal record. 'Done a year for GBH,' he said. And then it was like watching a fruit machine pay out, that last flick of the bounce bar and the three oranges span and stopped together and illumination lit Sammy McGuigan's face as the payout began.

'Oh aye Wilbur McCabe, Wilbur! He's a good lad is Wilbur. What d'you want Wilbur for?'

'Just a wee chat, that's all,' said McCann.

'I've not seem him in a while mind,' said McGuigan, becoming crafty. 'Found God. Hear tell he's gone a bit doolally.'

'Doolally?'

'Oh aye, given up the booze.'

'Where'll I find him?'

'Celestial Church of Christ, Ravenhill Road,' said McGuigan.

---

9 The murders in the Rose and Crown were carried out by Loyalists who threw a cannister bomb into the pub, killing five Catholics.

'You're having me on,' said McCann.

'Straight up son, God can happen to anyone.'

'And McCabe's electrical?'

'What about them?'

'How are they with the fundraising for you, Sammy?'

'Fundraising?' he said innocently, as if it were a word he associated only with the likes of Oxfam and the Save the Children's Fund, flag days and the sound of collection boxes rattling in the city centre.

'I wouldn't know if those fellows give to charity.'

'Not any charity Sammy, it's your charity I'm talking about.'

'Ah now Inspector we're not a charity, we're a movement,' he said.

'And you never passed the collection box their way?'

'We may have done but they never put a coin in. I'd not say they were supporters,' said Sammy.

'I thought it wasn't voluntary,' said McCann.

'Not voluntary, no McCann, every loyal citizen should contribute, but it's up to them if they choose not to do so.'

'And take the consequences?'

'Oh aye.'

'Meaning what?'

'The takeover by Republican popery, McCann. That'll be the consequence of not making your contribution to the defence of Ulster.'

Afterwards McCann took a stroll from the bar round into one of the arcades off Royal Avenue, to his favourite shop, hoping to catch it before it closed.

'Now this one's a beauty.' He picked up the fly and turned it over and read the handwritten label:

'Crystal nymph.'

The assistant leant over the glass counter and held the fly up in the bright light, the two men leaning in to examine the fine blaze of coloured feathers that made up the lure over the cruel barb. McCann could hear the murmur of traffic in Donegall Square, but in here the sound was muffled. The shop smelt of the country; of waders and oilskin, the rods neatly stacked in the polished wood cabinets behind glass. McCann had shopped here ever since he had come to Belfast, it was something he couldn't stop and now it was something he needed to do to calm himself, to take some kind of control.

'I tried the orange dog biscuit but it didn't take,' he said, remembering his last disappointing day fishing on the river.

'Could have been the weather. You'll need the nymph on a grey day, the dog biscuit's no good. You definitely need the sun to catch the colours on it though; a fine day with high scudding clouds and the odd burst of sunshine will bring this fellow alive. Or maybe it's thunder and lightning you need; the bold flash of red kite feathers and the double hook beneath. Or how about the general practitioner, there's something a wee bit more fancy to coax them? I had a fellow in who'd been up on the Bann above Carnroe and took a five pounder with one just last week Inspector.'

'I'll think about it,' he said. 'Have you not something special?'

And he described the weir, the river, the fall of the light and water and what he wanted to achieve when he next went down there to fish.

'I'll see what I can do for you anyway Inspector. Is Thursday all right?'

'Thursday's grand,' said McCann.

Chapter Seven

As the Land Rover climbed up the hill the engine whined, struggling to lift the armour and the five officers inside past Ulster flags and burned out cars, a row of shops: a bookies, a chip shop, a ladies hairdressers, a pub turned fortress, a newsagents and sweet shop. At the top of the hill they swung round one last roundabout and stopped in front of a terrace of grey painted houses. As they got out a ferocious barking erupted and McCann nodded to two of the men to cover the back. The driver stayed with the vehicle while he walked up the path to Wilbur McCabe's house, Thompson at his side. This high up the morning rain in Belfast had turned to sleet. He could smell the coalsmoke in the air, blown in the wind. Ignoring the bell, he rapped loudly on the door, turned his back to it, looking briefly down off the hill at the straggling outskirts of the city dropping away to the lough below. Up above the mountain was obscured with a low mist. There was no reply, so McCann rang the bell and a tinkling rendition of 'abide with me' filled the air.

'This is a waste of...' he began to say, just as the door opened and Wilbur McCabe stood there. He stared blankly at McCann for a moment, intelligence numbed by television and the sleepy fug of the interior. McCann flashed his card and Wilbur showed them grudgingly into the low-ceilinged living room. The room was spotless; there was a yellow tiled fireplace in which smoked a low fire. China horses pulled brass hay-wagons on either end of the mantelpiece and a big painting of a ship at sea in a storm, tossed on green breaking waves hung against the floral wallpaper. Through the window he could see his men at the rear, their green police capes turned up against the weather.

'That's a terrible day,' said McCann, rubbing his hands.

'Aye its bitter right enough,' said Wilbur, manoeuvring awkwardly in the small, cluttered living room.

'Any chance of a cup of tea?'

'The missus is out,' said Wilbur. McCann let the awkward pause in conversation extend until Wilbur relented and offered to put a brew on, allowing McCann to sit down, sinking into the armchair till his legs were almost horizontal, like he'd been sucked in.

Wilbur busied himself in the kitchen. While they waited in silence, Thompson idly lifted the lid from a brass pot on the mantelpiece, peered at an open letter on the dining table, till Wilbur came back with a heavy brown teapot and three mugs.

'Well now,' said Wilbur, settling at the table and pouring the tea. 'I'd been expecting you fellows to come and call. Will you be taking sugar and milk Inspector, or having it neat?'

'A wee drop of milk and three sugars.'

'Right you are Inspector. And for the sergeant?'

'I'm fine sir,' said Thompson.

Once the mugs had been distributed and the first sips taken and the necessary commiserations for the loss of his niece given, McCann said: 'They say you were some kind of bodyguard for Elizabeth McCabe? Is there any truth in that?'

'Bodyguard!' McCabe choked on his tea, put the mug down, wiped his mouth with a large white handkerchief. 'A bodyguard! Who told you that? You're away with the fairies McCann. I could no more be a bodyguard than fly to the moon. I've been on the compensation these last years, on account of my leg.'

'Compensation? For what?'

'My leg was twisted at the Europa.'[10]

'You were at the Europa?'

'Aye, in the bar the last time and was thrown through the window by the blast Inspector. I was up in the Royal for three months. I've two nine-inch pins in my leg. Can't carry no weights neither. And you say I'm a bodyguard. Fat lot of good I'd be, pal.'

And he eased himself upright, over to a shelf by the door, pulled out a tin tea caddy, rootled out the necessary papers to show McCann.

'That's OK Wilbur. That's OK, I believe you. But why'd Peter say you were there to protect Lizzie? Maybe it seemed like you were, the amount of time you were spending with her. Waiting at the school gates for her and all. What was that about? Why couldn't Peter or Mrs McCabe collect her? Why couldn't she make her own way home come to that?'

'I loved that girl, Inspector, I would never have left her in harm's way.'

'You've got previous Wilbur. I've looked at the records.'

'Previous? I was in the wrong path Inspector, but now

10 The Europa Hotel was the most frequently bombed hotel during the Ulster troubles.

that's behind me.'

Wilbur reached inside his leather jacket and pulled out his wallet, bulging with dog eared paper and took out a cutting; six lads with matching jackets, check shirts, guitars.

'We were big back in the day Inspector,' he said. 'Down the Ards peninsula, Bangor, Warrenpoint, even did gigs in the Republic too, down to Drogheda, we were well known.'

Something stirred in McCann's memory. Perhaps maybe he'd even been there, seen them play.

'Did you play Armagh?'

'Of aye, those police dos. I remember them right enough. We had some wild times then, eh Inspector?'

McCann remembered those kinds of nights too, uncomfortably; the big country and western sounds, the girls round the door in their short skirts.

'But this kind of thing it's way off my territory. Would you look at me for God's sake Inspector!'

Maybe it was because of that, because he couldn't get what he wanted now, because she was taunting him and he got frustrated, thought McCann. And looking over at Thompson, he could see her with her calm blue-grey eyes on him, perhaps thinking the same thing.

'The day she went missing, where were you? Did you meet her Wilbur?'

'I was in the Prince till nine, played brag in the back room. And by the way pal, if you're here in an official capacity I'll be wanting my solicitor present.'

'There's no need for that. This is just a preliminary chat. It's off the record. If you've nothing to hide you'll not be wanting a solicitor. Who'd you play brag with anyway?'

Wilbur reeled off a list of names. They'd be the names he always used, thought McCann. They'd be solid, reliable, they'd back him up like in a rugby scrum.

'Give us a clue, then Wilbur, for Christ's sake man, someone killed your niece. Why'd they do that? Why would Peter ask you to meet Lizzie? What was that for?'

Wilbur shook his head, lit a cigarette.

'Was it protection? He thought you could protect her because of the people you knew, the circles you moved in. You were in the Crumlin Road with Lenny Murphy and Willy Moore. You were in there with UVF royalty,[11] you could call in favours, couldn't you?'

Wilbur hung his head.

'I should've been able to keep her safe but it didn't work out that way at all Inspector.' And suddenly McCann found himself almost sorry for Wilbur.

'Who made them pay then Wilbur? Who took your niece?'

'I don't know.'

'Don't know or won't say, Wilbur, which is it?'

'It's don't know.'

McCann's mouth was dry from the cigarettes he'd smoked, from the air in the small hot room. He took a slurp of his tea. He could feel the pressure in the room now, that he could be closing in on something, though Wilbur would no doubt say afterwards that he'd been harassed and falsely accused. On impulse McCann reached inside his coat and pulled out an envelope, spread the photos out, one by one on the table before

---

11 Lenny Murphy and Willy Moore were members of a notorious paramilitary gang that became known as the Shankhill Butchers. They were held in Crumlin Road gaol.

McCabe, amongst the empty teacups.

'This is what he done to her,' he said.

McCabe glanced down, looked away. Thompson seemed shocked, seemed on the point of moving forwards to stuff the photographs back in their envelope. McCann could see the effect it had. Maybe he'd gone too far? But he could not read that sudden pulling back of Wilbur's head. Was it revulsion, or was it unwillingness to look at the consequences of something in which he had been involved?

'I don't know nothing about that,' said Wilbur. 'The person that done that must be some kind of animal.'

'Who? What person?'

'I don't know. If I find him he's a dead man.'

'Are they out looking for him now, Wilbur?'

'What would you expect?'

'Are you scared of someone Wilbur? Is that it?' And suddenly the anger overwhelmed McCann so much that he began to raise his voice, had to stand up, pace to the door, light a cigarette to calm himself, his hands shaking.

'I'm not scared, Inspector. I trust in the Lord. He can come for me now and I'll die a happy man.'

'But who'll come for you if you tell on a nonce?'

'I tell you I don't know any nonces. If I was you Inspector I'd be looking elsewhere. It's the work of the devil, Inspector, he's the power. The great Satan, the purple hand of Rome, Inspector, some Romish plot to enrage us so we lose control. Have you been up the seminaries? There's more perverts there than I've had hot dinners,' said Wilbur darkly. 'That's more like it. That's where you should be looking Inspector.'

'If it's not Wilbur and maybe nothing to do with protection rackets, what other possibilities do we have?' asked McCann, back at the office.

'How do we know it's not Wilbur? He'd the easy access,' said Thompson.

'Just speculating sergeant, that's all,' said McCann. Clarke had joined them for the review, slouched in his chair, fiddling with a ruler on his desk, flipping it over and catching it like a bored schoolboy.

'Maybe some fellow on the Republican side, tit for tat,' he said.

'I doubt they'd do that on a girl that age,' said McCann.

'Maybe some fellow that's gone over the edge. Or a unit that's taken losses and wants to hit back.'

'Maybe its personal,' said Thompson. 'Someone who's lost a wife or brother or son?'

'They'd need the means, they'd be organised. Look at the van they used.'

'I could take you over to Castlereagh,' offered Clarke. McCann was surprised.

'They'd maybe know more than we do. Maybe have some ideas.'

Later, in the afternoon, McCann and Clarke drove past the City Hall and down to the river. The centre of town was crowded with shoppers taking advantage of the first days of spring, with long queues at the security barriers and the bus stops. People were clutching bags of purchases from the sales, wrestling with buggies and children. Overhead the sky was blue, swept by the occasional light fluffy cloud. McCann tried not to smoke, leaving the half empty packet of Weights shut in the glove compartment and the lighter zipped inside his jacket pocket, edging forwards through the traffic down to the docks and the bridge over the river. Beside him Clarke lounged in boots and denim, a dark jacket with the collar up around his face, his head almost below the level of the dashboard, his eyes scanning, always watching, left, then right, without his head moving at all. McCann wondered how he did it, without his eyes working loose in their sockets, without giving himself a migraine, wondered how he could remember the faces and then spot them in the crowds. It stood to reason though that murderers would be out looking for bargains just the same as anyone else, that they'd be tempted out from their burrows on the Falls and Shankill by the promise of a new suit for a wedding or funeral, a parka to replace one that'd had to be burnt or disposed of. Even children's clothes because these fellows might have children of their own. Maybe the two sides would cross each other's paths in C and A or Anderson and Macauley, buying underwear, or ties?

'Maybe he's getting a suit?' said McCann.

'Who is?'

'The fellow that done it.'

'Aye, could be,' said Clarke.

'Or socks?' said McCann.

'Swimwear, beach towels,' suggested Clarke. 'Getting ready for summer.'

Then they were crossing the river and McCann could see the brown water down below and the channel ferries tied up after the night's crossing, before they joined the road out to Castlereagh.

'This boss of yours,' asked McCann. 'Is he any good?'

'He's the DI running the ANT[12] teams,' said Clarke. 'Unmarked cars, surveillance. He knows where people are.'

'It's not where people are that we want to know about,' said McCann. 'It's maybe where they aren't that's more interesting. We want to know of anyone dangerous who's vanished. Who's gone on the run or been disappeared.'

The Special Branch had their HQ at Lisnasharragh, a sprawling headquarters complex just off the main Castlereagh Road. It was a nondescript part of town, merging easily into comfortable suburbs of neat red-brick houses with views over the Black Mountain and the city below. Not wealthy, but well-built and loyal, the union flags fluttering here and there in the breeze to mark the territory.

The lights at the junction were at red as McCann approached, so he accelerated past them into a gap in the traffic and up to the steel gates, past the sangar,[13] inside the barbed wire to the security area where they got out and stretched. The barracks was like a small city of office blocks, Nissan huts, manicured grass and flowerbeds with crocuses nodding in the breeze. As their papers were checked a white Saab came up, driven by two young men in civilian clothes, unshaven, dressed like Ulster lads except for the heavy jackets, the expensive shades. They stared at McCann. Clarke nodded to the driver.

'They're from the ANT team,' he said.

'Bit conspicuous, aren't they?' said McCann. 'Shades like that. The eejits will get themselves killed.'

---

12 ANT teams were unmarked police vehicles used for anti-terrorist surveillance operations.

13 A sangar was a fortified sentry post.

They drove through to the back of the barracks, around several roundabouts. There were grey police Land Rovers everywhere, armoured cars, a squad of men in PE kit. It was all a far cry from C Division where McCann spent his days.

'Jesus this place has grown,' he said.

Inspector Munton was a slim fellow with close cropped hair, thin arms, dressed in the faded denim some of the branch seemed to favour. His office was utilitarian; new fake wood office furniture, a glass fronted cabinet with some shooting trophies, a couple of framed photos of rugby teams. He was friendly.

'McCann is it? C Division? You'll be with Deevery?'

'Aye,' said McCann, settling himself down on the seat he was offered.

'And Clarke, good to see you again son. Hope the Inspector's treating you right.'

Why wouldn't I be, thought McCann?

'Very well sir, yes,' said Clarke. 'It's been interesting getting back to Division.'

'I bet it has,' said Munton, chuckling.

McCann explained what they wanted and Munton listened politely.

'Yes, I see,' he said. 'You want to find someone who might have been involved in the murder of Elizabeth McCabe, maybe a paramilitary with a record for that kind of thing?'

'Or someone unstable enough to be tipped over into an uncontrolled revenge attack,' added Clarke. 'They could have disappeared, been disciplined. Maybe one of your informers who seems to have just dropped off the map?'

'Even if I knew that I'd not be able to tell you that kind of information,' said Munton. 'I'm very sorry but you appreciate that the identity of our informers must be kept a hundred per cent secure. If ever their identities got out they'd be dead men,' he said.

'And you can't trust the RUC is that it?' said McCann.

'That's not the case McCann. It's just intelligence protocol. It's basic, elementary practice.'

'OK, but then can you tell us if you've lost anyone, without telling us who they are?' said Clarke, reasonably.

'You've just to nod or say yes. It's not that difficult,' said McCann.

'Sadly, we lose men all the time, for one reason or another. We work in very difficult circumstances. There are always risks.'

'We are the police force. We look for people. We're maybe better able to find them,' said McCann. Munton thought for a moment, then went over to the filing cabinet, unlocked it, slid out the top drawer, extracting a file.

'We've this fellow. Fintan O'Connor. He's been on the run for four months now since the attack on Belleek and we'd like to find him.'

'Previous?'

'Oh aye, from a strong Republican family down in Tralee, father was Dermot O'Connor, OC in the Kerry Brigade of the IRA. Close family. His sister was killed in a drive by shooting on the Falls, UVF raked the bar they were in with machine gun fire. But he'd already started before that. Fintan was charged with membership of a proscribed organisation when he was sixteen, messed about running their training camps down there in Magilikuddy Reeks.' He slipped over four or five blurry black and white photographs taken with a long lens, of a group of armed men advancing across a field, each succeeding photo more enlarged than the last, till the lead man came into view. Just a young man, with long hair, a sergeant Pepper moustache, walking at the head of the group.

'When he came out the Gardai[14] think he was involved in a raid on the post office in Monaghan, raising funds for the cause. The gun they used was also used in the attack at Beleek three months later, so either Fintan was there or his gun was and he was an accessory. We hear tell he's a wild lad.'

'Anything sexual, anything inappropriate?'

Munton paused.

'Nothing. Oh no nothing like that at all Inspector,' said Munton, and McCann wondered why the denial had been so emphatic.

'So where is he now?'

'Last heard of he was freelancing with the Newry Active Service Unit. But he could just as well be in the city along with a couple of hotheads from Londonderry.' McCann was impressed with the detail they had on the man, the thoroughness and confidence that came from it.

'How do you know?'

'I can't tell you that, but let's just say we have people inside the IRA in Newry.'

'They could be lying to cover him,' said Clarke. 'If they wanted to take the heat off him they'd put it about he'd gone AWOL.'

'Or if they wanted him for something special,' said McCann.

'Let's not speculate,' said Munton. 'I mean he could maybe

14 Gardai – the police force in the Republic of Ireland.

have been executed, punished. Anything could have happened to him.'

'Or he could be the fellow that done Elizabeth McCabe. There'd been enough provocation hadn't there? More drive by shootings like the one that killed his sister. Maybe he just blew up, took out the first person he could find that would even the score? The Republicans are turning to tit for tat, hitting our people where it hurts hardest, isn't that right?'

'Well the wildest units, maybe. Newry, South Armagh. You could away to Long Kesh[15] and see if you can get any sense out of the commander there, that's if you want to waste your time,' said Munton, looking at his watch like he felt they were wasting his time too.

They drove out of the city, past the Lisburn Road barracks, protected by a high palisade of wire mesh and a heavily fortified sangar. Clarke was silent and thoughtful as they turned at the ice rink at Balmoral and headed under the railway line up to the motorway.

'Best let them know we're coming?' suggested Clarke.

'Give him a shock,' said McCann, accelerating up onto the slip road and into the motorway traffic coming out of Belfast, then out into the fast lane, past the Dunmurry Industrial Estate where Peter McCabe had his business. A shower of rain had lifted but the hills to the right were still dour. It would be a week or two until the new grass would show through.

'Music?' suggested McCann.

---

15 Long Kesh (Officially known as Her Majesty's Prison 'The Maze') was the prison where most paramilitary prisoners were detained. It was opened in 1971 and closed in 2000.

'OK,' said Clarke, reluctantly.

And so they drove out through Lisburn with the soft sounds of the Beatles playing 'Good Day Sunshine,' pulling off the motorway at Moira, through the checkpoints, till they could see the watchtowers of the prison up ahead.

'Here we go,' said Clarke, the car pulling in through the first of the security gates, a tunnel of corrugated iron on either side, into the security area. Both men got out, McCann showing their papers, lighting a cigarette while the car was checked, the boot opened, the seats pulled up, the underside checked over, bonnet opened, four or five squaddies wordlessly going about their business. Then they were through and once the car was parked, they were searched; the linings of the coats, the inside legs of the trousers, the soles of the shoes, scanned with a metal detector.

'I'm Inspector McCann from C Division RUC and this is DS Clarke,' explained McCann. 'We are here in respect of the murder of Elizabeth McCabe.' He hunched his chin into the collar of his coat, stubbed his cigarette, anxious to get on.

The Republican Commander was tall, almost bookish, with gold rimmed spectacles and large, soft brown eyes. His beard was well trimmed; it was almost as if he had stepped from some well stocked private library for a moment to share a few words with them.

'Gentlemen,' he said and sat down carefully, crossing one tweedy leg over another. McCann noticed the shoes too, highly polished, heavy brogues, such as a fellow would wear on a country estate.

'You'll have heard of the murder of Elizabeth McCabe,'

said McCann, without any other preliminaries.

'Aye,' said the Commander, his eyes twinkling with a certain perverse amusement that was hard to read.

'She was fifteen years old and found off Kennedy Way in Andersonstown. She'd been hit over the head with an iron bar, killed outright.'

'I was very sorry to hear about it,' said the Commander. He briefly scratched one eyelid, as if dealing with an itch, but otherwise sat perfectly calm and still, his hands clasped in his lap, legs slightly apart.

'And she'd been sexually assaulted,' said Clarke. The Commander's eyes widened.

'I didn't know that,' he said.

'We were wondering if there's anyone you'd have had cause to discipline for the likes of that,' said Clarke. 'It'd be off the record. We've all an interest in stopping this kind of thing,' said McCann.

'Oh come on boys I think it's the other side you'd best be looking at for that,' said the Commander.

'Fintan O'Connor,' said McCann suddenly. The Commander blinked, like some kind of salamander on a rock out of some nature film, the bit before the tongue lashed out for its dinner.

'Doesn't mean much to me,' said the Commander, idly scratching the back of his neck.

'His father was OC in Kerry. You'd have known him.'

'Would I?' The Commander smiled a beatific smile.

'Could this have been tit for tat?' asked McCann.

'We don't do tit for tat,' said the Commander.

'Not even for the Miami Showband, the Strand Bar?' said

Clarke, naming the most recent infamous massacres where the Commander's community had been targeted by paramilitary gangs.

'We'd only do military targets,' said the Commander. 'We're a disciplined force. You should know that. The police and their UVF killers certainly, major economic targets, but not young girls.' He smiled, enjoying the provocation.

'Military is it?' snapped Clarke. 'What about Bloody Friday,[16] what about the civilians killed then?'

'Collateral damage,' said the Commander. 'I regret that as much as you do. If the security forces had acted appropriately, no lives would have been lost.'

'C'mon McCann let's go,' said Clarke. 'I've had enough of this shite that I can take,' and he stood up, pushing his chair back. The Commander stood up calmly, offered his hand which Clarke ignored.

'Nice of you gentlemen to call,' he said.

Back through security they took their belongings from the lockers and walked out into the fresh air, McCann lighting up, looking up at the small patch of sky visible above the tall corrugated steel walls of the prison.

'Fat lot of use that was,' said McCann.

'He does not do sectarian killings,' said Clarke. 'That's their line now.'

'Oh aye,' said McCann. 'And it's only Protestants that have sex with underage girls.'

---

16 Bloody Friday was one of the most controversial episodes of the Troubles. On 21st July, 1972 the IRA exploded twenty bombs in the space of less than two hours in Belfast, killing nine people and injuring over one hundred civilians.

Chapter Eight

They'd taken over the school office as a dressing room for the reconstruction and McCann hovered around while they applied make-up and got the girl ready. Looking down the path that led to the school gates McCann could see the camera crew setting up and the glare of their lights, a UTV van and a couple of technicians in anoraks laying cables. Finally, the door opened and the girl playing the part of Lizzie walked out with the head teacher shepherding her. He had to admit they'd done almost too good a job, almost to the point where it would scare her schoolmates that they'd think they'd seen a ghost. He wished them good luck and they walked together out to the school gates. He could see the Poet getting out of a squad car, putting on his cap, shaking hands.

'All set up, McCann?' The Poet asked, then the head teacher introduced the girl and they took some preliminary camera shots.

'I'll just need to freshen you up a bit sir,' said the make-up girl, pushing the Poet's cap back on his head so she could dab pink powder on his forehead. 'And a bit on the lips too.'

'I'm not having lipstick,' said the Poet, rubbing at his face with the back of his sleeve, leaving a smear of pink there and then trying to brush that off.

'No leave it on, you need it sir,' said the make-up artist. 'Are you ready?'

'Aye,' he said, putting his cap back on and looking into the camera as the lights came up.

'I'm Superintendent Jones,' he said. 'And I'm in charge of the investigation into the murder of Elizabeth McCabe. This murder threatens our community and the RUC will take whatever steps are needed to root out this evil malevolence from wheresoever it may have arisen.'

'Could you start with a bit of detail perhaps sir,' said the producer. 'Like the time of the murder, the route she took and of course you'll need the confidential number too.' The Poet paused, looked around for McCann, snapped his fingers.

'McCann give us the gen,' he said irritably, pulled out a pen and paper, noted the facts, started again when the red light showed the camera was filming.

When the Poet had finished, he lit a cigarette and smoked it with his back to McCann while the technicians crouched over the monitor, running back the interview.

'Sorry, we've got some snow on the tape. We'll have to run it again,' said one of the technicians.

'Snow?' said the Poet. 'It seems a fine enough day to me.'

Early the next morning McCann pulled over at the bakery on his way in. There was the smell of fresh bread, the baker stacking split tin loaves straight from the oven, a queue of workers by the till for sliced sandwiches, schoolgirls and lads for iced buns. McCann bought a bag of them, six or seven, lined up like soldiers in a white paper bag, paid and left the shop.

'Morning girls! I brought you some refreshments.' He brandished the bag as he entered the call centre. The room was hot and airless, though several fans whirred across the desks where the operators sat, stirring the dead air around, turning the corners of the pages of the call logs. The supervisor unhitched her headphones and looked at him with glassy-eyed tiredness. He could hear the others murmuring into their microphones.

'Anything come up yet?' he asked.

'Busy after the show,' said the woman. 'We've two or three calls that match up with a girl getting into a car with a man.'

And she handed him a clipboard of sightings, contacts following the reconstruction that had been shown on the previous night's TV.

McCann sighed. He'd get on it, but as like as not the girls would have been picked up by their parents, because that was what happened at the end of the school day and it'd be difficult to separate out the normal from the abnormal.

'There's just this one maybe you should take a look at. It's a bit off the girl's route though. Fellow saw a girl arguing in a van up the Crumlin Road.' And she handed him the slip of paper with her notes on it.

'Thanks for all of that,' he said, folding the call sheet up and tucking it carefully into his jacket pocket. 'And don't forget those buns.'

The shop was cluttered with newspapers and magazines, a counter full of chocolates, a big fridge freezer of lollies and ice creams and behind the counter a wall of jars filled with sweets. A gang of schoolchildren were arguing how to spend a few pennies, under the impatiently watchful gaze of the shopkeeper. He nodded at McCann to suggest he ignored the kids, but McCann said it was OK, he'd wait as he wasn't in a rush, feigning indulgence for the youngsters' indecision. When the last of them had scuttled out, he produced his warrant card and the fellow came out from behind the counter, pulled the snib on the door and flicked the card saying 'open' over to 'closed'.

'I did see that girl,' he said. 'The one on the television.'

'Which one?'

'Out of the Academy.'

'Elizabeth McCabe?'

'Aye that's the one. I was out the front bundling up the unsold papers for collection when I saw this van pull over just up past the shop. Thought it was odd as no one would stop up there with the double yellow lines and there's nothing much left to stop for anyway '

McCann had thought the same, as the shop clung to the end of a terrace of poor Victorian houses, mostly boarded up awaiting demolition. Cars on the road outside generally raced nose to tail from the City Centre to the security of the suburbs.

'At first I thought the fellow had a flat, so I thought I'd go and help.'

'Leaving the shop?'

'Aye just for a minute. It wasn't far and I could have always dropped back. But in the end it wasn't necessary because the fellow drove off.'

'What kind of van?'

'Hard to tell. Ford maybe. I'm no expert, me.'

'Colour?'

'Kind of greyish white, like some kind of dark milk.'

'And what happened when you got up to the van?'

'Well that's just it. I saw the girl in the passenger seat.'

'How did she seem?'

'Well I think she was trying to open the door or something.'

'And the driver?'

'I couldn't see,' said the man. 'Parka jacket, I could see the sleeve holding her arm.'

'Then what?'

'They drove off as I came up to them.'

'Which way?'

'Up towards the mountain,' said the shopkeeper. 'I'm sorry there's not more I can say.'

'Well, I'm grateful to you,' said McCann, picking up another packet of Weights, a Mars Bar and the evening's Belfast Telegraph.

'Terrible business,' said the shopkeeper, handing him his change. McCann wasn't sure if he meant the murder was terrible, or that business was terrible, or even that his own investigation was terrible.

'We've no more description to go on?' asked Clarke. 'No one else that saw them?'

'Nothing more come in as yet. What about the branch then, Clarke? They got anything we could use?' asked McCann. Clarke shifted in his seat.

'There's a surveillance point on the top of the base at Taggart Memorial Hall. They've spotters up there.'

'Spotters!' said Thompson, looking up from her desk, where the contents of Deevery's folder of paedophiles lay spread around.

'They've telephoto lenses. They're looking out for targets moving up and down to the Falls and Andersonstown.'

'See if they can get us anything Clarke, can you?' asked McCann, glancing down at Thompson's desk.

'I've been going through the records,' she explained, handing McCann the beige folder that had contained details of sex offenders, now much thinner than when Deevery had delivered it. 'I've taken out anyone that's in custody or died, or moved away and these are the fellows we're left with.'

'You could put Deevery onto that,' suggested Clarke. 'Seems like the kind of fellow that could put a bit of pace into things?'

'What, like a bowler in cricket?' said McCann.

'Knock them for six.'

'He'd certainly do that,' said McCann.

'The Superintendent's said he wants the pace stepped up,' said Clarke.

'When did you speak to the Poet?' McCann was surprsied, angry even, that Clarke had been going behind his back, had the brass neck to tell him in front of Thompson. The last thing he needed was people in the investigation floating ideas with the Poet, raising new doubts in his boss' mind.

'He's worried about Lisburn apparently. Explaining it all to the Army and the Minister. Up there they already think that RUC means 'Really Useless Constabulary and the longer we're on this the more they'll think that. We need Deevery on board. We've not got the men for it otherwise, McCann.' Clarke was animated, leaning forward, his arguments reasonable. McCann nodded impassively, like he was made out of granite, seated on his desk with his sleeves rolled up, his thick arms crossed.

'I could follow up on the van on my own. Do the garages,' offered Thompson. 'Honest, Inspector, it's just routine.' McCann hesitated, knowing that nothing was routine, or if it was pretty soon it could turn into something else when you were least expecting it. He didn't want that happening to her.

At home that evening McCann went through into the kitchen. It seemed more of a mess than usual; unwashed plates from the previous night still on the counter and a frying pan full of congealed fat alongside his whiskey glass and the empty bottle, the bin overflowing onto the sticky linoleum floor. He looked in the fridge. There was a half empty can of beans, half a pack of sausages going hard and red at the edges, in the breadbin a sliced loaf with a faint whiff of mould about it. His stomach rumbled and he made himself an instant coffee, lashed in a couple of big spoonfuls of sugar, went back out into the living room. It was cold, the heating off, the big glazed windows looking out on the gravel path, a certain darkening in the street outside. Then the phone rang.

McCann cradled the receiver and immediately he heard the pips going he relaxed, guessing who it would be on a Friday night. He could even imagine his mother fumbling the hoarded coins out of her purse, laying them out on the ledge in the phone box before putting the first one in.

'Hello Ma,' he said, wondering why it had taken so long for her to stop the insistent beeping of the pips. Maybe she'd dropped a coin and had had to stoop to find it on the floor. But then there was a surprise.

'Michael?' said his father's voice. 'Michael is that you?'

'It's me. What's up?'

'Your Ma's taken a turn.'

'A turn? What kind of turn? Have you called the doctor?'

'Aye.'

'What is it?'

'It's a wee stroke. Nothing serious.'

'When did it happen?'

'Tuesday.'

'Tuesday!'

'She didn't want to worry you,' said his father.

'So how is she now?'

'Poorly.'

'What do you mean, poorly? Where is she? Is she at home?'

'Aye, the doctor says she's to rest, that it'd be better if she was in the hospital but she refused to stay, so they've got her in bed here.'

'I'll be down,' said McCann, thinking hard, wondering could he extract a day or half a day from the investigation, racing on in his mind to the next steps that would be needed.

When the photograph from the spotter came the next day, the evening sunlight was reflected back off the windscreen of the van and at such a distance it was hard to make out if it was Lizzie. The figure at the wheel had his face shrouded by the hood of his jacket, like death itself, all features invisible. The only thing they could agree on was that he was a big man, if he was a man at all.

Chapter Nine

The phone rang at half past four in the morning, just as McCann had plunged into a dry-mouthed half-sleep. The phone's volume seemed to increase as he became fully conscious, its jangling call amplified by the bare walls and hard floor. He stumbled from his bed.

'McCann,' he grunted into the receiver. There was a silence then on the line, a nuisance call maybe, a real nuisance at that time of the morning and McCann was about to slam the phone back down when a voice said:

'You gentlemen will find something of interest down the back of Donegall Avenue.' And then another silence, as if the fellow was listening for the effect and then a click, just as McCann was wondering was he awake or still in a nightmare.

The torchlight played along the narrow alley into the back yards, with their coal bunkers and bicycles, clotheslines overhead, the houses still mostly dark. McCann advanced cautiously, a constable from the night shift a pace behind him. At each bunker he paused, played his light inside and moved on, until at the third bunker he stopped. The girl was lying awkwardly across the coal, discarded and crumpled. He waved the constable forwards.

'This one's been shot. See there? Just below the hairline? Back of the head.' And he shone the torch to illuminate the glistening blood matted into her hair, the collar of her blazer, flowing away into the coal beneath.

He scrambled over the loose coal to take a closer look, leaning forwards, put out his hand gently as if to touch the girl or comfort her, then he seemed to sag, overbalanced and put his hand on the coal to steady himself.

'I'd leave that, sir,' said the constable. 'Till forensic gets here.'

McCann stumbled out of the coalhole, sucked in the dawn air outside, lit a cigarette, his hand sticky with blood and coal dust.

The police radio burbled in the Land Rover at the end of the alley and McCann ran back.

'They've a name sir,' said the driver. 'Last night on the missing person's we've this girl. Mairead O'Shea, fifteen years old. Failed to come back from school last night, no explanation, no warning. Division have been on it checking she's not staying with friends or anything.'

'Description?' snapped McCann.

'Five four, brown hair, wearing a green blazer.'

'That'll be the one then.' he said. He swung out of the Land Rover and back over to where the constable was standing guard, his torch beam silhouetting him. McCann stood behind him for a moment, deep in some kind of private prayer or reflection.

They spent a few minutes running police tape around the crime scene, tying it off on drainpipes and fencing, closing the alley to intruders until they heard the sound of a vehicle approaching along the road, the high whine of another Land Rover at speed and the squeal of tyres as it turned into the alley and stopped, the doors opening, disgorging the forensic team with their swabs and cameras. Dawn light was now filtering into the darkness at the back of the terrace. He could hear the first train of the day passing behind the wall, taking commuters into Great Victoria Street station, the lights from the carriage windows flickering back against the brickwork of the houses. McCann lit another cigarette, briefly calmed by the ritual of it, the routine.

'Well, here we are again Inspector,' said the forensic officer cheerily. He noticed her pink wellingtons, a pleasing familiarity in a bleak scene and the fact that she had applied lipstick with cruel haste. She paused before him, carrying the two aluminium cases that held her equipment.

'My picnic boxes!' she cried loudly. 'Take me to the cadaver McCann.'

McCann led her round to the bunker where the body lay. She stumbled on the loose coal underfoot, tugging at McCann for support.

'Ah yes. Now look at that would you?' Her torch beam flickered around, illuminating the ghostly face, the tangled limbs, then a glint of something on the girl's school jacket.

'What?'

'Saint Louise's,' she said. Her light illuminated the school crest, the flash of gold embroidery.

'Shot too,' she said, her torch playing round the walls of the bunker, across the coal.

'We've got a pair. One Protestant, one Catholic. It really is tit for tat this time. We'd best clear everything out just to be sure there's no cartridges, stray rounds. You've your shovels with you, McCann? That'll keep you fit Inspector, a good bit of shovelling eh?'

'Job for the constable here,' said McCann. He turned and walked back up the alley. As the light improved he could see more clearly that the yards were set with wet stone slabs, some of them closed with rotting gates, others open to intruders. Along the back of the alley there was a high fence of railway sleepers topped with barbed wire decorated with fragments of litter, newspaper and plastic bags that dropped down to the railway cutting on the other side.

He called to the constable to follow him, led him round to the front of the terrace. It was still early morning, with the curtains mostly tight drawn as McCann knocked, quietly at first, then loudly.

The door opened and a woman in a pink dressing gown and curlers appeared, half asleep, slightly stooped, then stepped back at the sight of the uniforms.

'Missus, did you know you've got a body in your coal bunker,' said McCann.

'A body! Ah dear God!' She rubbed her eye with the back of her dressing gown sleeve, the sleeve pulled over her hand like a glove to keep herself warm there on the step.

'Did you hear anything at all, last night?'

'I never heard nothing,' she said. 'I'm on the sleepers and you could drop a bomb on me and I'd never know.'

On the drive back to Division McCann radioed in that Clarke and Thompson should be brought in, so they'd be ready to go once he returned. When he arrived he found them already there; Clarke nursing a steaming coffee in a Styrofoam cup and Thompson yawning, still brushing her hair, wiping away traces of make-up.

McCann explained the situation.

'Sammy McGuigan behind this one, do you think? Maybe can't control his men? An eye for an eye for Lizzie McCabe maybe?' he asked Clarke. Thompson seemed shocked; her eyes wide

'You'll get nothing out of him Inspector, you know that,' said Clarke.

'Let's bring him in anyway,' said McCann. 'Give him a roasting.'

'Who reported it?' asked Thompson.

'I had a call, at home,' said McCann.

'At home! What did it say? Anything that'd give us a clue. Any password. Anything?'

'Just the address.'

'Man or a woman?'

'Man.'

'We'll have the tape,' said Clarke.

'The tape! Of what?' McCann was astounded. Of course he should have known the military would have enough resources now to listen in to whole sections of the city. Maybe that explained how Clarke had been so quick off the mark, despite the unsocial hours.

'So how did they get my number?' growled McCann.

'It'd only be the Superintendent and the desk. It'd be restricted, wouldn't it?' said Clarke.

'You boys have the contacts. You could have passed it on.'

Clarke shifted uneasily, not liking the way McCann had of

suddenly turning the temperature up. Typical of the uniformed branch, believing that the Special Branch knew everything, and weren't fussy about what they did with that knowledge.

'Why would we do that?'

'You tell me. Who gave them murdering bastards my home phone number? It's bad enough taping my calls Clarke, without every psycho in the country able to call me at any time of day or night.'

'Aye well,' said Clarke, not knowing how to respond. 'That's a bit of bad news for you right enough, Inspector.'

McCann sent Thompson out to the new victim's school, leaving Clarke to contact the branch for the tape of the call, while McCann himself dealt with the parents. Thompson turned off the ring road at Divis Street, past the Royal Victoria Hospital, then into unfamiliar territory, past a large church with the tricolour flying, a bookmakers, a bar, another tricolour, up the Falls Road. She knew Saint Louise's from the old days; she'd driven past it many times in the days when you still did. She'd seen the girls at the Ulster athletics competition and her daughter had raced and jumped against theirs. It was different now to be visiting under these new circumstances and she checked the road ahead for any sign of danger, any hold-ups where she might be recognised and maybe pulled from her car.

Apart from the large crucifix over the entrance lobby, there was little to distinguish St Louise's from her daughter's school or Elizabeth McCabe's, so recently visited. There was the same familiar murmur from the classrooms, the same polish on the parquet floors, the same bare corridors. The head teacher's office was in a modern block with aluminium windows, but the paintwork was faded, peeling here and there.

'Hello, Mrs Hagan,' she said. 'We spoke on the phone. I'm so sorry to be bringing bad news.'

'Dreadful. Its just disgusting isn't it?' said the head teacher after she'd absorbed the information, anger and sadness distorting her face. Thompson sat at the head teacher's elbow while she sifted through the records of progress for Mairead O'Shea's last year; the too frequent circles in the register rather than attendance ticks, the report of the family liaison officer. But now the records would end – there would be no more ticks, nor circles in the register for Mairead O'Shea. She recovered school photographs, a list of the girl's contacts and her teachers and set in train the steps needed for a reconstruction, as McCann had instructed her. A parallel investigation, a different girl.

While the headteacher made coffee in the small kitchen off her study, Thompson looked around the walls, adorned with pictures of the school and its achievements: lines of girls in their athletics outfits, arrayed in ascending order of size, all smartly turned out and smiling, the photos of visits by the bishop, shaking hands, pictures of girls abseiling, canoeing, in some place with a wide sweep of water, a distant glen with a great stone house behind. The head came back with two steaming mugs of coffee, placed them quietly on the table, unwrapped some biscuits.

'That's the Black Lodge. We send some of our girls there. Sometimes it helps to settle the more difficult ones,' she said.

Thompson finished around lunchtime. Leaving the school gates she saw a group of thick-set men, smoking, standing as if waiting for a bus. She felt a sudden pang for her own daughter – would she be safe? A desperate need to know if she was. And a certain gratefulness to the men too, a feeling of re-assurance that what they were doing was better than nothing while there was a madman about.

She returned to Division. McCann was curt, abrupt. It hadn't been easy at first at the O'Shea household, he said, as they'd had to get a military escort up to Turf Lodge. Then they'd been beset by questions and accusations from the distraught parents: 'Aye they were regular folk, but Shinners[17] nonetheless. Devastated all the same though. We'd to get the priest along but he refused to go in the Saracen, said he'd make his own way, so they all ended up in a taxi together.'

'And nothing you could see? No clues or leads out of that?'

'Nothing we could see. How about yourself, up at the school?'

She explained to them about Mairead O'Shea's record, the arrangements she'd started to make, handed over the photographs.

'There was just one other thing that might be relevant. There was a photo on the wall of the girls at some study centre up in the Glens. The "Black Lodge," it was called. She said they'd sent some of their more difficult kids up there, including Mairead.'

'Jesus why'd you not tell me that before?'

'Because I've only found it out, Inspector.'

---

17 'Shinners' – a colloquial expression to describe supporters of Sinn Fein. Turf Lodge was a strongly Republican area and McCann would normally have been met with suspicion and hostility regardless of the purpose of his visit.

'We'd best get out there then,' said McCann, setting his coffee aside, shrugging on his coat.

But out in the corridor they encountered Deevery, tried to brush past him with a nod but he gripped McCann's arm.

'Did you hear the news?'

Deevery stopped quite close to him, turned to face him.

'What news is that Deevery?'

'There's been another murder.'

'I know,' said McCann. 'We're on it now.' Deevery's eyes flicked over to Thompson, then back to McCann. He stepped back out of McCann's space and McCann could see his hard, bright eyes calculating a bit, seeming to assess whether it was decent to ask the obvious question regarding the girl's religion, but McCann saved him the trouble.

'She's Catholic,' he said, imagining he saw a tiny hint of repressed satisfaction there as he told Deevery what he knew of the body in Donegall Avenue and the taped message, all in a low murmur, Deevery nodding and saying, 'Yes, yes,' like he was pleased that some kind of order had been established, that justice had been done, like it was what he would have expected. But when McCann had finished, nothing came back; Deevery was silent, expressionless.

'Well, I'm grateful to you McCann, for sharing that with me,' he said at length and they walked together to the end of the corridor, through into the old barracks, the first bit of natural light coming in, together with the noise of rain on the skylight roof and the scent of wet streets outside. But the passageway was hot, with a blaze of TV lights, microphones waving in the air, the blinding white light of flash photography, a crowd moving towards the conference room. Up ahead he could see the Poet with his cap gleaming with gold braid like an Indian headdress.

'McCann, McCann,' he called, waving at McCann over the heads of the crowd, indicating he should catch up. Drawn along in the melee, McCann found himself swept to the raised table at the front, blinking in the harsh light. His throat was dry and he looked around for water, but the table was bare except for a single microphone and the RUC shield. The Poet nodded to him and gestured to one of the plastic chairs laid out there for the senior officers to meet the press. He recognised the reporters from the Irish News, the Belfast Telegraph, the Newsletter, the Irish Times, the crews from RTÉ, UTV[18] and the BBC jockeying for position with their lights and microphone booms. He could see Deevery, standing at the back expectantly, leaning against the wall, like a good show was about to start.

'Gentlemen, I'm going to be quick,' the Poet addressed the crowd. And he outlined the barest facts of the new murder, such as McCann had rung through to his office. The first question came from the Irish News.

'Can the Superintendent explain what steps are being taken for the security of the Catholic community in the light of a further sectarian murder?' The Poet leaned towards the microphone in a practised way, explained that the security of both communities, Catholic and Protestant, was his primary concern and the concern of all of his officers. He had, he said, been in discussions by phone that very morning with the minister regarding the strengthening of army patrols at school

18 RTÉ – Raidió Teilifís Éireann, the national broadcaster in the Republic of Ireland. UTV is Ulster Television.

gates. There was a slight altercation at that, with the fellow from the Irish News questioning how the army could be responsible for security at the same time as carrying out murderous attacks on the very people it was meant to be protecting. The fellow from the News Letter demanded to know why patrols had not been strengthened after the murder of Lizzie McCabe, and was it not just another case of the Protestant community being left unprotected while nothing was too good for Catholics and Republicans?

'One question at a time please gentlemen,' said the Poet, holding his hands out, palms flat as if to calm troubled waters. But the reporter from UTV butted in to ask if there was not a concern that some kind of paedophile was on the loose and that girls wouldn't be safe until he was caught. The Poet passed the microphone down to McCann's end of the table.

'Inspector McCann would be best placed to answer this,' he said. McCann coughed and looked out at the audience but the TV lights shone straight into his face, as if he were looking into the headlights of a fast approaching car. He cleared his throat again and looked directly ahead into the lights.

'I'm afraid it's too early to say much about that,' he said, to a brief murmur of disquiet. Nonetheless, it was true. They'd nothing; no firm leads or suspects, no motive, no opportunity, and they'd barely started on Mairead O'Shea. The fellow from the News Letter was incredulous: 'It's four days since the murder Inspector and nothing to show for it?'

'There's matters I can't discuss at this stage,' mumbled McCann, but the Poet had called the microphone up to his end of the table to say irritably that the Inspector's investigations would be prejudiced if their full details were known. But now the fellow from the Belfast Telegraph was on his feet: was there a danger that a new, darker turn was being taken by the troubles, with tit-for-tat killings of children and young people on either side? Someone else shouted: 'What advice has the Superintendent for the parents of young girls?' The Poet glanced at his watch and smoothly drew the press conference to a close. McCann tried to get away through the crowd. But the Poet lunged after him.

'Ah McCann, McCann, just a moment Inspector,' he said and laid his hand with a certain firmness on McCann's arm. 'There's someone I'd like you to meet.' And McCann found himself ushered over to greet two men in suits, one of whom he vaguely recognised from television.

'This is George Irving,' said the Poet. 'He's the Secretary of State's new PPS.'

'Pleased to meet you, sir,' said McCann, clicking his heels as if standing to attention. Perhaps it was too much of a caricature of obedience though, because the Poet glared at him and said: 'The Minister's very concerned about this new development and its potential to escalate matters. Is there anything more you can tell us Inspector?'

McCann knew how to handle them anyhow, the Chief Constables and the Deputy Chief Constables, the Superintendents and their assistants. You'd to keep below the radar, not be noticed, keep them out of your space, out of your head. But not too much, so they'd not suspect that's what you were at. If you weren't careful they'd dig down demanding reports, briefings, giving you 'support' and generally getting in the way of investigations.

'Maybe there's something *you* can tell me,' he said instead, his irritation overcoming his better instincts.

'In what way Inspector? What do you mean?' asked the fellow from the ministry, smoothly polite.

'Speak up McCann, Mr Irving's a busy man,' snapped the Poet.

'We all are,' said McCann, digging himself deeper in.

'Are you implying that the government is involved in some way, that there's something we wouldn't share Inspector?'

'Not implying anything at all, sir. I'm just asking that's all, if there's any context.'

'McCann will have to pursue all the hypotheses of course,' said the Poet, turning to Mr Irving in a lighter, explanatory tone, gently touching his arm, trying to move him forward away from McCann before more damage could be done, giving McCann one last backward glare as the two men inched away through the crowd.

'Well, that went well didn't it?' said Deevery, pushing past McCann. 'You're still the boy at the diplomacy, aren't you?'

And then Thompson was at his side.

'Rather you than me, Inspector,' she murmured, then leant in to him and asked: 'Are we still going out to the Black Lodge?' But Deevery had moved closer, overheard what was said.

'That'll be a nice wee trip for the two of you then,' he said, and winked knowingly.

Chapter Ten

The Black Lodge was a fine Edwardian mansion with high gables and granite walls, reached by a driveway that curved up to the front door. Several cars and a Belfast Education and Library Board bus were already parked there when McCann and Thompson arrived, inhaling the heavy sea air, mixed with a scent of pine, as they climbed the steps to the front door. The director was waiting for them.

'Inspector McCann? We had your call. A terrible business. We'd been expecting that someone would be down when we heard about Lizzie McCabe and now that other girl too.' The director was a slender man, tall, in a tight grey suit. 'It'd be normal for you to check up and yes we're ready for that, we're anxious to help in any way,' he said, rubbing his hands as if to warm them, then ushering them inside, standing aside to let Thompson go first.

The corridors inside were wide, with parquet floors, leading into open, light filled rooms with high windows looking out over the forest and the sea. They paused to observe two groups of schoolgirls in one of the rooms – the green and the blue of their uniforms like tribal markers – preparing a role play, two girls blushing and hesitant rehearsing their lines before their peers. It was a strangely peaceful sight, thought McCann, to see the girls together, to hear the low murmur and shuffle of a class, the sense of learning under the quiet tutelage of their teachers.

'The students usually stay a few days, sometimes a full week. In the holidays we have longer courses for some of the hard cases,' explained the director.

'Hard cases?'

'We've had all sorts out here; kids from the Ardoyne, Creggan, Tiger Bay.[19] School refusers from both sides. It's the biggest part of our work. We've money from the government to try to keep them in school and out of the way of the troubles. You'd not believe some of the stuff they get up to. Sometimes they can't even be in the same room together, without straight away they're into spitting and fighting and name calling.' The director smiled weakly, seeming both bewildered and amused by the behaviour he'd seen.

'Did you know Lizzie McCabe or Mairead O'Shea?' asked McCann. The director paused in the corridor.

'Lizzie McCabe, yes, she was the daughter of Peter McCabe, one of the founders, so we saw quite a bit of her. A lovely girl, an able girl. Peter would bring her down from time to time for her personal development. Said it would look good on her CV to be doing something for the community. It's terrible for Peter that this has happened.' He trailed off, unsure how to finish, jiggling the keys for his office in his hand.

'And Mairead?' prompted Thompson.

'Mairead was here too. It was just too much when I heard

19 Ardoyne and Creggan are Republican areas, Tiger Bay is Loyalist. The mixing of groups from different sides of the sectarian divide would be unusual.

that another of our girls was killed. You'd wonder when this madness will end.'

They settled in the director's office, a large room on the first floor that would originally have been a sitting room, with splendid views of countryside and sky and the sea beyond. A narrow corridor led through to another office from where they could hear the sound of a typewriter. The director stuck his head round the door and asked that tea and coffee be brought through.

'This won't stop the work of the centre though Inspector. If anything, the fact that girls who have been here may have become victims of the troubles will make us redouble our efforts. We're committed to carrying on,' he said, as if he'd been able to work out what his line would be for the future, to make sense of what had happened.

'So how many staff would you have?' asked McCann.

'Academic staff there's myself and four others – on secondment from the schools on either side. And then we've quite a few sessionals, who come in when there's a lot going on. Over the summer for example.'

'We'll need a list of everyone and their CVs and contact details,' said Thompson, a notebook already out on her knee, pen in hand.

'And the management of the place? How's that done?' asked McCann.

'There's a board, a joint board with both communities represented.'

'We'd like a list of the members.'

'And volunteers?' asked Thompson.

'We have visiting speakers who come up, representing the

different communities. We like to see the place as a neutral meeting place. It's a very new initiative, supported at the highest levels in fact.'

'We'll need a list of them too,' said McCann.

'And your other staff? Groundsmen and the like? Who have you got?' prompted Thompson.

'Dear God you don't think anyone here could be responsible?' asked the director. 'It'd be the end for us, given our mission and what we're trying to achieve.'

'It's routine in these cases, sir,' said McCann. 'We look at all the contacts the victims had.'

'Of course, everyone's checked out,' said the director. 'We wouldn't let anyone in who had any kind of criminal convictions, or even rumours of any of that kind of thing. You can check in the records.'

He seemed flustered, but maybe only on account of not understanding the filing system or where the records were kept, thought McCann, watching him hovering around the administrator as she opened and closed the drawers of the filing cabinets, while Thompson studied the notice boards with their photos and schedules.

'It's not a school though is it, so there wouldn't be a requirement for checks, would there?'

'Not a requirement as such, but we make a point of it. You can see for yourselves,' said the director, pointing at the growing pile of staff records emerging from the copier. 'You'll find us clean Inspector. It's just unthinkable anyone here could have been involved.'

McCann came over towards him, sat down casually and began to riffle through the first of the records, his foot swinging to and fro. Thompson drifted up on the other side.

'And there's been no trouble has there, of that kind?' she murmured, almost casually.

'Allegations?' suggested McCann. 'I mean your paperwork may be hunky dory but that could mean nothing in the scheme of things, couldn't it?' he said, dropping the file back on the pile. The director turned to him: 'Aye well when you run a place like this there's always a risk of allegations from either side,' he said.

'What kind of allegations?'

'Nothing of any substance that's not been dealt with, Inspector.'

But McCann was looking at one of the photographs on the wall, of a gang of teenage girls in a disorderly line, grinning and laughing, some on their knees, others with their arms around each other, a group of smiling men at the back.

'Would any staff have access to the records of the girls attending?' asked Thompson.

'What kind of records?'

'Home addresses and the like?'

'No, not that I'd know of.'

'But they'd know the schools?' said McCann.

'Oh yes, they'd know where each group came from.'

'And it'd be easy to find the school. Maybe wait outside? Find the girl?'

'It would,' admitted the director.

They spent the rest of the afternoon working on the staff rotas and schedules, identifying when the two girls had attended the Black Lodge, using the photocopied information, backed up by a few questions to the administrator. By the end of the day they had the dates when Elizabeth McCabe and Mairead O'Shea had been at the Lodge, the names of the staff who had worked on their courses and the visiting speakers who had come in.

'There's two teachers that worked with both girls.' Thompson leaned over and read out the names, marked with a cross, her head close to his.

'McAllister and O'Leary. Let's take a look.'

But McCann hardly seemed to hear. Instead he was studying the list of visiting speakers.

'Sammy McGuigan,' he said. 'Can't be the same man, can it? What are they doing inviting Sammy up here?'

'There's not a lot of space in the staff accommodation, Inspector.' The teacher offered McCann a battered armchair with a blanket over it to hide the bulging springs. In front there was a low table set with unwashed mugs and a teapot, an old brown television propped on a milk crate with a clothes hanger stuck in the back for an aerial, a cheap bookcase overflowing with books, leaning forward as if it was about to topple over.

McCann settled himself in the armchair and Thompson remained standing while Mr O'Leary perched on his bed, its springs creaking, gesturing awkwardly for Thompson to join him, but McCann stood up apologising and offered her the armchair which she refused, remaining standing instead. There was something random, temporary, about the room as if O'Leary expected to be not long there, but then that was the bachelor life, wasn't it? No pictures, photographs, other than some old dried flowers in a frame over the mantelpiece that might have been put up to hide peeling wallpaper. There was a clothes rail too, but the hangers carried only O'Leary's suit and some shirts, with a couple of pairs of brown shoes scattered underneath.

'What can I help you with, Inspector?' O'Leary asked.

'We're investigating the murders of Lizzie McCabe and Mairead O'Shea and believe that both of them attended courses you taught here at the Black Lodge.'

'Aye I read about Lizzie McCabe. That's a dreadful business. And now this other girl that's in the news tonight. Jesus Inspector you'd wonder what's going on, wouldn't you?'

O'Leary was a callow young man, turning thirty, the words pattering out with a smooth southern brogue, while a slight smile played about the corner of his lips.

'How well did you know Elizabeth and Mairead? Do you remember them?' asked McCann.

'Elizabeth? I remember her well' said O'Leary, 'But Mairead, well I'd need to think.' His eyes seemed to shift, become unfocussed, as if searching in his memory for a girl he had difficulty recalling. McCann slipped the two school photographs out on the table, side by side. Almost identical except that Lizzie McCabe's head was angled slightly to the left and Mairead O'Shea's to the right, both with their expressions innocently composed for the school camera.

O'Leary looked down, tapped Lizzie McCabe's picture.

'This one, everyone knew her. She was one of the volunteers from the Academy and came down with her father from time to time. Lively girl, had her own opinions.'

'Meaning?' asked McCann.

'I shouldn't speak ill of the dead, Inspector. None of us should.'

'Aye but if there's something relevant Mr O'Leary, you should tell us all the same,' said Thompson.

But O'Leary's mouth had become a thin hard line, his lips bloodless.

'And Sammy McGuigan?'

'Sammy who?'

'A visiting speaker from the UVF.' But before McCann could continue, O'Leary burst out: 'I never saw no one of that name Inspector. To be honest I couldn't tell you. We've so many courses coming through it's more than enough to just stay on top of the teaching.'

'And afterwards? After the courses. In the evenings? What did the girls do?'

'Well there was a television room, a games room. After supper they'd often be in there. It was in an annexe behind the old stable building.'

'Did you ever go up there?'

'No, I'd had enough of teaching all day, though I'd sometimes watch the news and that'd be it.'

'We'll need to see that annexe,' said McCann.

A narrow, concrete path led around the side of the accommodation block, past the bins, to the annexe, then turned into a well-worn track as it entered the woods, the ground slippery with rain between the rhododendrons. After a hundred yards or so the pathway opened out into a clearing occupied by an old Nissen hut, made of corrugated iron, the grey paint peeling on it.

'This isn't our finest asset. We've been meaning to do something about it for a while now,' O'Leary said, fiddling with the keys in the padlock that held the bolt on the door.

Inside the room was cold as if the windows had been opened for a long time to blow away the smell of something. The wooden floor was well worn but clean, a makeshift stage and the loudspeakers for some kind of sound system at one end, a kitchen area at the other by the door, stacking chairs arranged in a semicircle around a large TV.

'There's not much to see,' said O'Leary, standing by the open door jingling the keys in his hand.

On the way back through the wood McCann trailed behind and let O'Leary and Thompson turn the corner together. He flicked open one of the bins. Beer cans, a whiskey bottle, someone's old shirt that had been used for cleaning lay inside. He put the lid back, wiped his hands, looking around at the woodland which seemed to have drawn in closer while they'd been at the annexe; the glossy green leaves, the rhododendron flowers blooming in orange and red.

The other teacher came down the stairs to meet them, pushing a shock of blond hair from his forehead. Though it was midday, McAllister was still in his dressing gown, wrapped tightly round his thin body, dark bags under his eyes, his face pale. McCann introduced himself and Thompson. McAllister shook hands at the foot of the stairs, his hand pumping McCann's enthusiastically when he heard the purpose of their visit.

'I'll help you any way I can, Inspector,' he said, ushering them into a common room, a smell of fresh coffee in the air, newspapers scattered across the table. Thompson settled in her seat with her notebook and pen, while McCann handed the photographs to McAllister.

'Lizzie first; academy girl, fifteen years old and Mairead, same age, St Louise's.'

McAllister examined the pictures.

'You were on duty when Lizzie McCabe and Mairead O'Shea were here. The weeks of 9th February and 12th April. Before they disappeared,' said McCann. 'Is that right?'

'I was,' he said, fingering Mairead O'Shea's photograph. 'This one was from St Louise's,' he said. 'It's a rough school.'

'How was she in class then?'

'Fine with the Republicans, of course she would be. We'd a nasty wee fellow in to speak to the girls as I recall, with a face like a ferret, thin, like he'd not had a decent bite to eat for weeks. The girls lapped it up. The brutality of the Brits. He'd got a slide show up. Very technical it was too. Women disfigured by rubber bullets, children bandaged, photos of the army kicking in doors, armoured cars outside schools, all the usual Republican palaver.'

'And how did they take that?'

'Well you could hear a pin drop. The fellow could have been a recruiting sergeant for the IRA. And afterwards the girls were all over him. Could he tell him how they were organised? What could they do to help? Did they know so and so and what had become of him? I doubted how useful it was.'

'Can you remember the fellow's name?'

'Ah now there you have me Inspector. O' something or other, some typical…'

'Fenian name.' Thompson completed his sentence for him. 'Like O'Reilly for example? We've had the lists of speakers and there was a fellow called O'Reilly up here at the time.'

'Maybe,' said McAllister.

'Was there anything inappropriate there, between him and any of the girls?'

'Inappropriate? Well he was friendly and with the girls crowded round him it would've been a temptation.'

'And did he give in to that in any way you saw?'

McAllister was silent.

'What about the evenings?' McCann prompted.

'It was a bit awkward in the evenings, so we tried to break the ice with a few games, some music and dancing.'

'And alcohol?'

'Aye it got a bit wild sometimes.'

'Wild?' said Thompson, sitting forwards.

'I raised it with the director, in point of fact.'

'It must have been something serious or you'd not have done that,' said McCann, watching McAllister closely now, like a vicious hawk that had seen a weakness in one of its prey.

'Would the girls have been in uniform, Mr McAllister?' asked Thompson, changing tack.

'Depends on the school they came from. We like to encourage mixing, informality. A uniform's like a flag, it can cause problems. But then some of the girls would take it too far the other way if they were let out of uniform. We'd a dress code.'

'A code?'

'Aye. No short skirts, crop tops, high heels or boots, that kind of thing. No make-up. But the girls could be very competitive.'

'Competitive?'

'Trying it on.'

'With you? Was there any of that?'

'Absolutely not Inspector. I've my position to consider. I've a girlfriend of my own.'

They slipped out, thanking him. McCann felt they'd done a good job, had made a good team together. If Thompson had been a fellow he'd have said as much, maybe clapped her on the back, but well that would maybe have been misunderstood. All the same he felt appreciation for what she'd done. The two of them together had made a better job of it than if he'd been alone, or God forbid with Deevery in tow. Outside, McCann smiled, tapped out a cigarette till Thompson pointed to the no smoking signs, but McCann lit up just the same.

After saying goodbye to the director, they went down the steps to the car park which had emptied while they had been interviewing, so only the director's car and their vehicle remained. The evening was darkening, a cool, moist breeze off the Irish Sea rustling the tops of the trees, where the crows were fighting noisily for position. McCann walked round to the driver's door and stopped.

'Ah God,' he said. 'We've got a flat.' The wheel was right down on the tarmac, the tyre scrunched underneath. He bent down, touched the side wall, where a sharp cut had been made along its length. McCann straightened up, looked around. The only light in the house now was in the director's study. The field beyond the car park fell away to the river and the trees beyond, the ground in-between lost in deep shadow.

'Who'd have done that?' said Thompson, coming up beside him to take a look.

'Could've been anyone,' said McCann. But there was no one in sight.

McCann opened the boot, got the spare and the jack and

wheel wrench out from under the carpet, rolled the spare wheel into position, leaning against the bonnet, turned to get the jack to find that Thompson had already found the jacking point and was starting to raise the car.

'Did you put the handbrake on?' she asked. 'You get the wheel nuts off Inspector before I lift it any further.'

He'd got the wrench on them but the nuts had been put on in the garage by some mechanic with a power tool. He jumped on the wheel wrench with the full force of his boot but the nut wouldn't budge.

'Here,' said Thompson, 'Let me help.' And she came up behind him, put a hand on his shoulder.

'Now, let's jump together, Inspector,' she said, and the two of them fell on the wrench until the nut began to turn with a screech.

They drove back along the coast road, around great looping bays with cliffs behind, succeeding one after the other, giving wide views out over the sea. It was a clear evening, the water dark and driven with small even waves. As they swept through each bay, the view would turn and change with the curve of the road, first south into the Irish Sea, then north up towards Scotland. McCann could see a car ferry from time to time, plodding out from the harbour at Larne. At each bay it was slightly further out from Ireland, with a faint buoy of black smoke at its chimney and a line of lights along the deck. Then they were in Larne, a huddle of mean grey houses spread out along the road to the ferry port, an abattoir, a queue of cars waiting for the next ferry. They stopped at a level crossing and the boat train pulled in, its carriages half empty, rocking and swaying over the points. The girls would have come this way, not knowing what was going to happen, he thought.

'Give us a fag,' he said. Thompson tapped him out one, lit it and passed it over. McCann sucked the smoke down greedily.

'Jesus, Emily,' he said. 'I'm going to get the fellows that done this if it's the last thing I ever do.' And realised he'd used her first name.

'What happened in them parties, dear?' asked Thompson. The girl was seated on a low sofa in the head teacher's office at St Louise's, her knees prominent with the scabs of fresh scrapes on them, a pair of dirty white socks and scuffed shoes, a skirt a size too large and a school jumper a size too small. She had lank brown hair clipped back with a pink hairgrip over one ear and very pale skin. She shifted in her seat like some kind of wild animal straining at the leash.

'Tell us what happened after you finished for the day.'

There was a silence. The girl's mother was as large as her daughter was thin, wrapped in a red coat that she'd refused to take off, wellington boots on her feet. From across the table Thompson could smell stale sweat, tried to not let it affect her.

'Missus d'ye mind if I smoke,' asked the mother.

'That's fine,' said Thompson and waited while she rummaged in her handbag, pulled out an empty packet of ten Sovereign and crushed it up and threw it on the table between them, rummaged some more until Thompson reached into her own bag and offered her one of her own.

'Rothman's? That's nice,' said the woman, lighting up, drawing deeply on the smoke. The girl's face was turned away.

'So after supper, where did you go?'

'We went to play games.'

'What kind of games?'

'There was a pool table. But we played some kind of word game.'

'Scrabble.'

'Could be.'

'And who'd be there?'

'There was Mr O'Reilly.'

'Anyone else?'

'Another fellow. From the other side.'

'A Protestant?'

'Aye, he was…' And here she made a shy gesture in the hope her mother'd not be offended, to indicate he was overweight.

'They were together?'

'No, on different nights. They'd not get on.'

'And was Mairead there?'

The girl nodded glumly.

'Was there anything inappropriate at all that you saw? Anything involving touching?'

'Blind man's buff.'

The mother turned sharply towards her. Thompson had the impression that if she'd not been there there'd have been a slap dealt out.

'Who played that?'

'Mr O'Reilly and Mr McAllister.'

'Did Mairead play that.'

'We all did.'

'Did you enjoy it?'

'No. It was stupid. I went to bed.'

'And Mairead stayed?'

'Aye, she did.'

'And did Mr O'Reilly touch her at any time?'

The girl looked down, ashamed. Her mother nudged her shoulder.

'Tell the sergeant.'

'He touched her down there,' she said, putting her hand between her legs.

Chapter Eleven

It was a dirty morning, the sea in the lough flattened by rain, pale mud-coloured water merging with the mud of the flats at low tide. McCann wanted to be in early, to move forwards now there was at last a direction to the enquiry. But there'd been an edict that the Land Rovers were no longer to be used except in an emergency to collect him, in view of the risks, so he'd booked a cab from the right kind of firm. The driver was a silent, small man in a stained red car coat, unshaven who smoked constantly as he drove, making McCann want to do the same. There was a roadblock on the Shore Road and the delay made him impatient, angry with the routines of the military; opening car boots lackadaisically, going through the motions while time ticked away. By the time he'd reached division he was already late for the meeting he'd called with Clarke and Thompson. He went up the stairs two at a time and arrived out of breath and sweating to find Deevery ensconced in his chair in the office.

'Don't mind if I sit in on this one?' he said. Clarke was already there. The two men had been chatting together, stopped when McCann entered. Thompson was at her desk, going through the notes of the previous day and looked up. She told him about what the girl she'd interviewed at Mairead

O'Shea's school had said, the allegations against O'Reilly.

'O'Reilly? Give us all his description again,' said McCann.

She reached for her notebook, riffled through the pages, licking her fingers, rattled off the description given by McAllister and the girl.

'About thirty-five, slim, short sandy hair. Put up by the Republicans as a speaker at the centre. Seems like he may have liked the girls.' McCann let her take the lead. After all it was her work that had given them the clue and she deserved the credit for it.

'Anyone know this fellow?'

'Likely he's a Sinn Fein councillor, if he's in the public eye and they're letting him speak at the Black Lodge,' said Clarke.

'Sinn Fein IRA,' said Deevery, 'Two sides of the same coin. What were they doing letting a fellow like that near children?'

'They wanted them to hear both sides. Sammy McGuigan's been out there too,' said McCann.

'Sammy!' said Deevery. 'Ah come on McCann, Sammy'd not be involved in that.'

'Maybe he was doing his bit for the Peace process,' said McCann, like he was a comic delivering a deadpan punchline. But Deevery didn't see the joke.

'There's fun and games going on out there,' said Thompson.

'What kind of fun and games?'

'Scrabble, Blind Man's Buff.'

This time Deevery let out a great bellow of a laugh.

'Come on, love, since when is playing Scrabble a crime?'

McCann was on the point of backing her up against Deevery; there was something about the Black Lodge that didn't feel right: the isolated location, the faint air of disorganisation, the odd juxtaposition of Sammy McGuigan and this Sean O'Reilly, from opposite sides of the conflict yet both seeming to have had access to the girls, on different days. But he held back because there still wasn't enough that was solid to go on and he didn't want Deevery seeing him backing her up, though his instinct made him want to so strongly it almost hurt.

'Bleak Lodge? Isn't that one of Dickens' greatest works? Mr Gradgrind and all that? Marvellous stuff!' said the Poet, stepping down from his desk to join McCann in the romper room.

'*Black* Lodge, not Bleak House,' McCann corrected him. 'It's a study centre at Cushendun. Both the girls went there.'

'And you think it could be involved in some way?'

'It's not just a coincidence. We've some suspicions of impropriety. We're on it now.'

'Good, good. It's important to have a direction of travel rather than just tootsy-footing about McCann.' But then a cloud seemed to pass over the Poet's expression and he clicked his fingers as if trying to recall something from the whirling fog between his synapses.

'Black Lodge? The Black Lodge, McCann? Now half a moment, before you go rushing in there like Perseus on his winged charger. Wasn't that the place that was opened last year with all that fanfare by the minister? "A new beginning" or something like that didn't he say, bringing young people from both communities together? Though goodness knows for the life of me I can't see how you could have an old beginning, can you McCann?' And the Poet walked towards the half-opened door to the corridor where he kept his secretary wrapped in scarves against the icy draft.

'Deirdre could you pop your lovely head in here for a moment,' he said.

Deirdre appeared in the doorway, hesitant to enter until the Poet brought her in.

Yes, she remembered the opening of the Black Lodge, she said, because her husband had been with the minister on special protection there. He had told her all about it; the minister had cut the tape, there'd been speeches from both communities, handshakes and there'd even been a fair to middling reception, judging by the quality and quantity of the drink that had been available.

'Ah now McCann you see the detail that a woman's eye can bring to things, illuminating the scene for us when we just have some dull headline recollection, but dimly perceived, yes.' The Poet tailed off, for a moment seeming to forget the purpose of his enquiry.

'Yes, yes, well thank you Deirdre and maybe you can close the door on your way out while McCann and I discuss the implications.'

With the door softly closed behind her, the Poet took up his customary position on the throne in the romper room, looking down on McCann, with one foot in a highly polished brogue and loud paisley sock jiggling distractingly.

'Y'see McCann, the minister seems to have, wisely or un-wisely – it's not for us to say – pushed his boat out on this one. He'd be a very disappointed man if his initiative turned out to be a dead end. Sorry, let me rephrase that. Let's call it a blind alley. I'll have to think about this one. Just leave it with me will you?'

McCann hesitated, on the point of arguing. The Poet was

famous for delay. Decisions, he would say, came of themselves like magic when you least expected them; like a bolt of lightning through thunder clouds, presaging some grand clearance in the weather and sunny days beyond. But he hadn't time to wait for that so he stood up and murmured: 'Very good sir,' in a tone that meant the opposite.

On his way out, McCann paused by Deirdre's desk to collect his leave card.

'I'm having tomorrow off. Got a few wee things to do.'

'Anything nice, Inspector?'

'Away out of this place,' he said, as if that were nice enough.

Thompson came back from lunch and found the office deserted, with no sign of Clarke, Deevery or McCann. She looked around on McCann's desk for his diary, amongst the ashtrays and unwashed mugs, the clutter of paper. Nothing personal there, which was unusual for an Inspector, unless you counted a couple of lead fishing weights and a couple of flies in their Perspex boxes. No clue where he was or what he was doing. No clue of a life outside or any relationships or family. She bent to look in the drawer, but stopped herself before opening it. Frustrated, she went to the window and looked out at the grey courtyard below, where she could see a man in overalls supervising a smashed Land Rover being winched off the back of a low loader. She tapped the window to get his attention, opened it to speak to him when he looked up.

'You got a minute?' she shouted down.

'Could do. Depends what for.'

'Help me out on a visit?'

'What kind of a visit?'

'Repair yard. Resprays maybe.'

'How long would it be?'

'Depends,' she said. 'Need some advice.'

Tom Biggar made a show of looking at his watch, but really he was pleased to see a female officer that needed his services, so he wiped his hands and agreed to accompany her.

They had checked a couple of repair yards before they reached Alpha Motors. The firm occupied part of a disused railway yard and the track leading to it was crammed with cars and vans in various stages of reconstruction; wings or bonnets missing, or primed and taped for spraying. As Thompson walked up, Biggar bent here and there to look into an engine compartment, or to check the quality of the paintwork on a newly sprayed vehicle.

'Barley Mow,' he said, wiping the beads of rainwater from the bonnet of a van by the entrance.

The sliding corrugated doors of the garage were shut, but the padlock undone. From inside they could hear the high whine of a spray compressor. Thompson pressed the bell by the door and a loud jangling was followed by silence as the equipment was turned off and a fat man in stained overalls slid back the door, wiping his hands, his belly bursting from between the buttons.

Thompson showed her warrant card and they stepped inside. The workshop walls were hung with car doors and wings in various stages of repair. Tins of paint, spray equipment, panel beating rams and shapers for metal, grinders, sheets of fibreglass and resin lay all around. It was like an Aladdin's cave, she thought. Or Fagin's den, because as she looked around a lad of no more than fourteen glared from underneath a van, skinny and lithe, his face lit by the glare from an inspection lamp.

'We're looking for a couple of stolen vehicles.'

'Let me stop you there missus,' said the fellow. 'There's no stolen vehicles come through here.'

'I'm not saying there is, Mr...'

'Malone.'

'But we'd like to have a look around.'

'What for? You'll not find any stolen vehicles here.'

'Then you'll not mind if we take a look.'

'You might need a warrant.'

'Oh aye we can get that. But it'd save time all round if you'd let us have a look. Is that an MK1 Cortina you've got there? Not seen one of them in a while.'

'It is that.'

'I had one of them but could never get on with it. Mind if I just have a look,' said Biggar and went over to where the car was jacked up, borrowed the inspection lamp from where it hung, flicked it on and shone it up into the engine compartment, noting the place where the filestrokes had neatly taken off the engine number. When he straightened up he gave Thompson a quick nod.

'Who's the owner of this place?' she asked.

'The owner?'

'That's what I said. I assume it's not you?'

'Jesus no, I just work here that's all.'

'There's not a Mr Alpha then?'

'There is not.'

'So who manages the place?'

'There's a fellow comes in to do the books.'

'What's his name.'

'Gerry.'

'Gerry who?'

'Just Gerry. Comes up from Belfast regular.'

'How regular?'

'Once a month.'

'We'll need to see the books,' said Thompson. 'Make sure everything's in order.'

Sammy McGuigan sprawled on his seat in the interview room, legs like tree trunks, tight in the faded blue denim trousers, sleeves rolled up to show the bulging white forearms covered with black hair, beneath which his tattoos undulated as he clenched and unclenched his fists. He seemed to occupy the room with almost complete familiarity, as if it were an extension of his own home or the bar at the Washington, almost making the two detectives feel as if they were intruding on his space rather than vice versa.

'It's like an equaliser isn't it Sammy? First Lizzie McCabe and then Mairead O'Shea to even the score,' said Clarke.

'Oh it's an equaliser right enough. I mean it's a shame a wee girlie like that has to die, but they should of thought of that before they done Lizzie McCabe shouldn't they?'

'We know you know some fellows that could have done it,' said Clarke.

'Who?' snapped McGuigan. 'Give us some names.'

'We're asking you, Sammy. That's why you're here. Some of your boys out of control maybe? We know you have the people that are capable.'

McGuigan looked at Clarke expressionlessly. McCann tapped out another cigarette, lit up, blew out the smoke.

'Who? Give us some suggestions, sonny,' said McGuigan.

'Don't you 'sonny' me, pal,' said Clarke. 'Jesus, McCann where'd you find this fellow? Is he just out of police college or what?' said McGuigan, in mock exasperation, appealing to McCann.

'Sammy would you just answer the questions and not ask them and you'll be out of here,' said McCann wearily.

'Have you asked the Shinners too, McCann? They've more of a taste for wee girls.'

McCann went to the window and pulled the blast curtain back, looking down through the glass, smeary with the plastic that had been pasted over it to prevent splintering were a bomb to be set off outside. It was raining and the skyline of the city seemed to be blurred and melting in the rain, the dome of the City Hall wavering and wobbling in the distance like some kind of mad blancmange in his distorted vision.

'What were you doing out at the Black Lodge, Sammy?' he asked quietly.

'What about it? What's all this about McCann?

'Tell us how many times you've been up to the Black Lodge. Was it a regular little peccadillo or what?'

'Pecadillo? What the fuck are you talking about?'

'You been up there talking to the girls Sammy. You were seen.'

McCann went at him hard, knowing any advantage he had could be quick to evaporate.

'And what of it Inspector? What if I was up there? This may surprise you McCann but our organisation is as interested in peace as anyone is. Conflict is bad for business, bad for Ulster, bad for Ulstermen, so when the Peace Foundation suggested making a small contribution to the work of the centre I was only too happy to oblige. Oh yes.' And Sammy McGuigan moved his buttocks on the small upright chair, with a faint, satisfied sound like releasing a small amount of wind, before warming to his theme. 'It's important them youngsters understand our position, everyone's position, even the Republicans with their nonsense. I'm an open minded fellow McCann...' He held his hands out, drew breath for a moment.

'So you were there on the 9th of February,' asked McCann. And before he could answer McCann said:

'When Lizzie McCabe was there?'

A look of caution passed over Sammy McGuigan's face.

'I could have been,' he said. 'But so could a lot of other people too.' Then, suddenly angry: 'Where's Deevery? Does Deevery know you fellows are up to this?'

Later, McCann made a call, though with little expectation of success, especially when he heard the phone ringing on without answer. He was on the point of giving up when a gruff male voice answered.

'It's Inspector McCann here, from Crumlin Road. Is that Mr O'Shea?' There was a silence then at the other end of the line and McCann heard breathing, the distant sound of an argument in the background.

'It is,' the voice said. McCann fiddled with his cigarette, desperate to keep the fellow talking, desperate not to say anything that would provoke the fellow to drop the receiver back on its cradle.

'I know it's a difficult time for you, with the death of your daughter Mairead,' he began. 'But I've just one wee question about something that's come up that could really help us with our investigation.' There was no noise from the other end of the line so McCann rushed on: 'Your daughter stayed at the Black Lodge for a while before she died. I wonder did she mention anything unusual that happened while she was there.' There was another aching pause. He heard the fellow shouting to someone out the back that he'd be a minute, that he was on the phone. McCann willed him not to say he was speaking to the police, willed him to keep things confidential. The voice came back, low and guarded.

'What kind of unusual?'

'I was hoping you'd tell me that.'

Again, the heavy silence. McCann watched the second hand of his watch, ticking round. There was something the fellow was wrestling with, but what was it?

'There was some fellow she was very taken with,' whispered the voice, barely audible.

'Did you get a name?'

Another silence.

'Was it Sean O'Reilly?'

But the line went dead.

Thompson and McCann pulled in at Newry barracks to pick up an army escort to bring O'Reilly in. Clarke had by now found his name in special branch files and it was a quick step to match the name with an address. On the way into town they'd seen the estates on either side of the main road, sprawling away up the valley. New corporation houses with concrete walls and grey roofs, arranged in interlocking crescents that provided perfect cover. No sooner had a patrol entered off the main road than the residents had the time to flee out of the top of the estate and block off the road behind them, or fire down from the woods above, picking off the security forces as they moved between the houses.

The army captain in charge was implausibly young, a thin black moustache quivering over his upper lip, but smart enough as he snapped at the heels of his men climbing into the back of the Saracen. Thompson was friendly, shook hands with the captain.

'We want it surgical this one. Quickly in and out with no collateral. We've to speak to O'Reilly,' said McCann. 'We want him on our side, so no rough and tumble.'

'Well I think there's little chance of avoiding that,' said the captain, smiling drily, trying to break up the nervousness that was creeping upon them. The radio burbled, some incomprehensible army jargon and he checked his watch.

'OK let's go.'

Inside the Saracen the noise was tremendous and McCann and Thompson hunkered down in the gloom, just the glow of a single red light illuminating their faces and those of the squad of troops. The only other illumination was a tiny shaft of grey natural light from a hatch covered in wire mesh high in the rear of the armoured car. The men held stoically to the grab rails as the vehicle swung left, then right, bumping over humps set in the road and then climbing in a series of semi circles up the estate. The rear doors opened and the squad vanished over the threshold into the light, taking up covering positions in flowerbeds and garages, or out through the back of the estate along the edge of the wood.

'You're good to go Inspector,' said the captain. McCann jumped down into the road with Thompson and the two of them walked up to the front door of the house. Far below, on the main Warrenpoint road, he could see three more Saracens pulling to a standstill at the entrance to the estate, and a group of youths assembling on cue, milling along the footpaths, funnelling down the hill to block their retreat. In the front garden were children's toys; a trike rusting, half a pram. A couple of car wings under a tarpaulin. McCann knocked and a man answered the door.

'Mr O'Reilly?'

A thin fellow with a narrow, intelligent face and sandy hair stood before them.

'Who wants him?'

McCann pulled his gun, stepped behind him into the house.

'I'm arresting you on suspicion of the indecent assault of Mairead O'Shea. Anything you wish to say may be taken down in evidence and used against you. Can you please accompany us, sir?'

The fellow nodded wearily, like it was an everyday occurrence, a normal day's work to be arrested by armed police in his own home before he could even get the day's milk in off the doorstep.

'I'll get my coat,' he said. But Thompson had already got it for him, was draping it round his shoulders.

They brought O'Reilly straight back to Belfast, fast along the motorway with an escort front and back.

'Very nice,' said O'Reilly, twisting in his seat to see the

vehicle behind. 'Like I was the queen or something. You'd wonder where the taxes go wouldn't you?'

But neither McCann nor Thompson responded, so silence descended until they approached the city and turned towards Castlereagh and O'Reilly became agitated.

'I'm not going to Castlereagh. You have no right. I'll not go without a solicitor. It's my legal right.'

'You'll have your solicitor,' said McCann wearily as they swung over the river into East Belfast with its narrow streets of terraced houses with their union flags flying, their red white and blue kerbstones.

'Or maybe you'd like us to drop you here and find your own way home?'

Deevery was waiting for them at Castlereagh, a short mac on against the rain, rocking back and forwards on his heels. As the car pulled in he stepped up and pulled open McCann's door even before it had stopped.

'What are you up to McCann?' he said. 'Have you cleared arresting this man with the branch? '

'If there's suspicion of a crime we've an obligation to act.'

'Not if it jeopardises other security operations. Anything involving bringing in paramilitaries like this man has to be approved by the branch.'

'I'm not prepared to see more girls attacked,' said McCann.

'Well McCann that's very principled. Very high and mighty indeed,' said Deevery. 'But we are talking procedures here. And I'm telling you you'll need clearance before you lift anyone.'

Thompson's eyes asked a question of McCann. How come

Deevery seemed to be taking charge?

'Clarke had no objections,' McCann said, 'He gave us the address. He'd have cleared it.'

'Clarke! Sure he's just the tea boy. You'd need to clear that higher up.'

'We'll give Munton a call then, shall we,' said McCann. So they hung about outside the custody suite while Deevery put the call through. There was a long pause and Munton must have said the right thing, because Deevery came back and said:

'OK McCann, but you won't mind if I sit in on this too, do you?' Then added as an aside to Thompson: 'You'll not be needed love.' McCann was ready to argue. Thompson would have been more useful than Deevery, in fact if there was a spectrum of usefulness Thompson was at one end and Deevery at the far extreme of the other. But she gave him a warning look, a small barely visible gesture with her hand, like she was calming a child that needed to learn to control his temper.

'Have you ever heard of the Black Lodge?' asked McCann.

'The what?' said O'Reilly.

'The Black Lodge at Cushendun. It's a peace foundation, established by a fellow called Peter McCabe. Takes troubled kids away from their home environment.'

O'Reilly looked over towards his solicitor, a youngish fellow in a smart suit, his coat folded carefully on the table in front of him. The solicitor nodded.

'Yes I've been up there once or twice. It's a new departure for us.'

'Who's us?' Deevery's voice cut in harshly from behind McCann, from where he'd been standing impatiently while the prisoner had been brought in and the paperwork set up.

'The Republican movement. We've always believed in dialogue and understanding, the Armalite rifle by itself is useless without changing hearts and minds. The Black Lodge was an opportunity to do that.'

'Was it? In what way?' Deevery's voice cut in again over McCann's shoulder, tinged with cynicism and disbelief.

'We could talk to people on the other side in neutral surroundings, try to educate young people about our struggle and the way we saw things.' O'Reilly was young, McCann would have put him at just under thirty, with that kind of open, infectious enthusiasm you'd often get with political people, that disconnect between the things they said and the consequences that arose from them and their actions.

'I'd imagine that'd be hard, to educate some of those people?'

'Oh aye some of them wouldn't listen. It wasn't easy. But some of them would be more sympathetic.'

'Girls from your own community for example?'

'Oh yes, we'd have a good reception. A very good reception.'

'And how many times did you say you went down there?'

'Let's see, maybe three or four.'

'Can you remember the dates?'

'Well maybe it was in January last year, early in the spring. If I were at home rather than this place I'd be able to tell you exactly. I'd have it in my diary.'

O'Reilly looked around the interview room, its concrete walls, the single barred window letting in a wan shaft of light.

'Were you there during the week beginning 12th April?'

'My client can make no firm admission of having been there without access to his records,' said the solicitor, sitting forwards to intervene.

'When Mairead O'Shea was there.'

'On what grounds is this allegation being put to him?'

'We have witnesses who say Mr O'Reilly was present when Ms O'Shea was at the Lodge, who says they may have had a relationship.'

'What witnesses? What relationship?'

'I'm afraid we can't reveal that.'

'You are aware that the mere fact of interviewing my client in this place will have a potentially negative and prejudicial impact?' added the solicitor.

'Yes and we will take all possible steps to minimise that,' said McCann.

'The fuck you will,' said O'Reilly, suddenly angry. 'Everyone'll know I've been lifted. There'll be doubts about me now when I go back to Newry. Sure you fellows can't understand that, maybe don't care. In fact, I bet you like it that I'll be distrusted back home after this, that it'll make us weaker. You'll even put it about what I've been in for.' O'Reilly began to rant, leaning forward in his seat, pointing his finger at McCann.

'So you did meet Mairead O'Shea?'

There was a silence then. O'Reilly swallowed.

'Were you involved in the social events in the annexe?'

'The annexe?'

'Yes there was a Nissen hut where the students would hold socials some evenings.'

'I never heard of that.'

150

'We've evidence that you did participate. That you were close to Mairead O'Shea, inappropriately so.'

'Inappropriate?' said O'Reilly. 'That's ridiculous. Sure she's half my age.' But he flushed a little awkwardly at that, moved his feet on the bare concrete floor.

'We've evidence there was dancing, alcohol, that things may have gone a bit further.'

'But she's dead so you can't say that. You've nothing to go on.'

'You were seen, Mr O'Reilly. Seen by someone behaving inappropriately.'

'What do you mean by that? My client would need details of the allegations before responding,' said the solicitor.

'Whoever said that was lying,' said O'Reilly, then he seemed to glare at Deevery, looking over McCann's shoulder. 'This is just typical. Everywhere we go we seem to get fitted up.'

'Was she older than she looked? Leading you on? Maybe with a wee short skirt up round her arse?' Deevery growled suddenly. 'Lipstick maybe, them high heels?' He stood up, pirouetted, showing an imaginary pair of heels be-neath the heavy turnup of his trousers. 'Is that what it was, eh? Showing her panties and you couldn't resist?' He loomed towards O'Reilly across the table, putting his full weight on it so the steel legs slid on the concrete floor and O'Reilly and the solicitor had to reach to prevent the papers slipping to the floor.

'My client would admit to nothing. You have presented no evidence of his involvement in any such alleged activity,' said the solicitor.

'The fuck there isn't,' shouted Deevery and suddenly his

face purpled and he leant forward, his mouth inches away from O'Reilly's ear.

'You've been doing it with underage girls haven't you?' he said, waving his hand behind him to show that McCann should move back and keep out of his way.

'No way Inspector. I'd never do anything like that.'

'I must protest. The manner of the questioning is inappropriate,' said the solicitor.

'I'll give you something inappropriate to remember, pal, if you don't shut up,' snarled Deevery.

He walked round behind O'Reilly, then shouted into his ear: 'What about the girls, eh? Luscious wee teenager was she? Lipsticked maybe, sheer stockings, a tight wee mini-skirt...' Deevery paused, O'Reilly remained silent, until Deevery grabbed his hair and slammed his face hard down on the table top, blood bursting from his nose, a look of horrified surprise on his face, the solicitor moving ineffectually to intervene.

'Let's take a break,' said McCann. Deevery let go of O'Reilly's hair, his head lolling forward, disorientated and bleeding so the drops fell on McCann's shoes.

'Good idea. We'll take a break so you two jokers can think a bit more carefully about your answers,' said Deevery, nodding to McCann that he should follow him out.

Outside in the corridor he shouted for tea from the custody sergeant and took a seat.

'Jesus that was a bit rough,' said McCann.

'Rough? You've not seen rough yet,' said Deevery.

And when the tea came, he turned to McCann.

'That Clarke's a smart lad, isn't he?'

'Seconded from the branch,' said McCann.

'The branch is it?' said Deevery, smiling in a weird kind of way that was not really a smile at all.

'I'd like to make a complaint about Deevery, about his methods,' said McCann.

The Poet was seated behind his desk. Behind him the framed photograph of the Queen and the Duke of Edinburgh smiled down. He looked at McCann without expression.

'What methods?' With repetition, the word seemed to have become loaded with innuendo.

'Who brought him in, over my head?' asked McCann.

'Not over your head McCann, alongside, that's all. Look on him as an extra pair of hands, a different set of tools and techniques, no doubt distasteful, yet which can also be very effective. There's a war on McCann. And since his appointment Deevery has already made some useful arrests. I'd give him time.'

'He's deranged,' said McCann. 'Like something out of *The Godfather.*'

'I'm not even sure what you're talking about McCann.'

'He's mental, like some kind of mafia hood. The folk in Derry will be relieved he's down here now.'

'Londonderry,' corrected the Poet, 'It's Londonderry, not Derry. It's important to maintain that at least, McCann. I thought you understood that.'

'His methods are counterproductive,' said McCann.

'If you're unhappy with it McCann you can always ask for a transfer.'

'I'm not leaving,' said McCann. 'It's Deevery who should go. He's a disgrace.'

The Superintendent went over to the window, pulled the blast curtain back a fraction and looked down into the courtyard below.

'You need him McCann. You're overstretched as it is and an experienced man like that can give you support where it's needed, free you up to properly lead the investigation. We've to find the culprits and put them away. God knows McCann, we don't want dangerous murderers on the loose.'

'Deevery will not help me,' said McCann.

'Listen McCann,' said the Poet wearily. 'There are men getting into their vehicles down there tonight, married men with children, wives and families, going out now on duty and not knowing if they're coming back. Not knowing if when they get back from work their homes won't have been hit, their children attacked, blown to bits so their wee limbs have to be picked out of their front gardens and you come in here worrying about Deevery's methods. Wise up McCann,' he said. 'Before someone does it for you.'

It was late when McCann drove himself home. The lights from the car roamed across the shuttered streets, illuminating the occasional stray cat darting from bin to bin, the streetlights mostly out, the city in ghostly black and moonlight. McCann drove on. On a corner some crows had got a plastic bag out onto the street and were ripping away at it. Suddenly McCann had to pull over, rammed the car up onto the curb. Why had there to be crows as well? Jesus that was too much. He felt like he was suffocating, like the air had been taken out of the car. He wound the window right down, pulled open the door, leant out breathing in the night. He wouldn't look at the crows or what they were eating but he knew they were there and what they were up to. Suddenly he'd a mind to get back in the car and drive right over them, just start the motor and reverse right over the ugly creatures but they'd be too quick for him. Primitive and greedy, but crows were clever beasts all the same. Bringing him back to scenes he'd rather forget, when he'd been first there after a bomb and had fought the crows to collect the parts of human beings.

Then he saw the lights of another car approaching, the glare of them coming up the road and the wings of the crows flapping away illuminated in the headlights, the bag of stuff scattered in the roadway. The lights illuminated him in their glare as the car slowed. Then he heard a woman's voice.

'Inspector? Is that you Inspector McCann? Are you OK Inspector?'

He straightened up, turned towards the light.

'Aye fine,' he said. 'Wee bit of a bug sergeant,' he said. 'Soon be over it.'

'I could give you a lift,' said Thompson. 'You look a bit done in.'

She switched the headlights off and for a moment McCann was plunged into blissful darkness until his eyes adjusted and he saw her walking towards him, dressed in civilian clothes, high heels, the glitter of an evening dress beneath her coat.

'I'm alright,' he said. He could smell perfume and alcohol from her. 'Have you been out on the town?'

'Aye,' she said.

'Do you want a nightcap?' asked McCann.

'A nightcap?'

'Just suggesting,' he said.

Every surface in the bar seemed to be sticky to the touch. The black plastic on the bar stools, the Formica surface of the bar, even the whiskey glass McCann was holding seemed to stick to his fingers. When he leaned on the bar his shirtsleeves came away with a ripping sound, as if being unglued. Maybe it was drying sweat that was gluing him to the bar top.

'How many of them can you drink?'

'Try me,' she said.

Thompson leaned sideways, supporting herself against the bar, one hand propping her head up, from time to time stirring a cherry around in her cocktail glass, or tapping imperiously on its rim when it was empty. The whole bar seemed gloriously insulated, bathed in a kind of sulphurous yellow light through which drinkers and waiters moved as if underwater, all noises muffled by the thick adhesive carpet, the red embossed wallpaper, the heavy drapes across the shuttered windows. It was the kind of place where nothing said would be overheard or even remembered.

'She was my best friend. My only buddy,' said Thompson. 'It was a massive attack; the whole of the Armagh brigade, mortars, automatic weapons. She never stood any chance at all.'

'Let's drink one to her,' said McCann blurrily. Yes, they could both have another one. They deserved it. It would do them both good.

'Let's see, I'll have a...' Thompson waved her hand airily to attract the attention of the barman, who appeared from nowhere, as if he had been hiding beneath the bar to await her call.

'I'd like something stronger,' she said.

'Double Jameson,' suggested McCann.

'Fine. Whatever,' said Thompson grandly. 'I'll have

one of them'

'Ice?'

'Just as it comes, Peter. It is Peter isn't it?'

'Aye,' said the barman.

And when the drinks came she and McCann clinked their glasses together.

'Cheers,' he said.

'Down the Swanee,' she said, gulping the drink down, started to cough, put her head down into her handkerchief, her blonde hair covering her face.

'What's that on your shoes?'

'My shoes?' He looked down at the toe of his shoe and there was something there, so he took a paper napkin off the bar to it, gave it a wipe and had a look in the light.

'Is that blood, Inspector, blood on your toecap?'

He sniffed the napkin. Dog mess would have been better than human blood on your shoes.

'I must have cut myself,' he said.

'With what? A carving knife? A black and decker?' McCann mumbled something about preparing a steak at home, not knowing how to cook. He could see she didn't believe him. She leant forwards.

'It's up your trouser leg too. Splattered it is, absolutely splattered.'

He could see the distaste in her eyes, the disappointment.

'That was Deevery. I couldn't stop him. I never could,' said McCann.

'Tell me about him,' she said, leaning forwards closer to him, sipping the whiskey.

So then he told her about Deevery, how far back it all went.

He could still remember every part of that evening as if it was yesterday, had played and replayed it in his mind. He'd arranged to meet Mary Channon at the party. They'd been out a few times together and already they were in step, excited by each other's company. Deevery was at the door, the glow of the light illuminating him as if in a magic halo, dressed in the latest style; a pair of tight grey trousers and a black shirt with a red bandana knotted in the style of Elvis Presley. His hair had been black in those days, luxuriously brylcreemed and curled.

'Well would you look what the cat dragged in,' said Deevery, above the noise of the music and the noise of the fellows inside shouting to make themselves heard above the music.

'I'll expect you'll be looking for Mary? She's out the back with some guys,' he said.

It was already so crushed that McCann had to squeeze along sideways with his back to the wall to find her. He'd had a lump in his throat just at the sight of her, the sheen on her hair, the way she had turned to smile at him. They fought their way out to the table where the drinks were laid out. She'd asked him for a smoke and they'd gone out the back together, pushing through the house and out through the kitchen and then up some steps onto the lawn at the back. It was still warm, quite dark apart from the light from the kitchen window. He gave her a cigarette from the pack he'd bought specially.

'Dunhill,' she'd said. 'Very smart indeed,' and she looked around the place, the lawn falling away into the valley beyond.

'Jesus, this is some spread,' she said.

'Cost them fifty thousand, or so they say.'

'Aye, well,' she said doubtfully. 'Money can't make you happy now can it?'

They went inside after a while and had a dance, McCann remembered struggling with the spins and turns to Eddie Cochrane until 'Now or Never' came on and he was able to hold her in a soft embrace turning slowly in the hot, noisy room, while the flashing lights made her face turn green, then orange, then red. And finally kissing upstairs amongst the coats that were laid on the parents' bed as the time spun on.

'I'd best be getting back,' she'd said in the end. He'd offered to walk her back to her parent's house, but it was a long walk she'd said, and took him in the opposite direction to his farm. Maybe one of the fellows could give her a lift back down and he could go down with her, he'd suggested, and make his own way home afterwards? And so they'd asked around and hung about waiting in the hallway until Deevery came by.

'Hear tell you need a lift, Mary?' he said, taking her elbow as if he owned her, turning her away from him. 'I'll run you down in the Volvo.'

McCann remembered thinking that maybe Deevery had had too much to drink, remembered resentment at his sense of entitlement. And then another fellow he knew came up and offered to take McCann the other way back up towards the farm where he lived.

'You go on,' said Mary to McCann. 'Makes more sense not coming all the way down to mine and walking back up to yours.' He'd hesitated even then, but she'd insisted. 'I'll see you Monday,' she said. The hall was crowded with people putting on coats, gathering belongings.

'Go on or you'll miss your lift,' she'd said, gave him a kiss

and a gentle push towards the door. He followed Deevery out and heard the engine of the Volvo revving, the wheels spinning as it accelerated out through the gates, had a glimpse of Mary's face looking back through the window. Maybe he'd been unclear what the rules were and overawed by the fact that Deevery had a car, and had been able to have a party such as this one, and yes, just a slight feeling even then that maybe she'd wanted to go with Deevery alone. So he watched the car swing out onto the road in a wide arc and accelerate away into the darkness moving at speed towards the village, before vanishing in the drop down to the river.

'Well,' said McCann, rehearsing the old tropes in his head. He'd been only young. Both of them were. All three of them. Had their lives in front of them. Except for Mary Channon who'd been killed in the crash. It was a mistake that'd be easy enough for anyone to make at that age. Not fair the punishment they'd had. It was disproportionate; Deevery's injuries, the guilt they'd both felt. The blame he'd put on Deevery, so bad he could hardly think about him without his fists clenching. They were desperate to get away from each other but always together; first the police training, and now the same Division. Well, that was the thing with Ulster, said McCann. It was such a small place you could never get away from anyone, from consequences, from history. It was all around you, closing you in till sometimes you could barely breathe. It was why so many of his friends were scattered far and wide in England, America, Australia, some of them even in Africa, Russia, Japan, like they couldn't go far enough to get away from it, though they'd done nothing to deserve that exile. Unlike him, and yet he was the one that stayed, like he wanted to carry that burden. Maybe wanted to do some good too, in what was left of his life. To even that balance. Some Protestant thing, that guilt was your birthright, that you bore alone face to face with the Lord in all your nakedness, and only He would know when you had made sufficient amends, though like as not he'd never tell you when you had.

When he had finished speaking, McCann looked into his empty glass and Thompson was silent. Then she said: 'Well, Inspector, you certainly know how to cheer a girl up.'

'It's the way I tell 'em,' said McCann, suddenly laughing, clapping his hands to dispel the gloom, before standing to get her a cab home.

Chapter Twelve

McCann had a slow start the next day, with a dry mouth and a splitting headache, lashing a couple of glasses of ice-cold water down with three codeine to contain it. He took his car over to the University, with the tape containing the recorded tip-off that had led to the discovery of Mairead O'Shea's body securely in the glove compartment. The wide streets were tree-lined, with comfortable Georgian houses set back from the road. A modern block housed the students' union and students spilled out down the steps as he drove past, eventually finding a space for the car at a meter some way off, so he had to walk back in the blustery spring sunshine, one hand clutching the tape in its plastic box deep in his coat pocket. Many of the houses he passed had plaques on the gateposts, advertising the departments of geology, history and other subjects that McCann barely recognised. He hopped up the stone steps to the door of the Department of Linguistics and rang the bell, which chimed in an old-fashioned way as he peered through the glass. He heard steps coming and a woman with sandy hair and a bright, lipsticked smile opened the door to him.

'Professor Lundgren?'

'Yes and you will be Inspector McCann. We were expecting you,' she said.

She led him through two sets of fire doors. He was surprised how big the place was out the back, wished he'd had a smoke before getting indoors, as she didn't look the smoking type and it wasn't the smoking kind of place he could tell.

'A rabbit warren,' he said.

'Sorry?' she said. And it was then he realised she was foreign.

'Place where rabbits breed,' he explained, his heavy police shoes squeaking now on the polished parquet as they made their way to her office beyond.

'This is the tape I told you about,' he said, passing it to her and settling himself in one of the low chairs she'd offered. She slipped it into a large tape machine on the desk, sat on the edge of the desk, while the voice said:

'You gentlemen will find something of interest down the back of Donegall Avenue.' The voice was languid, almost cultured, as if in no haste and without the fear of discovery snapping at him, quite unlike the recorded tip offs that McCann had heard before; no blurting of names and addresses followed by a perfunctory slamming down of the receiver.

McCann nodded, that she should play it again.

'You gentlemen will find something of interest down the back of Donegall Avenue,' was all it said, announcing the death sentence that had been executed on Mairead O'Shea. And then there was a pause on the tape, the sound of a door slamming in the distance and a short time afterwards, the receiver was replaced with a careful click.

'Posh,' said McCann, 'What's that gentlemen and something of interest? Isn't that weird?'

They played the tape one more time. It was hard to be sure

of the accent. The thought came to McCann that it wasn't a real accent, but a voice someone had put on, which wouldn't be unusual. But you'd need education to think of that, then to do it right. And underneath the smart accent there was a rural roughness from west of the river Bann in the voice that McCann found familiar. Was it the killer himself? It was as if suddenly he was very close, suddenly the game was beginning; the killer had wanted him to feel that excitement, to tease him and whet his appetite.

'There's not much here. But just the same we can slow it right down. We have a library,' Professor Lundgren said. 'Over two thousand voices. With our mainframe computer we can analyse the minutest differences and similarities. It's a really exciting time right now for this kind of work.'

'How long will it take?'

'Give us an hour,' she said. He was pleased by the exotic lilt and swoop of her voice, by the fact that maybe she'd have some skill unknown to the province and the objectivity to use it well. He watched her as she copied the voice onto a larger high-density tape, pleased by the careful steps she was taking. Then she pulled out something like a sound meter, spending a few minutes assembling the equipment, connecting a larger tape machine to the sound meter and the sound meter to a printer with an ink needle like the cardiograph he'd once seen attached to a seriously injured colleague in hospital. She slipped in the tape and played it once, checking the sound meter was working, the audiograph responding.

'Looks like rocket science,' he said. She looked at him sharply.

'This part is quite simple actually Inspector. It's the next bit that's magic.' She pulled the print-out from the printer and he followed her down the corridor, through a locked door into a much larger room, high ceilinged, bright and clean where a mainframe computer hummed busily.

'This is Seamus,' she said.

'Seamus?' Asked McCann, baffled, because the room was empty apart from the machine.

'Seamus the computer. He knows everything,' she said. 'We'll give him a taste of your friend and see what he makes of it.' McCann watched as she fed the audiograph into the machine, watched as it scrolled its way past an optical reader, waited as the machine digested the voice and its peculiarities. The machine began to spool out more printer paper with a clattering rattle into a bin by her side. When it had stopped she pulled out the paper, tore off the first sheets and examined the results.

'There will be some matches,' she said. 'Let's see, we've possibly got the upper Bann here.' She went to an index cabinet and pulled out two, three, then five or six cards, studied the results, discarding some cards, retaining others, which she passed over to McCann, each card headed with a place name. McCann flicked through the file cards she had given him and suddenly the place names there were familiar: Achnakerrig, Ballylisker, Auchnaterrin – all towns and villages within twenty miles of his own family home. But how had he not recognised the accent?

'There are some significant irregularities. This man, he maybe disguised his voice, we don't know how, but the recording equipment is very sensitive. It detects the underlying structure, the rhythm. You can be sure the caller is from one of those places, or near,' she said.

McCann thanked her, for giving him the excuse that he needed.

'I'm sorry I'm late,' said McCann, out of breath from the climb up the stairs at Division.

'Been up to the university,' he explained.

'University? Doing a course or what?' asked Thompson, baffled. Her face was pale, crow's feet around the eyes, which were a little bloodshot.

'Christ no! Me? A course? You've got to be joking.'

'Just thought you seemed the type.'

'What does that mean?'

'Single man, maybe, isn't that what they do?'

'I could never stand book learning. Complete waste of time,' said McCann.

'Any further on with the tape?' asked Clarke. McCann had barely noticed him, distracted as he was by what seemed to be Thompson's flirting, or maybe he'd just imagined that?

'Some fellow from out west they think.'

'Some wild country boy maybe? Maybe a punishment killing by the IRA?'

'For what?'

'Maybe O'Reilly told her something and she passed it on to the wrong people and had to be punished for that?'

'It wasn't O'Reilly. O'Reilly's from Newry and this fellow is west of the Bann. And educated, they're sure of that. Disguised his voice.'

'You could check O'Reilly all the same, see if there's any kind of match, just to be sure,' said Thompson.

'He's been released,' said Clarke. 'O'Reilly's solicitor demanded it. He said there wasn't enough evidence and that he'd take a private prosecution against Deevery for assault if he wasn't let out. Habeas Corpus and all the old human rights crap. So the Poet let him go.'

'For God's sake!' said McCann, exasperated. 'I'm away to the autopsy room. Get a bit of sanity. Anyone want to come?'

Clarke followed McCann to the autopsy room at the Royal, where Mairead O'Shea's body lay. The air inside seemed particularly chill and heavy with the smell of formaldehyde. The doors pulled shut behind them with a near-silent swish of their draft excluders across the rubber floor. The pathologist was already dressed in her plastic apron, boots, mask and surgical cap, some of her instruments laid out ready for action, the body zipped in a green bag on the inspection table.

'Inspector McCann,' she said cheerfully. 'You're keeping me awful busy these days.'

'It's not me that killed her, you know.'

She chuckled and said maybe he was being touchy because he had something to hide, as she laid out her implements from the steriliser the steaming scalpels, the saw and pliers, all the tools of dismemberment to hand, checking the scales that would hold the body parts, the batteries on the dictaphone, the time on her watch. McCann could see that Clarke had started to sweat, had loosened his collar. Somehow it made him feel better about his own queasy stomach.

'10:42, the body of Mairead O'Shea, female, fifteen years,' she began, proceeding with a murmured inventory. McCann found himself somewhere to sit, a high lab chair with its seat covered in plastic and perched himself on it, a respectful distance away, far enough not to see the detail when the cutting began, wishing there was a window he could look out of, at the trees and sky, or traffic in some normal street, but the glass was frosted and impenetrable. It was hard to tell if the world outside even existed at all as the investigation proceeded; a careful inventory of the bag, clothing, the steady flash of the pathologist's camera, the taking of the corpse's temperature.

'Any idea of the time of death?'

'Close to the time the body was found I'd guess, so she'd have to have been killed close by,' said the pathologist, starting to swab under the fingernails, take fingerprints, examine between her legs.

'Any traces she'd been assaulted?'

'I'll come on to that Inspector, but I'd say yes. There's abrasions, signs of struggle. Some disturbance of the under-garments.'

'By the same man?'

'Ah it's too early to say. You'll have to wait for the report Inspector. Once we get the samples analysed and you get me some suspects, we'll have a better view.' She leant forward with a small pair of scissors, neatly cutting off hair, sealing it away.

Clarke was leaning on the rail now, breathing deeply.

'You could take a break,' said McCann. 'Get some fresh air, that sometimes helps, sometimes makes it worse.'

'I'm OK,' said Clarke. 'Had a curry last night and think it was off.'

The pathologist washed the body carefully, working her way along each limb, noting any significant marks till she came to the neck, the side facing away from McCann.

'Entry wound is enlarged with some traces of powder, indicating gunshot at close quarters, ' she said. 'Come and take a look.'

The pathologist was peering at the wound on the girl's neck, bending down, as if trying to see inside it, delicately moving the matted hair back with a pair of tweezers, then easing the girl's body to one side looking for something.

'No exit wound visible,' she said, reaching for a pair of long handled tweezers, inserting them into the wound, rotating delicately, then gripping something she extracted the tweezers.

There was a clatter in the porcelain specimen dish and something rolled to and fro in it, leaving a trail of blood and tissue against the white stoneware.

'There you are Inspector,' said the pathologist. 'Devil of a job but I got it in the end.'

McCann forced himself to look. It was a bullet.

'We've to do analysis on the tissue, for fragments, traces,' she said.

'We'll get ballistics on it when you've done,' said McCann.

'That's from a Walther semi-automatic,' said Clarke. 'It's a police gun.'

'Aye but a few hundred quid will get you one anywhere, no problem,' said McCann.

That evening McCann passed through the Arcade to the fishing shop, pushing open the doors with keen anticipation, making his way up to the high glass counter with its array of flies and reels, bait boxes, floats and sinkers.

'I've to pick something up,' he said, but the fellow was

already reaching under the counter for it and had it prepared for him, taking the fly carefully out from its case, the twin barb gleaming sharp amongst the frothy profusion of feathers, concealed within the lure.

'I've done some canary, Canada goose, jade,' said the fellow, holding it up to the light so McCann could see, turning it over.

'She's a beauty,' said McCann appreciatively and took the lure delicately in his fingers, examining it from every angle.

'How much do I owe you?'

'To you Inspector, that'll be three quid.'

'Is that all,' said McCann. 'You can't make a living out of that.'

'It's not a living is it?' said the man. 'It's just for pleasure. It's a real pleasure to have a fellow with the interest you have in it.'

McCann smiled, said it was kind of him, that he appreciated that as he counted out the money. As he turned to go he suddenly tapped the side of his head, as if he'd remembered something else.

'I've a mind to see if there's pike too,' he said.

'Pike? Ah well you'll be needing a wire trace for them boyos and a couple of barbed three point hooks.'

'What've you got?' said McCann. 'Think I may have a fight on my hands with a bit of coarse fishing.'

And when he left the shop fifteen minutes later McCann had a plastic carrier bag in which was curled a metre wire trace and two big, ugly hooks and a short-bladed gaff.

Once home, he laid the purchases out on the counter in the kitchen, placing the delicate fly with its exotic plumage on the table while he put the kettle on, then laying the gaff, trace and coarse hooks carefully side by side, touching the serrated blade of the gaff with his finger tip and drawing blood. He went to the bathroom to find a plaster but the cabinet was full of old medicines, so he just held some toilet roll to the cut, watching the blood seep through.

Chapter Thirteen

McCann's car had shed its fan belt and overheated on his way to visit his parents, so he found himself travelling by express bus as far as Omagh. He dozed along the motorway, from time to time waking to see the flat fields speed past from the anonymity of the fast lane, past the Maze prison, across the sodden farmland. After Portadown the road narrowed and the stops became more frequent as they drew nearer. McCann wondered how his mother would be and how he'd deal with it if she was incapacitated, knowing his father would not be able to cope. He wondered if there was any sense starting to look there for the man whose voice he had on tape.

At Omagh he changed to the rural bus for Achnakerrig and Mountjoule. It was almost empty and bucketed along the country lanes with the hedgerows scraping across the sides, occasionally skidding to a halt behind flocks of sheep. Then as the bus passed through Drumnaferighty he felt the old tightness in his chest. The bus slowed as it approached the humpback bridge over the Rashbrook river, with the sharp bend after and the climb up towards Deevery's old house. It had been just after the bend where it had happened.

He'd seen the wreckage the next morning, could still recall the sickening remains of the car, compressed like a wreck in a

scrap yard. Craning his head as the school bus went past. And ·
in school the murmuring rumours:

'Jesus, were you at Deevery's last night?'

'Did you see him?'

'Did you see Mary?'

'He's not in school. Did you see the car?'

'God, no one would've got alive out of that.'

The bus bounced over the humpback, the driver sounded
the horn and swung around the bend. Then they began the
climb up past the house, the glint of the wide picture windows,
the red tiled roof, the twin garage, set in a commanding
position over the valley. He could see the tennis courts at the
back. He'd heard they'd sold the place afterwards and moved
to Derryveagh.

A few minutes later the bus deposited McCann at Sullivan's
Corner. As it pulled away he paused with his bag and lit a
cigarette. The sun came out and he could see the bugs diving
to and fro. There was a powerful smell of grass, of dung and
everything he remembered from his childhood. He slung
his bag up on his shoulder and commenced the climb to
Drumnaferighty. He was quite hot and unbuttoned his coat,
the road steep and roughly unsurfaced, twisting across cattle
grids and through five bar gates. On this final climb he always
had time to rehearse his lines:

'Guess what ma, I've got my sergeant's exam.'

'I've met a girl, ma.'

'Da, I'm on the special training course in Birmingham.'

'Da, I've my medal for bravery. The commander's medal.'

And then later it was:

'Me and Irene's thinking about taking a break.'

He turned the final corner to the farm where it sat on the mountainside, sheltered by a few trees leaning over in the prevailing wind so their branches touched the grey slate roof. He half expected his mother's voice, to see her out on the step in her pinafore and wellingtons, coming down the path unsteadily to meet him with her arms outstretched. But there were only the dogs, barking and coming to greet him. He had to rap hard on the knocker before raising the latch, the door grating on the rough stone floor as he pushed through into the dark interior.

'Da? Ma?' he called out, listening for any reply. But the only sound was the clock ticking against the wall in the gloom, a faint sigh from the fire as the white peat ash subsided in the grate. So he climbed the stairs to their bedroom, the small square window letting in the sun's rays across the embroidered bedspread, his mother asleep bolstered upright with a book slipped from her hands across the counterpane, her breathing faint and rasping. He rapped lightly against the thin wood of the open door, looking at her face, fallen away with age and sleep, the lines drawn down at the corner of her mouth, her hair strangely thin and untidy.

'Michael?' she whispered. 'That you Michael?' and she smiled and he hugged her, her body thin and light with the dwindling of age against his chest.

'Your father's out in the top field,' she murmured. 'He'll be down shortly.' She moved weakly, trying to get herself upright. 'You'll have to make yourself some tea. Then come and sit here and tell us all the news.'

He took the dogs out up the hill at the back, letting them run on ahead out of the low front door and away up the rough track between the dry stone walls, barking excitedly as they went, following them with long strides, breathing in the fresh air off the mountains. The track climbed steeply and turned around an exposed rock, the place where his father had at one stage tried to plant a few pine trees. But now as he passed the spot there was little to show; one or two of the trees had taken root and grown or half grown on the poor soil, their branches stunted, others had never got beyond the size of a small shrub. Here and there were dried stubs of what had once been trees, gnawed off by the sheep that had broken through the fences. His father had had a couple of years of subsidy and then the whole experiment had been called off.

Further on, he spotted his father in the top field bending down by a tractor, his boots deep in the mud. He called out to him but the wind carried his voice away, so he climbed over the wall and crossed the field towards him, his shoes sucking in the heavy soil.

'Jesus son, you gave me a fright creeping up like that,' said his father, wiping his hands on a bit of old rag stained with oil, straightening his back with more stiffness than McCann remembered, but smiling too.

Once back in the kitchen McCann unpacked the food he'd brought, his father handling the items like they were dangerous and unfamiliar; putting the tins on the first available ledge, the bread in the cupboard behind the breadbin, pocketing the matches. Already McCann could see an unfamiliar chaos spreading, that his father had come into the kitchen with his boots on, leaving mud across the floor that had always gleamed.

'Doctor says she may take some time to mend,' his father said as he stirred the sugar into his tin mug, with his rough hands still confident and strong. But when he looked up over the rim of the steaming cup at McCann there was an unfamiliar redness around his eyes.

'Will you stay for supper?' he asked. 'I could knock something up.' And he glanced desperately around the bare shelves.

'I'll make you something,' said McCann. 'We've some beans and bread and a couple of packs of rashers that'll go off if you've not put them in the fridge. I've got one of them Bakewell tarts, ma will like that.'

After supper McCann tried to discuss the future, his mother asleep upstairs, but his father would have none of it.

'I'll manage,' he said. 'Doctor says she's to rest. They'll be sending someone up from the welfare, he says.'

'It's not the best place is it?' said McCann.

'It's what she wants.' And then his father got up from his armchair and switched on the radio, listening to the news with the volume turned up.

McCann stretched his legs restlessly, stood up and yawned.

'I'm away for a last smoke on the step,' he said. 'Take a look at the stars.' He pulled back the bolts and stepped out into the cool night and lit a cigarette. Outside it was completely dark, with low cloud obscuring the sky. The trees rustled and swayed in a soft wind. He wondered about the tape in his bag and if he should disturb his father with it. If the man on the tape was from around the area, his parents might know him. He'd never brought his work to them, never mentioned the cases he worked on. They were his family and they'd enough to contend with, but now the murders had led him back.

He waited till the news ended and his father switched the radio off. Then he went back inside, got the tape machine out and put it on the low table by the fire.

'What's that contraption,' said his father, looking at him disapprovingly. The sheepdog lay comatose on the rug, his tail twitching.

'You're not putting music on now are you? Sure it's too late for that.'

And then the voice came on. Every time he heard it now it made him angry, tense with frustration, as the man who'd sent it would well have known. Hearing it here, with his father beside him made it real however; the man had come from here, or nearby. He could be outside, in walking distance or a short drive away. The dog's ears twitched and he rolled over, shook his head as if shaking away an angry insect.

'Who's that fellow?' his father asked.

'Some fellow I've to find,' he said. His father leaned forward, his elbows on his knees.

'What's he done?' McCann's silence communicated everything.

'What's that something of interest bit? Was it a corpse or something?' asked his father.

McCann rewound and played the tape again.

'Sounds familiar,' said his father. 'I could of swore that's Alan Colhane. Try it on your mother.'

So he tiptoed up the stairs where she was stirring, took the tray with the food barely touched from her lap.

'Do you recognise this ma?' he asked. 'Dad reckons it's Alan Colhane.'

'Alan or one of them Colhanes from Mountjoule. You know that kind of high squeaky voice,' said his father, shouting up the stairs to her.

'Could have been anyone at all from round here,' she said tiredly, then more urgently: 'What's he done? He's not done one of those girls in Belfast, has he? You're never working on that?' With her hand to her mouth in horror. 'Oh no son, that's a terrible, terrible thing.'

'Jesus,' she said, waving her hand weakly at the tape machine as if it were responsible for the crime itself. 'Take that thing away out of here.'

'Don't worry, ma,' he said. 'It's just a long shot.'

And indeed, that was true he thought as he walked down the hill to the Beacon Inn. The tape was like one of those hopeless pot-shots you'd take when the thing you were after was so far away you could barely see it, or that the shot would reach it, let alone hit it in the right place. But at least it had given him the reason to come back, to make up a little for leaving them.

After he'd been walking for twenty minutes or so McCann came to the bar where he knew there was a phone. Back in the day when they were first starting to drink it was pretty much infamous for the ease with which underage teenage lads could get a pint in its gloomy interior. But now when McCann pushed through the front door the place had been opened up, the light let in. He blinked as he walked to the bar, the bright optic lights illuminating a glittering array of spirits. The carpet was newly laid and in place of the narrow cottage windows there were big coach windows in leaded glass looking out on the road and tables laid out for dining, big solid pine affairs glistening with new varnish, menus standing on every table. And there were women in the bar too, the soft sound of music from hidden speakers.

'Well, well, Michael McCann is it?' came a familiar voice

from behind him, making him jump. He turned and almost immediately regretted his decision to come in there.

'Michael it's good to see you again.' A woman uncannily like Mary Channon herself, but stouter, swollen, with a double chin beneath the expensive muffler reached out her hand to him briefly, holding his sleeve for a moment. And behind her a man, Mary Channon's father, his face red and pockmarked, his hand soft and trembling as he shook McCann's own.

'Will you take a drink?'

'Let me,' said McCann. 'What'll it be?'

'Ach no son, this is mine,' he said, pushing forward to the bar, an embarrassed silence descending meanwhile between McCann and Mrs Channon.

'How've you been Michael?'

'Grand,' said McCann. 'I'm doing well actually Mrs Channon.'

'That's good. And how's your mother? Your father still around? I've not seen him for a while.'

McCann told her about his mother's illness.

'That's a shame,' she said. 'She was a lovely lady. Still is a lovely lady. I'm sure she'll be up and about soon.'

Mr Channon came back with the drinks, balanced on a tin tray that collected the overspill, Mrs Channon mopping the bottom of the glasses dry with a beermat as they were placed on the table.

'Do you still see anything of that Deevery? You and he were best pals, weren't you.' said Mr Channon, settled now, taking a big gulp of his drink and fixing McCann with his watery pale blue eyes, while his wife put a hand gently on his arm, as if to hold him back, had he still been capable of coming forward.

'He's a DCI now, in Belfast,' said McCann. 'Done well for himself.' Almost adding, 'I'm afraid.'

'How's that? How can a fellow like that do well?' queried Mr Channon.

'And how have you two been,' McCann asked. 'How's Tommy and...' he grappled for the name of Mary Channon's sister, their surviving daughter, feeling himself plunging down a black hole, but at least one that would be better than talking about Deevery and what he had done. Or what McCann *hadn't* done, if he was honest about it, which of course he wouldn't be with the girl's parents there right in front of him.

But they wouldn't be distracted.

'I always thought that Deevery was unhinged,' began Mr Channon. 'The whole family useless. Accountants, lawyers, giving themselves airs and graces, the one couldn't add up to save his life, the other with about as much understanding of the law as Attila the Hun.'

'John, please. Michael doesn't want to hear this again,' said Mrs Channon.

'I bet he doesn't.'

'I know. I know,' said McCann, desperate to get away now. 'But the past is the past. You've to look to the future.'

'What future? You boys took our future.'

'I didn't. I'm sorry for your loss,' said McCann. 'More sorry than I can say. But it wasn't me that was responsible. Deevery was doing the driving and you know that.'

'But you were going out with our Mary. You should've looked after her. You were one of the fellows that let him do it, knowing he'd been drinking. You were probably as drunk as he was, or so I heard. You could have stopped him son and you didn't. You just couldn't care less. Neither of you could.' The accusation stung McCann. Mr Channon's lips worked, loosely wet over his uneven teeth as he continued speaking, in a low accusatory murmur, his eyes fixed on McCann.

'I can see it, son, in my mind's eye every night. Mary in her party dress, the dark road roiling and twisting under the headlights, the surge of the engine, the night air rushing past with the scent of a summer that never came for her and then her screams as they came into the bend...'

'Ah now Mr Channon,' he heard himself say, because he'd had had just the same nightmares himself. The new carpet with its floral pattern seemed to start to spin like some magic fairground ride, with McCann on a roller coaster not knowing which way was up and which was down, the two of them looking at him like their eyes could drill holes in his soul.

'I know,' he said.

'I bet you do, son,' said Mr Channon. 'Sure there's nothing we can do about it now with Deevery and yourself both Inspectors in the police!'

And Deevery had made it worse somehow, when he came back from hospital with that big empty swaggering glare of his, like he'd a screw loose, the screw that fixed his moral compass to the rest of his head. McCann hadn't forgiven him, but pitied him nonetheless, seeing the fellow struggling to get back on his feet; at first Deevery had trouble writing, trouble remembering, even more trouble speaking than he'd ever had. They kept him down a year, to help him catch up. While McCann was away at Enniskillen, Deevery was still there at school, like a big overgrown lad, like some kind of imbecile. And the sixth form boys who didn't maybe know the story began to tease him, make him mad.

Then he heard second hand that Deevery had been bragging about what he and Mary had done together, about stopping off on the way before the crash. About how she'd always fancied him. There was nothing he could do by then.

McCann was surprised when he heard Deevery had joined the police. He found out when there was a big rugby match. McCann had come back specially for it, and there was Deevery somehow larger, more vacant than he'd been at school. But his swagger was back.

'McCann you cunt,' he said and swiped his arm so hard it hurt as the two teams went into changing. And the punch on Deevery's nose later was more than natural. It was just the beginning as far as McCann was concerned.

'I've a call to make,' said McCann, backing away from the old couple, making for the payphone. A powerful smell of stale smoke filled his nostrils as he pushed open the door and dialled through to Division, shovelling the coins in, asking to be put through to the office, hoping someone would still be there.

'Hello,' he said. 'It's me.'

'Hello Inspector,' Thompson's voice came through. 'Where are you? We were trying to find you.'

'I'm at my folks, in Achnakerrig.'

'Achnakerrig?'

'Out past Omagh, in the Sperrins.' There was a brief pause then and he felt in her hesitation the almost imperceptible prejudice of the city for the country.

'We've been looking all over. No one knew where you were

Inspector. There's been developments. You've to get back. The Poet is doing his nut. It's Wilbur McCabe. They've found his body on the beach at Warrenpoint. It's all over the afternoon paper.'

When he came away from the phone McCann pushed out through the side door into the car park, fumbled for a cigarette. His eyes ranged over the crossroads, the tarmac with its loose gravel, the long grass at the verge, the overgrown tangled hedgerows dark and brooding in the moonlight. Somewhere behind the hedge sheep were bleating. The sky overhead was scattered with innumerable stars. He looked at his watch, stood out into the road under the light from the bar. A car went past and he tried to wave it down, but the driver swerved around him and accelerated away. At the third attempt McCann stopped a car and climbed in. An old Austin, the doors tied with wire and a clutter of oilcans and bottles under his feet in the passenger seat.

'You in a hurry son?' asked the driver.

'Aye,' said McCann as the gears engaged with a jolt and the car surged ahead, veering wildly out into the middle of the road.

'Where are you going?'

'Omagh,' said the driver.

'That'll do grand,' said McCann, knowing there was a barracks there and they'd have a car that could rush him back to Belfast.

Chapter Fourteen

The Poet greeted him on the stairs on his return to Division.

'Ah McCann, like the evil draft of Hesperus, his poisoned wind sweeps the marbled halls!'

He gripped McCann by the elbow and propelled him away towards his inner sanctum, past his secretary, barking at her:

'I've a five spot with matey here, then I need to get out to Lisburn.'

McCann found himself once again sliding on the leatherette sofa in the romper room, with the Poet looming over him.

'This new body that's popped up? Seen it in the paper. I get all the papers first thing every morning. Have them brought round straight off the press to my house in Knocknakracken so I've a chance to read myself in before the day starts and now what do I find McCann? Another member of the same family killed! First one girl, then two and now this. Good God man, Maureen and the children were down on that beach where they found the body just the other week. It's a gorgeous place and now it'll be completely ruined for us. What would have happened if the children had found the body? It doesn't bear thinking about does it? I don't know what I'm going to say to them in Lisburn about this.'

'It's bad news right enough,' said McCann.

'What's the connection, McCann? What do you know?'

'Wilbur was employed to keep Lizzie McCabe safe, as a bodyguard,' said McCann.

'Well that didn't work very well did it then?' said the Poet. Then he spun round at McCann.

'So where were you anyway when all this blew up?'

'I had some family business. My mother had a wee fall. Some kind of stroke.' The Poet hesitated, adopting a sympathetic look with his head slightly downcast.

'Ah now McCann I'm sorry to hear that. Not a bad one I hope? These things can be hard, very hard. I'd an aunt, a favourite aunt in fact, from Tanderagee. Lived in a big house by the crisp factory there. Lovely place, lovely lady. Fit as a fiddle and then all of a sudden, bang! Down she goes! Never spoke again, just a kind of 'nrrr, nrr' sort of noise out of her. Frustrating for all of us. But you do hear of remarkable recoveries, you think 'well, that's it' and then they're up and limping about, some of the faculties come back. Let's hope for the best, shall we?'

'Yes.'

'But what I can't understand is why you didn't put Deevery on it in your absence. Deevery would have put a stop to all this. He's been having some exceptional successes since he joined us. Arrests coming in all the time. Why just last week he brought in the commander of D Company and I hear tell he's got the team that bombed McGliverty's mill. It's just the kind of thing they want to hear up at Lisburn. Sugars the pill, McCann, of this kind of setback. Hear Deevery's got some excellent contacts, excellent intelligence. Maybe I could put him on it full time McCann, what do you think? With this new body there might be a case for lightening the load on you. That new young girl you've got, that sergeant too. Hear tell she's a bit of a one. Gather they were both looking for you. No way of contacting you either. That's unprofessional McCann. You know you could have compassionate leave? Deirdre here will fix you up with the forms. I'm surprised you didn't take advantage of that. We don't expect our officers just to labour on, as it were. No, we're a compassionate force, McCann, willing to give support wherever its needed.'

But McCann could see the interview was already over because the Poet was calling to his secretary, asking her to fetch him his coat, cap and umbrella.

Standing in the autopsy room half an hour later with Thompson by his side, McCann wished he'd never met Wilbur. Just the week before the thing under the sheet had made them both a cup of tea, shown them the papers for his invalidity pension.

'Ah good morning Inspector!' said the pathologist breezily, business-like as ever. 'Did you have a good break?'

'Not so bad,' said McCann. The smell was already getting to him.

'It's not a pretty one,' said the pathologist.

'He was never a looker.'

'Well they've not improved his looks,' she said, peeling back the cloth in one sudden sweep revealing Wilbur, eyeless and tattooed, his skin unnaturally white, except for a huge area of gore covering his lower body.

'Been in the water a day at least I'd say. And his dick's been chopped off.' The pathologist leant forward, her face puckered in distaste. McCann felt hot, the skin on his forehead prickling. He loosened his collar but found it was already loosened. Thompson was leaning forward to get a closer look. He pulled out a handkerchief and ran it over his face, hoping the feeling would subside.

'Can't have been very nice for him,' said the pathologist.

'You mean he would have been alive?'

'Hard to tell now, but if he was, then the shock and the bleeding would've finished him in a couple of minutes.'

Hence the sea thought McCann; they'd maybe done it at sea to hide the noise and dispose of the evidence. There'd be water enough on hand to clean everything away. He held the rail that divided the autopsy room from the observation point, feeling dizzy, the metal icy in his grip.

'Are you OK Inspector?' Thompson touched his arm gently.

'I'm fine,' grunted McCann, thinking through the nausea that there'd be scope for some plain honest police work; there'd be proper evidence – buckets of it – because no matter how much blood had been washed away they'd find the boat and then it would not be a long step to finding the men that had done it. It had to be men, because you couldn't have done something like that single-handed. And there weren't so many harbours, not so many boats out along Carlingford Lough where the body had washed ashore.

'Jesus, why'd someone do that to anyone,' he murmured in Thompson's ear.

'Punishment for a pervert,' she said.

'But Wilbur's not a pervert,' said McCann, turning towards the door and the familiar lure of fresh air and daylight.

'I've something else for you Inspector,' said the pathologist. McCann turned back reluctantly. 'Seems like you've not got two murderers. You've just got the one.'

'How do you mean?'

'We've the results back from analysis of the samples on both those girls. Blood, semen, hair, fibres. Despite the different modus there's enough similarities to say it's the same chap, like maybe he was covering his tracks, trying to confuse you with the gun and the iron bar, changing his methods.'

McCann paused at the door, looked at her, then at Thompson, who looked as nonplussed as he felt. If the murder of Mairead O'Shea wasn't tit for tat for the killing of Lizzie McCabe, what kind of murder was it? Then he looked again at the body of Wilbur on the table before them.

'Can you see if there's any match,' he said. 'With this fellow. Or what's left of him, and anything you have from the girls.'

'Can do,' said the pathologist. 'Cheer up Inspector, should make it easier for you looking for the one guy and a suspect right here in front of us.'

Back in the office he found Clarke hanging what looked like a new raincoat over his own on the coat stand, Deevery settled in his chair with his feet up, reading the 'News Letter' where a headline read:

'Protestant Butchered at Beauty Spot.'

'Good morning gentlemen,' said McCann briskly. Thompson followed behind, Clarke raising his eyebrows to her as if to ask what she'd been up to with him.

'You'll have seen this by now,' said McCann, tapping the paper, lifting Deevery's feet from the desk and dropping them onto the floor so Deevery had to scramble a bit to get upright.

'Good news for undertakers,' said Deevery.

'Looks like someone's taking the war to the McCabe family,' said Clarke. 'First the daughter, now the uncle.'

'Two Protestants, one Catholic. Two to one's not a good result, McCann,' said Deevery.

'It's not a football match,' said McCann.

'A punishment, a sign,' said Deevery. 'Means someone thinks Wilbur done the girls, doesn't it?'

'We should get onto the boat they used, find that,' suggested Thompson.

'Give you another wee trip down the coast,' said Deevery. 'Nice time of year for it.'

'You could take the sergeant with you for company,' suggested Clarke.

'Make a day of it,' said Deevery, then leering: 'Maybe an overnight stay. It's a long trip. There's some nice wee hotels down by Annalong.'

The slopes of the Mourne mountains rose steeply into the mist to the right of the road, a tumble of dry stone walling and the occasional glimpse of the waves breaking on the steep rocky foreshore below on the left. The road was empty except for the occasional tractor or van delivering bread or transporting feed or animals. McCann chewed the end of a matchstick as he drove, trying not to smoke, trying to cut back at least for half an hour or so and to enjoy the solitude and the fresh air that whispered through the window he'd left ajar.

He followed the signs down to the harbour car park in Kilkeel, through the narrow village street of grey stone houses, coal smoke drifting from their chimneys. It was low tide in the harbour, the fishing fleet dried out, boats propped against the high stone pier awaiting the return of the sea, their spars criss-crossed at angles to each other and hung with drying nets. He locked the car, thrust the keys in his pocket and went down to find the harbourmaster, but the office was locked, a fly-spotted card indicating he was out to lunch and back soon. McCann strolled along the edge of the pier, stepping round the puddles in the stone flags till he came to a boat where a man in yellow oilskins was busy washing down the deck with a hose and broom. He stopped for a moment to watch him working. The man looked up and McCann nodded.

'Grand day,' he said.

'Aye it is that,' said the man.

'Harbourmaster about?'

'Jimmy? Jimmy'll be up at the Anchor,' said the man.

While the fellow returned to his scrubbing McCann retraced his steps up Main Street until he found the Anchor Inn and pushed through the low doorway. Inside a newly lit coal fire sputtered fitfully in a narrow grate. One or two early drinkers leant against the bar in silence, studying form, while the landlord polished glasses. The TV was on, but no one watched, the volume down low. McCann ordered a pint, leant on the counter, looked around while he waited for the barman to let the Guinness settle and to cut the foamy top.

'I'm looking for the harbourmaster,' he said.

A man in a donkey jacket, who'd been sitting with his back to him turned around then.

'You've found him,' he said. McCann nodded at his empty glass.

'Can I get you another?' he offered and the man accepted.

An hour or so later McCann had the names of several boats

that had been out on the night in question.

The next morning the fleet at Kilkeel was surprised to receive a visit from the Health and Safety Executive, a snap inspection by a man and a woman in overalls, the woman in pink wellingtons, who'd emerged from a smart new van with buckets and swabs and sample cases.

'There's been a terrible case of anisakis worm in fish caught off the Irish coast,' said the woman.

'Aye it's a kind of worm that can even live in the anchor chains, the caulking on the deck. We've to swab down and take samples of every boat to find the source,' said the man. 'It can be the very devil to eradicate.'

Sammy McGuigan was hosting a dinner on the eighth floor of the Europa Hotel, his table set for twelve, in the corner looking up Great Victoria Street. At that level the lights of the cars and corporation buses passing below gave a certain illusion of city sophistication, as if he were dining in New York, but minus most of the neon lights, the city below instead punctuated by deep pools of darkness where the streetlights had been shot out and buildings burned. But inside the cut glass and cutlery glittered on the table beneath the chandeliers.

It was an important dinner, to reward friends, cement loyalties, important to signify that Sammy McGuigan was on the cusp of becoming legitimate. It had been a challenging time; there had been measures he'd had to take, for the greater benefit, and to make sure his reputation remained intact. A reputation as a man who got things done, a man who was always as good as his word. You had to take action to protect any besmirchment, any defacement of that hard-won reputation. But there was no question of his own hands being dirty when there were others who would gladly volunteer their services, he'd at last risen above all of that. 'Legitimate' was a phrase he liked to roll on his tongue, enjoying the feeling of solidity and importance it imparted.

There was a menu to match, five courses starting with oysters that Sammy had sent back because they were from Galway in the Republic and extracted whispered and panic-stricken apologies from the head waiter until caviar had been brought out instead, along with a complimentary bottle of Bollinger. By the time the main course came the incident was forgotten and the fellows were all roaring with laughter, great booming yo-ho-ho laughs that even the heavy security curtains couldn't quite muffle, the women shrieking, Sammy banging the table and crying out that such and such was a good one, wasn't it and that he'd never heard the like of it.

Sean O'Reilly was reading the Newry Times. He'd made himself a cup of tea in the kitchen at the back of the house where it was quieter and he'd the chance to study it properly. As a councillor he'd to keep up to date with everything, so he'd also a copy of *An Phoblacht*[20] and of course he'd contacts that would give him the true picture of the state of the armed struggle too; who'd been lifted, who'd been released, news of activity by the security forces alongside the everyday business of being a councillor. Trying to arrange housing transfers and repairs, roads mended, trees felled. You couldn't have one kind of struggle without the other if Ireland were ever to be

---

20 *An Phoblacht* ('The Republic') is the newspaper of Sinn Fein, widely read by active Republicans.

re-united. You couldn't ignore people's day to day problems. There were enough of them on the crowded estate: drugs, kids, joyriding, burglary too. That's why the armed connection was useful, to mete out a bit of rough justice from time to time as the police were no longer effective. They'd been driven out of the estates and rarely showed their faces. That was why they had to organise themselves. 'Ourselves alone', the old slogan still rang true. And on the estate it was like a new parallel structure had developed, a Republic in miniature, ready to take over when British rule finally crumbled.

O'Reilly stared into space smoking and found his thoughts drifting back to the Black Lodge. It was a bit of a cloud on his horizon, something he regretted. But still the fellow Deevery had done him a good turn in the end by belting him, giving him a chance to get out, and anyway they'd nothing on him that would stick now. He was in the clear, had been all along because there was no way he could have told what age the girl was when she'd told him she was sixteen, was there?

He tried to study the horses for a bit, maybe he'd go down and put a bet on, see if any of the lads were in the bookies, but found he couldn't concentrate. Restlessly he watched a little television and had another smoke while he peered out of the back kitchen windows at the woods that closed on the estate. He was almost sure the fellow was still up there because earlier he'd seen the car stop on the hill road and a chap ducking down behind the drystone walling as he made for the trees. And just now when the sun came out there'd been a flash, like the reflection off the lenses of binoculars looking down at his house.

Chapter Fifteen

'So the boat is registered to you, Mr O'Rourke. We have it right here,' said McCann, tapping the registration documents that'd been photocopied and brought up. The man sat on his steel chair, looking neither at Clarke nor at McCann, but at an empty point on the wall somewhere to McCann's right, his head slightly raised in a look of contemptuous disinterest.

'It was. But it's not mine now. I sold it to a fellow last week.'

'Who'd you sell it to?'

'Cash buyer, from Carlingford.'

'How much did you sell it for?'

'Eight thousand.'

'What did he look like? What was his name? Give us his details? Come on son, we'll do you for wasting police time. It's your boat and it was used in the commission of a crime and that's all there is to it. You can tell us lies and we can prove they are lies, maybe tomorrow, maybe the day after we'll find there's no money in your account, no eight thousand to be found, the fellow doesn't exist or if he does he's not bought your boat and it'll just be all a load of bollocks so let's cut to the chase, shall we? It was your boat and it was used on the night of the 24th in the murder and disposal of the body of Wilbur McCabe.'

'Not by me it wasn't.'

'Who was it used by then?'

'I've no idea. First I've heard of it.'

'Come on son. Are you seriously suggesting someone could take a forty foot trawler out of Kilkeel without your knowledge?'

'Why not? Sure, there's boats being lifted all the time.'

'And you'd no security? Left the wheelhouse unlocked, engine ticking over, under them circumstances? Helpful, but not very likely.'

'We note you don't deny the vessel was used in the murder of Wilbur McCabe,' said Clarke.

'My client just said that if it was used for such a purpose he had no part in it. That is not the same as admitting it had been used for such a purpose,' said the solicitor, sitting forwards. A smart young man in his early thirties, tweed jacketed. McCann recognised the firm, had had dealings with them before and regretted the fellow's presence.

'We've forensic on it. Blood matching Wilbur's blood type in the gunwales and in the bilges. Traces of human hair.'

'Does not mean my client was involved,' said the solicitor. 'Unless there is more evidence I must ask that he be released.'

'Released is it?' said McCann. 'I'll keep him for as long as I want. For the record too, Mr O' Rourke has provided no evidence that he is not the owner of the boat'

'Inspector, I must object to that. He has such evidence but you have chosen not to give him time or the means to produce it.'

McCann sighed heavily.

'Right. I can give you twenty-four hours to get it to us.

The name and address of the purchaser. Bank details. Proof of bank transfer. It's also an offence to transfer a vessel without registering its change of ownership.'

A look passed between the boat owner and his solicitor. The man slid his chair back, gestured for the solicitor to do the same so that they could whisper together out of earshot from McCann and Clarke. McCann looked at Clarke and winked.

'OK,' said the solicitor, after four or five minutes of whispering.

'I was approached by someone. Said they needed the boat for a wee job.'

'And you just gave it to him?'

'He made threats Inspector, to me and my family.'

'Duress means my client cannot be viewed as an accessory,' said the solicitor.

'Too dark to get a description or a name of the man I suppose?'

'You've got it Inspector.'

'How'd you know he could carry out the threats?'

'I couldn't take the risk he wasn't. I've a wife and family Inspector.'

'And they can vouch for you on the night in question no doubt?'

'You've got it again Inspector.'

McCann shared tea with Clarke in the canteen.

'What do you think, Inspector?' asked Clarke. 'Is he lying or what?'

McCann lit up, blew the smoke out over Clarke's head before replying with a question of his own.

'Have we anything on him other than owning the boat? Any paramilitary associations, any previous intelligence?'

'There's nothing,' said Clarke. 'But that doesn't mean there isn't any involvement. He could be involved but we've just not heard anything.'

'And how likely is it, the story, from what you know of the Newry IRA that they'd be up to lifting boats, lifting and murdering Wilbur?'

'They're well capable,' said Clarke.

'And Wilbur would be a target, well known in the para-militaries.'

'Aye but not active,' said McCann. 'That's what I can't understand, why they'd kill a fellow like Wilbur.'

'Unless it was someone tipped them off that Wilbur was diddling girls, or maybe that Wilbur killed Mairead,' said Clarke. 'That would give them a motive to take him out.'

'But why would someone tip them off if Wilbur didn't do it? That's what I don't get.'

'Maybe Wilbur did do it? Have you checked the forensics?'

'I'm waiting for that,' said McCann. 'But won't be easy with his bollocks in the Irish sea.'

McCann was thoughtful, pushed his plate away restlessly, the congealing beans and chips suddenly unattractive, thinking that maybe that was why Wilbur had been castrated, so there'd be no way of proving if he was guilty or not.

McCann hung around outside the crematorium, expecting a crowd, but was surprised when just a handful of people showed up, just a single black limousine and the vicar in his Riley. He saw Mr and Mrs McCabe step down and Wilbur's widow, a small woman in a tight black dress and heels, her face covered with a black veil and supported by the McCabes on either side. The hearse carrying the coffin followed; the name 'Wilbur' on one side in flowers and 'For God and Ulster' on the other and at the back a Union Jack, tapestried from pansies, roses and white carnations.

The bearers slid the coffin from the hearse and shouldered it through the gate and up the path. McCann stood back to let it through. Elegant and dignified, the three figures walked stiffly past, Peter McCabe treating him to a slight, imperceptible nod and a murmur of 'Inspector McCann' in greeting. Rather than intrude, McCann hung around outside, smoked a couple of cigarettes, stubbing them out on the crematorium wall, watching the traffic passing on the busy road.

When the funeral party emerged into the sunlight barely twenty minutes later, Wilbur's widow was convulsed with tears.

'It's a shame and a disgrace,' he heard her voice. 'What they done to Wilbur. Not just done to him, but what they done to his reputation.'

McCann moved closer and heard the vicar consoling her:

'He is in the arms of the Lord,'

'Fat lot of good that'll do him,' blurted the woman while Mrs McCabe tried to usher her away towards the waiting limousine.

McCann moved forwards, positioned himself like a good undertaker, obsequiously downcast yet available on the edge of the group. Peter McCabe gestured to him.

'There's the fellow you should blame,' he said. 'Blundering in, so the whole estate knew Wilbur was a suspect. Not leaving the poor man alone. God knows Wilbur felt guilty enough about what happened to Lizzie without finding himself a suspect.'

But Wilbur's widow had swung round towards him already, her face blotched by tears and for a moment he was afraid she would strike him with her handbag or the palm across the face. But something seemed to stop her and she murmured his name.

'Inspector McCann? Inspector McCann,' as if it had triggered something in her memory and she broke free and came towards him even as he tried to slip away, waving her arms at him like someone drowning.

'Inspector McCann! Inspector McCann!' Her voice became more insistent and he could hear her heels tip tapping on the path behind him. He glanced left and right and made it across to the traffic island away from the crematorium, the snarling bulk of a big Fison's lorry drowning out her noise, covering him as he dived over to the far side of the street. But she called to him from the island.

'Inspector McCann, wait. Wait Inspector McCann.' And then she stepped straight out into the traffic, in her tight black skirt and smart high heels, her arms still wind milling to maintain her balance.

'Did you not get my message?' Breathless, almost asthmatically, raising her veil to show the make-up running, holding his arm by the fabric of his green police jacket.

'What message?' Something about her made McCann soften. Her awkward lopsided grasp of his tunic, the desperation with which she had teetered after him and now the shortness of her breath, the faint sense that she, like himself, was past all attractive possibilities in life, all of these inclined him to listen

199

and to bend his head to her above the noise of the traffic.

'You see Inspector I tried to tell them confidentially about what Lizzie said, but it was not passed on.'

'What Lizzie said?' he repeated dully, then suggested they take a cup of tea together in the café opposite.

'That'd be nice,' she agreed. And she waved away the McCabes who were trying to follow, to show they'd to go on without her.

Inside the tea rooms there was a dense layer of steam hanging, dulling the lights and making the walls stream with moisture. McCann found her a chair and pulled it out for her, asked her what she wanted to have, read a few lines from the chalkboard for her as she said her eyes weren't good. He ordered a slice of marble cake and a mug of tea for her and got himself a fry up, delaying the conversation while he found the cutlery, condiments and napkins.

'I've something to tell you that wee Lizzie told me that I think you'd best know about,' she said as they settled at a free table. She'd lowered her voice and McCann struggled to hear over the noise of the geyser dispensing tea at the counter, accompanied by clouds of steam.

'Wilbur was worried about Lizzie you know.'

'On account of the threats to Peter's business?'

'Threats didn't worry Wilbur at all. Sure, he'd lived with that most of his life. That's why Peter had him to keep an eye on Lizzie. Thought it would discourage anyone from trying anything. Wilbur was very close to her. No, not in the way you think. Wilbur absolutely doted on her, we both did.'

'No kids of your own then?'

'We couldn't Inspector. That's why we were so close with

poor Lizzie. Wilbur would be distraught that it's come to this. It's just disgusting what they done to her and now them animals suspecting him for it, butchering him for it when there's no one loved her more than Wilbur. More even than her own parents. Lizzie trusted us completely. That's why she told me first.'

'Told you what?'

'I'll trust you to keep it safe, because it'll be the worst for you if it gets out. Like it was for Lizzie and Wilbur.'

McCann sat silent, expectant, nodded at her to go on. Watched as she took a deep breath and lowered her voice further so it was barely audible: 'There's a fellow called Sammy McGuigan, big name in the paramilitaries that Wilbur knew from way back. Well Lizzie was volunteering up at the Black Lodge, it's some kind of a study centre up the Antrim coast.'

McCann nodded, said he knew it.

'Well this Sammy turns up at the Black Lodge lecturing the girls, Lizzie has a bit of a row with him. You see she was getting old enough to have views of her own and was trying them out the way young folk do, you know not knowing when to keep your mouth shut and what not to say to particular folk. Sounds like she was giving Sammy some stick from what she told me and I don't know maybe he enjoyed it, misunderstood her because she could be awful forward, putting a contrary argument just for the sake of it and maybe he thought she was flirting? I mean God knows where these men keep their brains. Anyhow it was the end of the course and they was all waiting on the step for the bus to pick them up and go back to Belfast, when Sammy apparently swings up in his car and offers her a lift and because he's old friends with Wilbur from way back, she says 'yes' like an eejit and then she only gets into the car with him.'

'Into his car?'

'Aye I know. She'd not a lot of sense God love her, but of course it was more than Sammy could resist having her there in the front seat with him and he only tries to touch her up.'

'What did she say exactly?'

'It was all the usual craic; all the old: "I've to get something out of the glove compartment" and, *"I'm sorry oh look what I've dropped!"* and next thing she knows he's got his hand up her skirt. Lizzie just went mental, got out of the car and made a run for it at the lights in Carrickfergus, she said.'

'Jesus. Why didn't you tell anyone? Pass it on? Why didn't you tell her parents?'

'Lizzie begged me not to. Didn't want the fuss or the embarrassment. She just wanted to forget all about it. But all the same I thought someone should know about it so I rang Division. Crumlin Road Inspector. I done my best to warn them but nothing was ever done, least nothing decent. Then she was killed.'

McCann looked at her then. His own nick had been warned. She raised an eyebrow to him.

'So, God help me I told Wilbur then. I wish I'd never told him,' said Mrs McCabe. 'I wish I'd never told him what Lizzie said. Because it must have got back to Sammy that Wilbur also knew what he was up to, God knows how. And maybe that's why they done him in too.'

'But why did Wilbur not tell me, when I came round?' said McCann, trying to keep the desperation out of his voice. 'Why did no one mention this after Lizzie was killed?'

'I was out when you did the interview with him. Told him

afterwards, when I knew you'd been round. I knew it was important, and important that I'd told the police too. Wilbur was teetering on the edge with those boyos at the time; sometimes he was in and sometimes he was out. He liked to pretend he was in with them because he thought it gave him some kind of credit, but in the end it amounted to nothing. Less than nothing. Maybe he thought he could deal with it himself, in his own way. Maybe he thought it wasn't important, that fellows tried it on with girls all the time and there'd been nothing significant about that. But after I told Wilbur he must have told someone else because next thing I knew Wilbur was dead too. It was like Sammy was so powerful there was no one could stop him, like it had gone to his head, all of their heads Inspector. He was above the law or anything. It was a pity I wasn't home when you came to see Wilbur after Lizzie's death because I would of told you all of it then. Immediately I heard you'd been round I told Wilbur what I've told you now. I think he was trying to find you Inspector when they done him in.'

Grief, anger, bitterness, frustration filled her eyes and she gripped McCann's arms so tightly he could feel her nails through the tunic.

'Oh Inspector, you've got to do something now.' McCann's tongue felt thick in his mouth. He grabbed at his tea, slurping some over the side of the cup onto the tabletop.

'That's clumsy,' she said and began wiping it up with the napkins. Years ago, he would have patted her arm and said, 'We will deal with them missus, whoever done it, don't you worry about that.' But now he just looked into her face.

'Let's go outside to get some air. You can tell me what else you know.'

'I know nothing more Inspector. Thought I knew, but now I know that I know nothing.'

'Come on, let's get a wee bit of fresh air,' he repeated and bustled her out between the narrow tables, tossing a note down to pay.

They went into the park by the reservoir. There was a cool wind coming down off the mountain, turning the water black. The summer blooms were out, flattened in the wind as they walked, her arm still clutching his as if it offered her some kind of protection.

'So why did you tell me?' Asked McCann. 'It's a brave thing to do, if it's what led to Wilbur being killed.'

'I was always taught not to tell, but well you've got to or you'd go crazy Inspector, with the two of them dead. First Lizzie, then Wilbur. That poor wee Catholic girl too. Maybe you're used to it in your position, all those deaths,' she said. 'All those people keeping quiet, keeping their heads down.' She paused reflectively, hesitating whether to start a turn around the reservoir. 'And I seen you at Lizzie's funeral Inspector, I could tell you were upset. And it's good you came today. It means you are a good man and you won't let it rest, will you?' Her eyes gleamed as if she knew the curse she had put upon him. Her shoulders lifted a little, she rummaged in her bag and pulled out a handkerchief, blew her nose and said: 'Those flowers look nice Inspector, don't they?'

'Late this year,' he said. 'It's been a cold spring.'

'I'll be seeing you then Inspector,' she said suddenly and began to walk away. As he tipped his cap to her departing back she called out: 'Maybe over the water but not here after all of this. It's not safe for me now, however honest you seem Inspector. Once burnt, twice shy as they say.'

'Give us the station log,' said McCann. 'For February.'

The desk sergeant gave him a smile.

'For you Inspector, anything is possible,' and she went through to the duty room at the back, came back a few minutes later with the ledger, laying it out on the high front desk for McCann to peruse. There were hundreds of hand-written notes, in different inks, initials and times against each, a catalogue of misdemeanours, an encyclopaedia of frailty and wickedness. From the book it should be possible to see who had called and who had taken the call. He flipped over the pages, running his fingers down the entries around the time Wilbur would have contacted the police.

'This the only one?'

'For February?'

'Aye.' His feet hurt from standing.

'You could take a seat in the back Inspector.'

'I will that,' he said gratefully and settled himself in the warm comfort of the duty room, the ledger laid out on the table, a good light overhead. But there seemed to be nothing. Could Wilbur's widow have been mistaken? Could Wilbur maybe have told her he was going to the station but gone somewhere else instead, to the wrong place where they'd an interest in concealment and the means to achieve it?

It was only as he was leaving the station that he had another thought and turned back from the door to the duty sergeant.

'Here,' he said. 'Give us that ledger again will you?'

'You've not had enough of me then?'

'Oh, I can never get enough of you dear, but it's the ledger I want,' said McCann. He took it back to his office, up the stairs, his fingers feeling along the spine of the book as he went. Once in his room he put on the desk light, took out a magnifying glass and examined the ledger carefully, turning each page as he did so until he found the place where, if he opened the book out wide to expose the binding he could just see sharp white edges of cut paper where a page had been expertly razored. Of course there'd be dozens of people that would have checked the day book; people asked for it every day, if they were up in court or writing up their notes, there were a hundred reasons why people would want to see it. But it wasn't a good feeling that someone close could not be trusted. So when he returned the book to the duty sergeant he asked for a list of everyone who'd had it.

'I'll see what I can do,' she said. 'Tomorrow OK?'

'Tonight,' said McCann.

'This is about all I can remember,' she said later, as he was going off duty. There was a list of ten or twelve names, including Clarke, Thompson, Deevery, even the Poet himself.

'The Poet?' queried McCann.

'Aye I was surprised too,' she said. 'That he'd be interested in anything at our level.'

But there was nothing unusual in that, thought McCann. They'd complaints and allegations all the time now and the top brass were sometimes tied up in it just as much as the serving officers.

The next day Deevery came into the office in a jovial mood and put his arm around McCann's shoulder.

'Are you coming to the benefit McCann? Pick yourself up some nice young lady and put a spring back in your step.' McCann winced at the contact.

'You could be dancing the conga!' And here Deevery wiggled his hips, reaching out with both hands as if for an imaginary woman in front of him in the conga line, suggestively thrusting his crotch forward. 'What about it McCann? That'd cheer you up! C'mon and I'll sell you a ticket,' he said, reaching into his jacket and pulled out a bunch of tickets.

'Everyone's going, it'll be a grand night. Ten pounds,' said Deevery. 'All in a good cause.' McCann hesitated. 'You could buy the ticket for the cause and not go McCann. Sit at home and do the crossword, or whatever it is you do when you aren't inspecting. Two for fifteen pounds then. There's a free bar with dancing. You could win the raffle McCann. There's a Ford Cortina first prize, holiday in Florida second, trip to a show in London's West End third.'

'Give us two then,' said McCann. 'Seeing as there's a reduction and it's in a good cause.'

'Two?' said Deevery, surprised.

'Aye two,' said McCann and peeled off the notes.

It was a stupid thing to have done, to have bought two before even asking her and now he had the two tickets getting dog-eared in his wallet. Humiliating to turn up alone or worse, to not turn up and have to make an excuse. So the days went by and then he started to wonder if there would be too much distracting gossip if he asked Emily Thompson and she said 'yes,' or gave him the brush off, even complained. Maybe it'd harm her chances with the kind of younger men she should have been going with. But then – and much to his surprise – she came up to him in the canteen and asked: 'Just wondering if you had a spare ticket for the ball, Inspector.' Though she could have been just taking pity on him, having understood his predicament.

Chapter Sixteen

He felt a certain pride and apprehension as he drove in through the gates of the mansion and the security team came over to the car. They'd military as well as uniformed police with the search area discreetly hidden behind the cover of the gatehouse. He was proud that Emily Thompson was sitting beside him, quietly self-contained and smiling, her perfume still faintly discernible above the smoke from his cigarette. Already there was a queue of cars going through security and up ahead he could see the Secretary of State's black Austin Princess with the flag flying on its bonnet.

'They're taking their time,' he said, knocking the ash out of a crack in the window, watching the lights from the torches like so many fireflies, buzzing to and fro over the Minister's car then on to the car behind. He switched the engine off while they waited their turn and in the silence he murmured: 'I've evidence that Sammy McGuigan interfered with Lizzie McCabe before she was killed.'

Thompson didn't respond.

'Lizzie told Wilbur's wife and she told the police.'

'And who dealt with that?' She asked quietly, smoothing her skirt.

'We don't know.'

'It'll be in the day book.'

'It's not. Some pages have been cut out.'

'Very handy.' she said.

'And Wilbur McCabe, after his wife told him what she'd reported and nothing happened, he reported it too.'

'To whom?'

'We don't know that either because he was killed soon after.'

A horn tooted behind them and McCann realised the line of cars had moved forwards while he'd been talking, the search team waving them ahead, the lights of the Minister's big car sweeping away ahead of them in a wide curve to the house beyond.

When they arrived at the entrance McCann leapt out to open the car door for her, but she'd already got out. He could hear the sound of a band starting up; a few heavy bars from the bass guitar and the voice of the singer echoing and booming from inside as they climbed the steps, turning for a moment to admire the view of the lough glittering in the moonlight below.

'Good evening Inspector,' said the constable at the door and saluted while McCann fumbled for their tickets. They went through into the hallway, where the chandeliers blazed, then into the bar area beyond, bedecked in red, white and blue bunting, candlelit and already crowded.

'What'll you have?' asked McCann, his eyes ranging across the crowd, spotting Deevery, Clarke, the Minister, his wife and his minders, the Poet stepping forward to greet him, sporting a splendid dress uniform.

They went up to the bar, pushing through the outer reaches of drinkers, McCann nodding here and there to people he recognised. Clarke came up beside them in the crush.

'The lads are all over there,' he said. 'I'll get you a drink Inspector. A pint of double? And sergeant, what'll it be?'

'I'll get these,' said McCann, helping carry the drinks over to one of the tables, already crowded and laden with glasses and bottles.

'I remember the time me and Deevery arrested a fellow out on the strand at Magilligan,' one of the men was saying later, his collar loosened, legs splayed out.

'Oh that was a grand story, I heard,' said Clarke. Off duty he seemed like just a normal lad, thick black hair, smart evening dress that bulged and rippled on his broad shoulders.

'Fisherman he was,' continued the man, 'Owned one of them trawlers worked out of the Foyle, down the coast.'

'Sure them fellows have been in it up to their necks since partition,' said McCann. With a drink in hand he felt more in the mood for it. Thompson sat close beside him listening, he could feel her presence there.

'Aye they were in every kind of racket, drugs, guns, it didn't matter what.'

'Anything's better than John Dory. Them's ugly fuckers,' said one of the men.

'Anyhow, Deevery got the wink this fellow was bringing in Africans.'

'Africans!'

'Aye Africans, in the night.'

'Suppose you'd not see them then, in the night?'

'They'd been seen right enough. The Gardai'd lifted a van-load of Nigerians in Donegal and Deevery'd had the tip-off another load was on the way.'

The storyteller raised his hand. He'd everyone's attention now. The fellows were laughing and smoking and pulling on their pints. Thompson was smiling, tapping out the ash, her hand elegant with a tiny gold chain around the wrist.

'So four of us went down the dock to lift them, but when we get there he takes off down the Port Road, through the lights and away out along the coast. Deevery puts the siren on, puts his boot on the floor, a big handbrake turn on the dock, but the rear wheels slid off of the side of the dock and there we were hanging suspended with a twenty foot drop to the boats below, the blue light flashing away.'

'Jesus so how did you get going again?'

'We got the two branch men out of the back.'

'Weighing you down, were they?'

'Aye, lardy boys, but strong with it. We got them to lift the back of the police car till the wheels got back on the quay and we all piled in. But by that time your man was halfway back to Magilligan with his load of negroes. But Deevery didn't give up. He was like a man inspired. The James Hunt of the force if ever I saw one, down the Port Road the wrong way like a maniac, out onto the A2, then at the roundabout by the Esso station he suddenly turned sharp left out along the coast road, down along behind the dunes. The speed he was going he was up on them in no time at all. The van turned out onto the beach and it was low tide, out across the sand and Deevery heads them off. Five big negroes leapt out and started running away in different directions.'

'Did he get his man?'

'Not without a fight. He started chucking mackerel at

Deevery from out of the van.'

'Mackerel? You're having us on!'

By now hysteria had broken out, the audience clutching their sides with painful, drunken sobs of laughter.

'Away to fuck with you, you just made that up,' someone said.

'So help me God. Deevery shouts out, "Put them fish down," and pulls out his gun and just then a big mackerel hits him smack in the eye and his gun goes off. Which knocks a bit of sense into the fellow. But he'd achieved his objective which was distraction, because by then the black fellows were gone and never seen again.'

McCann listened and laughed, he joined in as he always did, watching Deevery reconstructed as the good old boy, Thompson and the young constables laughing too, feeling himself more alone and distant from it all. He stood up clumsily, pushing his chair back, almost knocked over a drink, apologised. Thompson touched his arm and murmured maybe it was time to go and dance, but the talk of Deevery had annoyed him and he growled: 'I'm just away for a bit of fresh air,' and shoved out through the throng, across the crowded dance floor, seeing the revolving door lit up ahead like a beacon guiding him towards the starry night outside. He pushing out through the heavy mahogany doors revolving slowly at first, then accelerating so that they almost threw him out onto the steps outside. He stumbled to the border of one of the flowerbeds, looked around, sat down and lit a cigarette, his body cooling.

Then Clarke emerged from the doorway behind him and looked around, made his way over.

'Needed a bit of fresh air too,' he said. 'That Deevery annoys me. You don't know him the way I do,' said McCann, shaking his head as if trying to clear the memory of Deevery away.

'I know,' said Clarke. 'I was listening McCann. Putting them at their ease. You make people easy, they make mistakes.' McCann looked over towards Clarke as he lit his cigarette, the lighter illuminating the lower half of his face. Had he heard him right, he wondered? Or was Clarke putting him at his ease, to watch him make mistakes too?

'Aye, well,' he said and stubbed his cigarette out on the sole of his shoe, the sparks showering like a small firework for a moment before the darkness closed in and he could barely see Clarke beside him. But now Clarke leant in to him and murmured: 'That O'Reilly we were watching for you. Met someone interesting,' he murmured. Then he leant over and slipped an envelope from the pocket of his jacket, pressed it into McCann's hand.

Back inside he found Thompson, still laughing with the lads, a line of shorts assembled on the table before her and Deevery himself now holding court, his face red and puffy with the drink, occupying McCann's empty seat. She looked up briefly as he searched for a free stool. Deevery leaned over her, grasped at McCann's coat sleeve, gestured he should come closer, made one of the constables give up his seat so he could sit down beside him.

'Been hearing about you son. You and the Poet.' And one eye seemed to coldly see right through McCann while the other smiled in a conventional, social way, his hand pawing at

McCann to sit himself down.

'Jesus Wilbur McCabe though? I knew the family,' said Deevery. 'Knew them well.'

In the background McCann saw Clarke asking Thompson to dance, leaning down to hold her hand and help her from her seat and lead her onto the floor.

'Leastways that'll be the end of your investigation I imagine,' said Deevery.

McCann sucked on his cigarette, drew down hard so it burned bright, took the hot smoke down into his lungs, stubbed it down in the ashtray, the butt end crumbling, blowing the smoke in Deevery's eyes, watching the dancefloor from the corner of his eye.

'There's no need, is there McCann? They got their man with Wilbur McCabe. There's nothing more for us to do in that respect. You can take it easy.'

'Take it easy? What about what they've done to him?'

'That's nothing compared with what Wilbur done to them girls,' said Deevery. 'I'd not waste your time on that son. It's rough, but effective justice. I reckon there's a couple of thousand wee girls sleeping easier tonight along with their parents on account of what they done to Wilbur. Far better the fellow is dealt with like that than twenty-five years watching television in his cell and doing the Open University, waiting for parole so he can get out and do it again. It would mean more to the parents, they'd be grateful for what happened.'

'Not for the McCabes,' said McCann.

'Deserves it more for that the dirty cunt. Doing it in your own family! That's the only way to make sure he doesn't do it again.' He leant back, a smile of satisfaction on his lips, then gestured at McCann's empty pint and made a sign for another one. 'It was all smoke and mirrors anyway, McCann. Now you see it, now you don't.' He moved his hands as if he were shuffling a deck of cards over the dimly-lit table. McCann could barely hear him over the noise of the music from the big six-piece band. People were dancing around them, starting to push the tables back, waving their hands in the air to the Hokey Cokey. He caught a glimpse of Clarke, with his hands round Thompson's waist. McCann was suddenly angry with this shadowy world of backroom nods and winks, the casual way Deevery seemed to be slurring over the mystery of the girls' last hours.

'But Mairead O'Shea too?' he said.

'What about her? It'll be the same story. Motive, sex. Opportunity, Wilbur had links with the Lodge through his brother and Lizzie McCabe. Means, Wilbur had access to vans and weapons too from his time in Crumlin Road.' Deevery's hands sliced the air decisively with each point.

'There's no forensic linking him.'

'Nor will there be unless you can find his bollocks in the Irish Sea,' said Deevery.

'If he was involved he wasn't the only one,' said McCann, shouting now to be heard above the music.

Deevery leant forwards, his hand over his ear, cocked against McCann's mouth to catch the words.

'Like who?'

'Sammy McGuigan, Sean O'Reilly. Their names are still in the ring for the killings.'

'And you've nothing come back from the surveillance?' Deevery leant forward, gripped McCann's sleeve. He could feel the tightness of his fingers through his suit.

'Nothing,' said McCann.

Deevery was silent. Suddenly he put his face close to McCann's and gripped his tie. 'If you've nothing more, I'd leave them out of this McCann.' McCann glared back, then pulled his face away, slammed his forehead into Deevery's nose, ripped his hands off his tie.

'You can't tell me what to do,' he said thickly. He was dimly aware of restraining hands and voices: 'Easy now. Easy now. If you boys have a disagreement could you take it outside.'

The band lurched into a chorus of 'I'm a lumberjack.' Both men turned to look at the stage where one of the constables was standing in a red Mountie's uniform. Everyone around them was now cheering and laughing and whistling and stamping their feet.

'Good on you McCardle!' Someone shouted and the band shifted into 'The stripper,' and constable McCardle began to unknot his tie on the stage, to wild cries of 'Get them off Cardy!' in an enormous wave of noise and drunken pleasure and the moment passed. Deevery was holding a handkerchief to his nose and saying:

'McCann for fuck's sake get a grip,' but then there was a brush of blue miniskirt against McCann's leg and a length of stockinged thigh, a strong perfume in the crush to see the show, and the moment passed.

'Here, you fellows don't mind if we sit down do you?'

'No. No, Sorry,' said McCann. 'Sorry. I'm away to the toilet,' and he stood up awkwardly, manoeuvring round the women's legs and heels, apologising as his coat trailed in the ashtray.

'It's my bladder,' he said. 'Need a piss every ten minutes.'

'I'm the same' said the woman. 'Never touch the beer. Not the capacity for it.'

'You two should get together then,' said Deevery.

In the toilet, McCann splashed his face with cold water to stop the bruise on his forehead spreading, to wash away the smear of blood, cursing himself. He could hear laughter and applause and then the band starting their final number; the big jarring chords, the final introductions of the departing musicians, the echo of the doo-wah in the purple bar outside. Soon the strip lights would come on and the doors would be thrown open to the chill air. He swayed in front of the mirror.

When he went back outside he tried to find Emily Thompson. He pushed through the dancers, went over to the queue by the Ladies' toilets and back to the group by the bar. Deevery's nose had stopped bleeding and he'd somehow found himself a clean shirt, a fresh short on the low table in front of him, guessed McCann was looking for her.

'Said she was disgusted,' said Deevery. 'Went away with Clarke. Said he'd give her a lift McCann. Bit above your class anyhow wasn't she, from what I hear and see.'

McCann knew it was time to go home. He could feel the edges of the evening getting rougher, snatches of conversation blurred and indistinct; the phrases with their ends wrenched off, meanings barely intact or somehow veiled and oddly malevolent: 'Wee feller... no hair at all, bald as a... put the cunt through the window... would you look at the state of that fellow got up like a... bladder fit to burst... near wet myself... up the Altnagelvin with a drip in him was the only thing keeping him going... white as a sheet, pasty like he'd seen a ghost… hold on here's the Inspector… let the Inspector rest his feet.'

McCann walked across the car park, his coat undone, crossed the road with its parked cars and down the steps to the beach beyond. Out on the sea he could see a couple of lights bobbing slowly northwards but otherwise there was nothing other than a tall bank of cloud where Scotland normally lay. The hotel was set back from the coast road, in a slightly raised position and the looming shape of the headlands on either side of the bay came into view. It was maybe right what Deevery had said, that she had been too good for him. She'd have left in the end so it was better sooner rather than getting deeper in. He'd ring her if she didn't ring him, to apologise and explain himself, tell her what Deevery had said and why he'd done what he'd done. The moon came out and suddenly the sea glittered beneath him and he could hear the sound of the water in the distance, drawing and chuckling on the fine pebbled beach. He picked his way across the narrow beach to the water's edge, awkward in his tight shoes, right up to the point where the stones gave way to a fine white sand, where the surf came in. Slowly he turned to the left, then right, peering along the water's edge. A burst of noise came from the hotel as a couple of revellers came out and was just as quickly extinguished as the heavy doors swung shut behind them. There was some banter and then the noise of car doors slamming, engines starting up and two sets of lights swung across the trees behind the hotel, out along the harbour wall. Some instinct of McCann's made him crouch down on his haunches as the lights swept over him. The two cars accelerated away, up the Belfast road and

McCann followed their lights along the dark road, round the first bend, then briefly they re-appeared before finally rounding the headland. Suddenly it was cold. He took a few stones from the beach, tossed them at the water, but they vanished without a splash, as if swallowed by darkness. He squinted at his watch but the moon had gone so he couldn't see, couldn't guess what time it was. Then came another burst of sound, the sound of heels unsteadily across the car park and a man's voice.

'Ach now Sheilagh, don't be so stupid.'

'I'm not stupid. It's you who are the stupid one.'

'C'mon Sheilagh.' The man's voice was pleading. McCann could imagine him pulling at her arm as she refused to get into the car with him and teetered off towards the sea. McCann began to walk away up the beach, but the sound of the argument seemed to pursue him.

'Sheelagh, don't be so difficult.'

'I'm not being difficult.'

'You are. Where are you going now? Come back!' McCann realised that as fast as he tried to walk away up the beach, the couple were keeping pace with him on the coast road above. He could see the woman now, the glint of her evening dress – as she strode along the sea wall and the man – much shorter – stumbling along after her. Swiftly he tossed his cigarette away into the sea, turned his back, so his black coat would merge in the black sea, making him invisible again, but now the woman was going down the steps to the beach, clutching her heels in one hand.

'I'm going for a swim,' she announced aggressively and stumbled across the pebbles, barely twenty yards in front of him.

'Sheilagh for God's sake don't be an eejit,' shouted the

man. 'You'll drown yourself.'

'So what?' shouted the woman turning to face him, then on seeing McCann she fell silent.

'It's ok,' said McCann, embarrassed.

'No. Actually,' said the woman, now embarrassed herself. 'Actually it's all right. I was only kidding. Just winding him up.'

The man scrunched across the stones towards them and stood a few feet off. He held his arms as if to say, 'What can you do with women?'

And she stepped across to him uncertainly, let him reach his hand out to steady her.

He watched them weaving unsteadily back up the beach together to the steps. At the foot of the steps she paused and leant on the man, putting on first one shoe, then the other, then following him obediently up the steps. McCann followed at a distance.

When he reached the road, they were turning in through the gates of the hotel, arms linked.

The night had darkened again and a thin drizzle blew in off the sea, obscuring the water, blowing across the hotel lights. Within an instant he was soaked, his hair plastered down. Instead of pushing back into the bar he found his car, fiddled with the keys in the dark till he was able to sit inside, slumping at the wheel, key in the ignition to get the engine on, to warm up and dry out, flicking the interior light on, remembering something, struggling for the envelope in his inside pocket, ripping it open in the yellow half-light. A photo of Deevery chatting with Sean O'Reilly, one of his prime suspects, like they were firm friends.

Chapter Seventeen

McCann came in early to show he had a head on him that could take the drink, but regretted it immediately because in the corridor he bumped into Deirdre who stopped him and said: 'Morning Inspector. The early bird then?' He had the feeling she could see the bruise on his forehead, despite the use of some old concealer he'd found in the bathroom. He burbled about the morning traffic, putting up a barrage of normality that was the opposite of what he felt, tailing off under her quizzical gaze in the middle of a sentence about the number fifty-nine bus, so weirdly that she peered up into his bloodshot eyes with a look of concern.

'Well the Superintendent said I'd to find you. Said he'd something urgent to discuss with you.'

'McCann, McCann. Ah McCann!' The Poet sighed histrionically, at the same time shaking his head from side to side so his gleaming, cleanly shaved jowls quivered with disapproval. McCann followed him into the romper room, while Deirdre retreated to her desk in the corridor.

'Shut the door, will you McCann. We don't want prying ears on this one. It'll be your embarrassment, although God knows you seem to be beyond embarrassment.'

McCann had a stabbing feeling in the left-hand side of his

head as if someone was driving a compass point through the top of his skull and twirling it to and fro behind his left eyeball. The right-hand side had no sensation at all, as if it were dead.

'Yes sir,' he said, judging the situation formal enough to require him to remain standing while the Poet stepped towards him.

'I have had reports McCann, of disgraceful behaviour at the police ball, at the benefit for dead officers and their widows and families.' He struggled to draw breath between each phrase, his face purpling and swelling. He drew level with McCann, his mouth close to McCann's ear. 'It's hard to imagine a more appalling scene. A senior officer head-butting another senior colleague in plain public view, like some young lout on a night out. I just can't understand what came over you man. Had you been drinking? Of course you had, I've no doubt of that. But that's no excuse. An officer should be able to hold a lot of drink and still disport himself like an officer.'

McCann nodded glumly.

'Yes sir,' he said.

'I know we are all under pressure McCann, particularly you, with these cases you're on. A most difficult, distressing situation and I know how hard it can be when you are not making progress or you feel that other officers are maybe holding you back, how easy it is to erroneously blame them for your own shortcomings. I've been there myself in the days when I was a young investigating officer, but you learn to take responsibility for your own failings, to ask for help before things get out of hand. It's the kind of professionalism I'd expect of an experienced officer at your level McCann, so I'm really disappointed.' The Poet eased himself down on his throne, gesturing McCann to take one of the smaller seats beside him.

'I wouldn't mind so much McCann but this seems to me to be the icing on a very unpleasant cake, attacking one of our finest men.'

'I was provoked,' said McCann.

'In what way? No provocation could justify such conduct. None at all. An officer should be able to withstand even the most extreme provocation.' The Poet clenched and unclenched his fist as he spoke. McCann opened his mouth to speak, to explain the circumstances, but the Poet held up his hand.

'No, McCann I don't even want to hear what kind of cock and bull story you've a mind to tell me. I'm afraid you've crossed the Rubicon now. It would not have been so bad if there'd not been members of the public there as witnesses. A good rumble between colleagues can sometimes clear the air. Why I remember when I was stationed in Armagh we sometimes had a bit of a scuffle on a night out and everything forgotten in the morning, but not with ladies involved. Of course, there's always ladies behind it isn't there?' And now the Poet leaned directly in front of McCann and his large questioning face looked into his, like some kind of monster looking into an empty cupboard in the hope of food. McCann stared expressionlessly ahead.

'I thought as much,' said the Poet with satisfaction, taking McCann's unwillingness to meet his eye as proof that his suspicions were well founded. There was a long pause, while the Poet seemed to be trying to marshal his thoughts and then he drew himself up and said: 'There'll be a disciplinary in due course. Normally I'd have to suspend you both, but that's impractical given the situation we're in. But as of now, I'm putting Deevery in charge. From what I've heard he's the victim here. There's been far too little progress on these cases. My patience was already thin, like gossamer, but now it is rent asunder and cold reality wafts its icy breath betwixt the tatters of it.'

He left the office, the Poet returned to his desk. Outside in the corridor Deirdre gave McCann a sympathetic smile and crossed his name through in the Poet's appointment book as he went past. He lingered on the stairs, not wishing to return yet to his own office to face Thompson, Clarke and Deevery. It was true he'd made little progress, but there'd be even less with Deevery in charge; Deevery who'd warned him off the suspects the night before. Deevery who had maybe received the tip-off from Wilbur McCabe's wife and done nothing with it, even tried to hide the fact by tearing the evidence from the day book. But maybe that was the way the force was working now and he was becoming too old school, not fully up to date with the new methods. He paused by one of the windows that looked out over the city and lit a cigarette, watched the grey clouds slowly drifting across the skyline. Well, thought McCann, it would not stop him, having Deevery in charge.

When McCann got back to the office, Deevery was already there.

'No hard feelings McCann,' he said and held out his hand to him.

'None,' said McCann and shook it, holding Deevery's arm with his other hand, while Deevery slapped him affectionately on the back in an apparent gesture of reconciliation.

'Is Thompson in?' he asked.

'Thompson's away up to Andersonstown,' said Deevery. 'She's no way finished with them school interviews.' Then, picking up on McCann's reaction, he said: 'Why? Did you want her for something else, McCann?'

But McCann had already gone. He called the dispatcher from a phone downstairs, found Thompson had gone out to an address in the west of the city. He scribbled it down and leaped down the stairs two steps at a time, his feet clattering on the bare boards, shoving his way past a couple of specials labouring wearily up the steps in their riot gear. At the foot of the stairs he turned sharp left, through the iron door to the armoury.

'Gi'us a walther 4.2 and aye a semi automatic too,' he said. The fellow moved with amazing slowness, as if underwater, towards the racks where the armaments were kept, whistling as he went.

'C'mon pal I've not got all day,' said McCann as the Walther was laid out for his inspection, its holster well worn and gleaming, the long barrelled semi automatic rifle following.

'You'll need to sign,' said the fellow, letting McCann initial for the weapons, his thumb showing him the place in the ledger with measured care.

McCann grabbed the weapons, buckled on the handgun, shrugged his jacket loosely over it and set off back down the stairs with the automatic. In the pound they'd already got a Land Rover out for him, a driver but no gunner, so McCann gave the address and sat himself in the back gunner's seat, banged on the side of the van and shouted, 'Let's go!'

Twenty minutes later they were in the heart of the estate, a maze of cul de sacs and footpaths where Thompson had gone. The driver swung round a series of sharp corners, looking for the street. McCann could see through the front windscreen a careering view of painted gable ends, mean corporation houses, burned out cars and overgrown gardens. They were in a no-man's-land of shuttered properties.

'Any sign of her?'

'Not yet,' said the driver. Then he felt a sudden wave of relief wash over him. He saw her coming out of a house, towards her parked Land Rover. McCann shouted to his driver to pull over beside her.

'We need to have a chat. Somewhere quiet, away from Division,' he shouted through the open window.

He had the drivers drop them both in the city centre and they made their way to one of the cafes that were popular with shoppers.

'I'm not the flavour of the month after last night,' said McCann, finding them a seat at the back where they'd not be overheard, ordering up coffee and cake for himself and a pot of tea for Thompson, carrying it back while she collected a couple of napkins.

Once settled in their seats McCann said: 'Deevery thinks Wilbur done the girls in and the Poet's backing him.'

'Is that why you belted him?' She grinned, amused by the senior officers' indiscretion, intrigued by McCann's loss of control.

'Deevery suggested Wilbur was the guilty man, that was the end of the story, without evidence, without doing anything to prove it. I think we should get forensic samples off Sammy

McGuigan too. We've got Wilbur's widow saying he tried it on with Lizzie McCabe, so there'd be grounds for that now.'

'Go over the Poet's head? Contradict Deevery?' She looked thoughtful.

'And the same for the other suspect, Sean O'Reilly. We've that girl you interviewed says there was touching going on, her father too, though he wasn't specific with names, suggested something similar. And McAllister worried about wild nights at the annexe.'

'What does Clarke think?'

'I think he's on our side, just. Branch have been helping out with surveillance on the suspects.'

'Still doesn't help belting Deevery,' she said.

'Meaning I'm being rash?' asked McCann.

'No, I'm sure you know what you are doing,' she said, stirring her tea slowly with the teaspoon, first one way then the other.

'Well I'm glad someone does,' said McCann. 'Because I need your help.'

There was a silence, then he asked: 'I hear you went off with Clarke last night?'

'I did.'

'What for?'

'You seemed otherwise engaged Inspector.'

'Aye, it got a bit out of control alright.'

'I could see, we could all see.'

'We went to the Strand Bar.'

'Why did you do that?' asked McCann, trying to keep the hurt out of his voice, that she'd gone off with the younger man, annoyed with himself for having given her the opportunity.

'It's not what you think,' she said, like she was reading his mind. 'I thought Clarke might be useful so I took the opportunity to find out a bit more about him.'

'Like you did with me?'

'And what's wrong with that?'

'Nothing. Nothing at all,' said McCann, holding his hands up, palms outwards.

'He told me something interesting about the Branch.' McCann could imagine Clarke bragging, getting close to her, knocking back the drinks, filling her glass. But then he could also imagine her drinking him under the table.

'He got very chatty,' she said. 'Said there was concern at the top of the Branch about operations that had got out of control, due to confusion and weakness in the lines of command. He said they had a phrase for it. Called it *monstering*, the way parents give birth to monsters they can't control. He said that was why they'd attached him to Division, to find out more.'

'*Monstering?*'

'Aye, that's what he called it.'

Now it was McCann's turn to be silent.

'So did you go home with him?' he asked.

'I told him to lay off. He was in no fit state anyway by then so I fixed him up with a cab, made sure he was in it.'

McCann smiled.

'Sounds far-fetched Emily.'

'What does? The cab or the monstering or the fact they trusted Clarke to do something about it?'

'All of that,' said McCann.

They picked Sammy McGuigan off the street outside his home, brought him over to one of the stations where Thompson was owed a favour, where they could talk undisturbed.

'We've evidence you gave Elizabeth McCabe a lift home,' said McCann.

The unfamiliar surroundings, the presence of a woman, McCann's weaponry, all of this had discomfited Sammy, making him cautious.

'I might have done.'

'Might have done or did give her a lift? Why're you being evasive Sammy?'

'Not evasive, just can't rightly remember.'

'And we've evidence you did. And that an attempt was made to assault her,' said McCann.

'What evidence? Sure the wee girl is dead, God rest her soul, isn't she? So there'd be nothing to prove that.' Sammy McGuigan looked up at McCann. The light from the desk lamp shone in his black eyes, making them glazed and hard to read.

'And Deevery,' asked McCann. 'Did Deevery ever ask you about Lizzie McCabe?'

Sammy McGuigan for a moment looked down, towards the floor, as if seeking some way out.

'Aye,' he said, reluctantly. 'He asked me just the same thing.'

'And…'

'And I told him just what I told you.'

'And what did he say?'

'He said just the same as you. That he'd the evidence against me. I mean fellows if you've the evidence, don't waste my time, go ahead and charge me.'

'Did he ask you for any forensics, any samples?'

'What kind of samples?'

'Hair, blood, semen, fabrics?'

'Ah Jesus Inspector why would he do that?'

'Because if you were in the frame for assaulting Lizzie once, you might be a suspect for her murder too.'

'Murder? Why? This is ridiculous McCann. Plain ridiculous.'

'Maybe you wanted to shut her up Sammy.'

'Why'd I do that if I'd done nothing with her?'

'Did Deevery ask you to help him, maybe say he'd overlook things if you'd co-operate in other ways? Were you helping him Sammy?'

'We will always help the RUC in any way we can. It wouldn't mean I done any of it. Now are we done here?' McGuigan stood up then, preparing to leave the room.

'Hold on,' said McCann.

'You've nothing on me pal,' said Sammy McGuigan. 'You've the wrong man.'

'Just one last thing,' said McCann, 'Before you go Sammy. If you're the wrong man you won't mind if we take a few samples. Take you down to forensics right now.'

McGuigan halted, his standing bulk now filling the interview room.

'Exclude you from our enquiries. It'll be better for you if we do.'

'I'll be happy to assist gentleman, if you'll just let me out of this circus,' said McGuigan, reaching for his flies. 'You can have just as much of this as you want, anywhere you like.'

Back at Division, O'Reilly's solicitor was waiting for McCann, seated in the reception in his suit, a smart leather briefcase on his lap. McCann explained the situation to him.

'We'll still need to take samples from Mr O'Reilly.'

'What kind of samples?'

'Blood, semen, bodily fluids. Fibres from clothing.'

'On what grounds? You've no grounds for that,' said the solicitor.

'It's routine. To exclude him from enquiries. It'll be to his benefit,' said McCann.

'I find that hard to believe after the treatment he's already received. The harassment and aggravation.'

'We could have an order made,' said McCann. 'Make it obligatory.'

'Oh aye, that'd be the icing on the cake. Not sure how the courts would see that in the context of the treatment Mr O'Reilly has already received.'

'Well I'd prefer it were voluntary,' said McCann.

'There's no chance of that.'

'Well it'll have to be obligatory then.'

The Solicitor looked flustered, angry, fiddled with the catch on his briefcase.

'This is not what was agreed.' McCann was baffled, conscious of some part of the story behind the story he knew, beneath its surface, some logic that was deeper and darker than anything he had yet imagined.

'Agreed! What was agreed?'

'Mr O'Reilly was a source,' said the solicitor. 'And as such benefits from immunity.'

'A source for whom?'

'I can't tell you that.'

Afterwards, McCann told Clarke of the allegations O'Reilly's solicitor had made. Clarke seemed thoughtful, scratched the side of his nose.

'That's an interesting one now Inspector,' he said. 'Normally I'd say that was counter intelligence, that O'Reilly's made that up.'

'Would Deevery be his handler then? We've the photo of the two of them together. Maybe blackmailing him in return for intelligence.'

'I'd say they're trying to fit us up. It's what we do to them whenever we can. To make them feel one of their own fellows has been turned so they trust no one. In the best cases they take out their own men, believing them to be touts, kneecap them, take them out of the field for us, no court cases, nothing. It's brilliant when it works but the chances are these fellows are doing the same to us; casting doubt on Deevery, hoping we'll believe them.' Clarke's face was in shadow, so McCann couldn't quite read his expression.

'You said "normally". Normally you'd say it was counter intelligence.'

'Did I say that?'

'You did.'

But Clarke had sown a seed of doubt in McCann's mind. As he went home that evening the seed germinated: how could Deevery even have heard what O'Reilly had done with Mairead O'Shea at the Black Lodge, in order to blackmail him? Was it even likely he was involved in such dirty tricks? Deevery wasn't in the branch, at least not as far as McCann knew, but he was bigoted and viciously cunning enough to care nothing for Catholic lives, might even take a perverse pleasure in such a plan. Had someone then got to Mairead O'Shea to have her silenced, to protect Sean O'Reilly's reputation? Had Deevery also protected Sammy McGuigan too over his assault on Lizzie McCabe, so he could get Sammy to do the things he wanted done? And finally, what would happen to McCann himself if he were to confront Deevery with his suspicions?

McCann felt dog-tired and his shirt felt sticky, smelt sickly sweet and musty when he took off his jacket. He went straight through into the bathroom and ran a bath, the water loud in the house, the steam coming through into the corridor as he let down his braces, unbuttoned the shirt, pulling the trousers off with the shoes and socks all in one go once the laces were undone, leaving everything in a pile on the floor. He sank into the deep water up to his neck, a fistful of Radox making the bubbles overflow along the sides of the bath.

'Oh dear God,' he said out loud. 'Dear God in heaven,' and he rubbed at his eyes with the ball of his hands, submerged like a pink whale, letting the hot scented water cleanse him and take away the aches at least for a minute or two.

After his bath, he pulled on an old pair of tracksuit bottoms, a rugby shirt and slippers and went through to the kitchen where he'd managed to get in a few things for supper: a tin of beans and sausages all in one, a fresh packet of white sliced bread and some fresh milk and bacon, a few eggs for the morning. There was even a pop tart for desert with a tin of custard. But first there'd to be tea so he made himself a full pot, put the tart in the toaster to keep himself going and then when that was done, he riffled out the magazine he'd bought from the bottom of his bag, settled himself in the armchair with his feet up and began to read: 'When there is a lack of food, young pike are often eaten by larger pike and often by their siblings, if conditions are not conducive to food production.' He read with interest, the magazine held open in front of him.

'Pike are very territorial and vicious disputes may erupt between pike, for example in drought conditions when territory is limited. They prefer to lie idle for long periods, but then lash out to capture their prey in sudden aggressive bursts of energy. Larger pike will control larger areas and will feed greedily, collecting as much prey as they can.'

McCann sighed, placed the magazine there on the arm of the chair by his half-drunk tea with the light on and the page open at the picture of the pike, its low snout, its long articulated jaws.

Chapter Eighteen

McCann turned back and forth in his bed, tossing the covers off against the heat of the night, but all the same his body seemed cloaked in a thin, adhesive sweat. At one point he'd got up and run a cold flannel over his face in front of the mirror in the bathroom. 'Like Banquo's ghost,' he thought, unconsciously mimicking the Poet, with whom he'd spent too much time with too little effect. He went back to bed and slept for an hour or two and awoke early, pulled back the curtains on a fine summer day with high white clouds in a blue sky, realised then what he had to do, called Thompson on the phone to explain the situation and arranged to meet.

He picked Thompson up where she'd been standing back in a doorway in civilian clothes, a shopping bag held in front of her like a talisman of some kind of normality. She climbed into the front seat swiftly without a greeting, stuffed the bag at her feet as he accelerated away down into the city.

'I've been thinking about the loose ends in what I've told you,' said McCann.

'Like how did Deevery first find out what O'Reilly was up to with Mairead O'Shea? And did he know it before she was killed, before we ever got wind of it?'

McCann, smiled like she was a bright pupil that had been ahead of him all along.

'So we'll speak to Peter McCabe then?'

'Aye that's the one,' said McCann. 'There's only him left.' He'd left Peter McCabe out of it until now, given the grief the family would still be suffering.

As they drove they began to see piles of broken furniture, packing cases, wooden pallets on the pavements, primed with tyres, as if awaiting the corporation refuse teams. Passing the closed, narrow streets of east Belfast the piles became too large for that, containing great beams of timber from demolished homes, whole tree trunks with their branches intact, leaves dry and crackling. The city was already preparing the great bonfires that would precede the impending 12th July holiday[21] and was alive with the tension and expectation that came with that. And then the terraces began to fall away as they joined the dual carriageway out to the suburbs, McCann driving in silence, like a husband and wife on their way to work, except that was just a dream.

The garden looked different from the last time he had visited the McCabes, with flowers blooming everywhere, their scent heavy in the air. The lawn had been recently mowed and the sprinkler set overnight to refresh the grass, its soft patter just audible above the rustling of the breeze in the treetops. He pressed the bell. It seemed a long time ago that he had first called here to give the news of the murder of Lizzie McCabe and since then there'd been two more murders. For a while there was no answer, the sprinkler continuing its work, while

---

21 On 12th July each year the Orange Order celebrate the victory of the Protestant King William of Orange at the Battle of the Boyne in 1690.

Thompson peered through the windows. McCann hammered at the knocker until he saw a figure in the hallway through the stained glass.

'Inspector McCann,' said Peter McCabe, the door open just a crack with the security chain still in place. McCann apologised for the intrusion.

'You'll know sergeant Thompson,' he said, pushing her forwards in the hope that a woman's face might defuse any hostility. McCabe stood back then to let them into the hallway, ushered them through to the living room.

'Before you start McCann, just let me say I'm still in a mind to make a formal complaint about your conduct. That visit to Wilbur, putting him under suspicion.'

'Well you'd be within your rights to do that, sir,' said McCann.

'And have you any ideas yet? About Lizzie, Inspector?' McCann stood awkwardly, not yet taking a seat on the sofa behind him, Thompson at his side.

'We do have a suspect for the murder of Lizzie.'

'Who? What kind of a fellow would do that? Who is he?' McCabe was suddenly motivated. 'Give me his name. I want to know his name.'

'I can't tell you that until formal charges are brought.' McCabe's shoulders slumped with disappointment.

'And Wilbur? Don't suppose there's any progress on that?'

'We think Wilbur may have been killed because he knew too much and that's all I can say right now. I realise your impatience, but these things do take time.' McCann's words felt like cardboard in his mouth. McCabe made a noise of frustration, like time was something he didn't have and if he had had it he wouldn't be spending it with McCann.

'I guess if Wilbur mixed with animals the way he did, sooner or later they'd turn on him,' he said.

'But there's another matter,' said McCann, easing himself down into the sofa, settling in, gesturing for Thompson to do so too.

'About the Black Lodge. We've a few questions for you on that.'

'Tell us about the annexe,' said Thompson.

'The annexe?' McCabe looked surprised at her sudden question, hesitated before replying.

'We did the annexe for the older groups, so they could have a bit more social space of an evening, I mean they were teenagers after all.'

'Is that where you had problems?' prompted McCann.

Peter McCabe's expression changed from surprise to caution and McCann knew they'd hit some kind of spot.

'Problems? Not sure what you mean, Inspector.'

'About drink and parties that went on a wee bit too long. A fellow called O'Reilly maybe, came in to speak to one of the groups, maybe got a wee bit too close to one of the students. One of your staff raised it with the director and we wondered if he would have raised it with you.'

'Yes, there was an issue,' said McCabe carefully.

'Did you take any action on it?'

'I did take action. Discussed it with one of your fellows that was up for the fundraising.'

'One of our fellows?'

'Inspector Deevery I think his name was. Big fellow with grey, curling hair at the back, red boozer's face on him.'

'And what did he say?'

'He was interested. Wanted the fellow's name, said he'd take it up with him.'

'And did he?'

'Well that's what I'm not sure about.'

'How do you mean not sure.'

'Because nothing happened. The same fellow was back up at the Lodge again a few weeks later.'

Deevery would have had some twisted plan, some logic, thought McCann, his mind rehearsing the hypotheses again. When O'Reilly fell for temptation with Mairead O'Shea at the Black Lodge, Deevery would have used it to blackmail him in return for intelligence on the IRA. Just the same as might have happened when Sammy McGuigan molested Lizzie McCabe while giving her a lift home from there, except that instead he'd be getting intelligence on the Protestant paramilitaries, control over one of their key men. Both O'Reilly and McGuigan would have known the epithet 'paedophile' and what it might mean for them if it ever got out in their communities. And Deevery had the evidence that he could release against them at any time. The two men, from different sides of the sectarian divide would both have been desperate to cover things up and to escape Deevery's grasp.

'Why did you not stop O'Reilly, take him off the course?'

Peter McCabe sighed heavily and there was a long silence as if he was wrestling with something.

'You see Inspector, I was advised not to. The Inspector said it was a matter of national security. That investigations were on-going. That I'd to take precautions but that was all.'

The poor man, thought McCann. In keeping quiet for

what he saw as good reasons he'd inadvertently condemned Mairead O'Shea to the same fate as his own daughter.

'Now McCann, this is just a fantastical tale,' said the Poet, his foot tapping up and down with nervous irritation.

'You're asking me to believe that Inspector Deevery was involved in some kind of conspiracy to blackmail para-militaries, that may have led to the deaths of two teenage girls? A dark and byzantine plot indeed, worthy of a Macbeth or a Prospero!' The Poet rubbed his hands with glee, pleased at his literary allusion and then became serious again. 'But quite ridiculous. Really McCann if I didn't know you better I'd have said you'd gone off your head.'

McCann had half expected this response from the Poet, had expected to be shown the door.

'So just who is it that's made these allegations?'

'We've Sean O'Reilly, he's one of the Republican council-lors who was up at the Lodge…'

'A Republican? And you believed him?' said the Poet, as if it were further proof of McCann's poor judgement.

'But there's other evidence too. We've Sammy McGuigan who admits what may have been a similar meeting with Deevery, though not that he'd anything to do with the girls.'

'Well then there can't have been a deal if there was no crime, no admission of guilt, can there?'

'You said yourself there have been unusual successes by Deevery against the terrorists. That implies he's opened up some lines of intelligence, doesn't it, sir?'

The Poet fluttered his fingers at McCann in a gesture of impatient irritation.

'If Inspector Deevery has had successes it's maybe because he's a fine officer, not because he's turning a blind eye to terrorist excess, doing deals with them, McCann.' The Poet's voice had adopted its customary high pitched whine of exasperation that McCann knew meant he had lost whatever thin line of credit he still had.

'There's more,' said McCann, saving his best point for the end. 'I've just been up with Peter McCabe. The founder of the Black Lodge. He's said Deevery ordered him to lay off on the grounds of national security.'

The Poet was momentarily taken aback by that. Peter McCabe was a player on the same pitch as the Poet, attended the same dinners with well-placed officials.

'Ah, I see,' said the Poet. And then he was thoughtful for a moment, before adopting a change of tone to that of a counsellor dealing with some tricky issue where the client was persisting with some fundamental misperception.

'Look, McCann, do you not think this could be some kind of vendetta against Deevery? I know you may feel bad that I've put him in charge, that's natural of course, but in the passage of time you'll recognise his qualities, learn from them. There's no point trying to damage his reputation, because it does you no credit. Why I remember when I first got knocked back for Superintendent and a useless little man – no, I shan't give you his name – got it instead of me, when everyone agreed I was the obvious choice. I was consumed with bitterness for a while, but things move on, I learned from it, knuckled down. In the end it did me good. Why don't you leave this kind of high flying speculation to the likes of Clarke and the special branch boys from Castlereagh? Stick to the knitting man. In my experience it's the slow, painstaking work that bears fruit. Are you still working on that van? Very mysterious, resprayed and no way of identifying it I gather? There's got to be something in that.'

'Yes sir. Barley Mow.'

'Good god what kind of a colour is that? Like the title of some Turner painting, or Constable maybe. I saw a fine exhibition of those when Margaret and I were over in London last weekend. Stayed in the Hilton. Lovely new hotel. Excellent breakfast. Allowed second helpings though Margaret had a gippy tummy afterwards.'

McCann recognised the Poet's tactic of introducing a personal anecdote that could extend across half a morning, leaving no opening into which his agenda could be pushed. He stood up, reversed reluctantly towards the door until the Poet realised that he had gone and fell silent.

'Mairead O'Shea,' said McCann.

'What about her?'

'We've talked to Sean O'Reilly's solicitor. He says you'd a deal with him.'

McCann took the fast route to it, cutting out any pretence at professional civility with Deevery the next time they were in the office together.

'A deal with O'Reilly? Oh I see McCann. Very funny. Very good indeed.'

'It's not a joke. You were involved in covering up the abuse of Mairead O'Shea. And Lizzie McCabe, too.'

Deevery made a short snort of contempt, as if he was clearing his nose.

'Now why would I do that, McCann?'

'Do you know Peter McCabe?'

'And if I did, what of it?

'Did he ever talk to you about Sean O'Reilly, or about potential abuse at the Black Lodge?'

'Never.'

'You never took a call from Wilbur McCabe's wife then?'

'What kind of a call? Look McCann I don't know where this is leading.'

'About concerns she had over the Black Lodge?'

Deevery looked puzzled then, scratched his head, shifted in his chair.

'What kind of concerns?'

'About assaults on underage girls,' said McCann bluntly, watching Deevery closely.

'And later maybe a call from Wilbur about the same thing, after you'd failed to act?'

'That'd be below my pay grade,' said Deevery smoothly. 'That'd get passed on to the protection team and if there'd been anything in it they'd have investigated.'

'So you never investigated it yourself? Never went down to the Black Lodge and met Peter McCabe? He also raised concerns with you, didn't he?'

'Now there was a matter with that Peace Foundation right enough now I come to think of it. I did meet Peter McCabe. Just tittle tattle, some rubbish allegations of one side about the other. We gave the foundation some money though. Some of the officers used to work up there, voluntarily like. What is this? Am I under suspicion? If I'm under investigation I want it done proper by the complaints and discipline branch, not by you McCann.'

'We're just checking some background and thought you'd be able to help,' said McCann.

'So you're saying you'd never heard any allegations about the Black Lodge from anyone?' asked Clarke, who until that time had kept mostly silent, so silent in fact that McCann had begun to wonder if he was distancing himself from it all, in case it all blew up in their faces. 'Are you saying Peter McCabe's lying then?'

'Well I wouldn't know about that,' said Deevery. 'I'd not be wanting to cast aspersions without the evidence for it.'

'And O'Reilly. You're saying you've never seen him before?'

'First time was when you lifted him for questioning. You were there. If I'd known him it would have been obvious,' said Deevery. And then he smiled, leant forwards.

'Sure McCann if I done a deal with him how come you were complaining to the Poet about me roughing him up? Would I have given the fellow a going over if I'd done a deal with him? I'd be trying to get him released, wouldn't I?'

'Aye, but that wee slap round the fellow's head had the same effect. Rendered everything in the interview inadmissible. Gave O'Reilly and his solicitor grounds to make prosecution difficult, even led to his release.'

'Come on McCann!' said Deevery. 'I know I'm clever, but the name's Deevery, not devious.'

'Then what's this?' said McCann, turning over the photograph that he'd been husbanding till then. Deevery and O'Reilly deep in conversation, the same grainy black and white photo that Clarke had shown him at the police benefit, with Deevery's head thrown back laughing at something the fellow had just whispered in his ear. Deevery glanced at the photo briefly, tossed it back at McCann across the table.

'Maybe I knew O'Reilly. With his record and connections, he was a person of interest we'd to keep in touch with. I know a lot of people. I'm good at my job. Had successes because of it McCann and maybe that's the problem here. Let me speak to the Poet on this. I'm not having this from you McCann.' Deevery got to his feet and McCann followed him down the corridor, up the stairs to the Poet's office. Deirdre rose from her desk to obstruct him but Deevery pushed past her into the romper room beyond.

The Poet came forwards from his desk, alarmed at the intrusion.

'I've a complaint to make,' said Deevery, McCann following a few paces behind, Deirdre still trying to block their passage. 'About unreasonable allegations McCann's been making against me, sir.'

The Poet reached into his pocket to pull out an enormous white handkerchief like a flag of surrender, then he sneezed into it and blew his nose like a foghorn at sea, inspected the contents and glared through watery, red-rimmed eyes at the two men.

'Listen the two of you. I've had about as much of this as I can take. While you two are fighting I've been carrying the can for all of this, up at Lisburn. You men wouldn't understand the pressure we're under. The Colonel raving on about how the RUC couldn't manage a piss up in a brewery, the new Chief Constable looking sick as a parrot.'

Deevery nodded.

'I understand that sir, but I can't accept McCann's attempts to impugn my honesty and the ethics of the force, sir. A naked and transparent attempt which frankly I'm surprised that Inspector McCann has had the temerity to give credence to.'

'But you met O'Reilly. You met my suspects before the murders. We've evidence for all of it,' said McCann, but the Poet raised his hand to silence him.

'Aye, maybe *met*,' said Deevery. 'Not met, as in did a deal with them.'

'You were aware of the allegations against the two suspects but took no action. Alice McCabe reported to Division that Lizzie had been assaulted by Sammy McGuigan.' McCann spoke swiftly, laying out as much of the evidence as he could before he was silenced.

'Could you keep quiet? Please, let Inspector Deevery explain,' said the Poet.

'There wasn't ever enough evidence to go on. It was second-hand. No one left who saw an actual offence committed,' said Deevery evenly.

'No smoking gun, no dog that didn't bark eh?' said the Poet.

'That's it. Well put, sir,' said Deevery.

'And then Wilbur.'

'Wilbur? Wilbur never came to see me. Don't try to pin that on me.'

'Gentlemen,' said the Poet soothingly. 'Gentlemen please. We're discussing the case and we don't want the waters muddied by aggression, at least not more than they are already. Seems like the two of you have both been working on it in parallel, overlapping. Shame there's not been better coordination between the two of you. Shame a disagreement seems to have arisen again.'

'And anyhow all of them are dead.' Deevery added, almost as an afterthought and before the Poet could finish, 'There's nothing can be pinned on anyone now.'

'Other than the fact we've two people that say you offered them immunity, offered to hush things up, in return for intelligence,' said McCann, pushing the boat out as far as it would go.

'Then it seems like there's no one in this Province I've not tried to blackmail,' said Deevery sarcastically. The Poet looked from one to the other, like he was watching match point in some Wimbledon final. When both men fell silent, he asked: 'Is there anything else?'

'Even if the allegations have some foundation, which they don't, it's all paramilitary counter-intelligence, a set-up to cast doubt on the security forces themselves. No, those fellows diddled the girls, likely had them done over to cover it up and now they should pay for it,' said Deevery.

'It's not fellows that done it, it's one man assaulted both girls,' said McCann. 'We've no forensics linking O'Reilly, none for Sammy McGuigan. None even for Wilbur McCabe. I've had the forensic reports back just now and there's nothing. We're still looking for the one man.' McCann reached into his pocket and pulled out the forensic report he'd received that morning, that had tried to match the new samples from O'Reilly and McGuigan with material found on the bodies of Mairead O'Shea and Elizabeth McCabe. The samples indicated a third man would have been involved in the killings; unidentified fabric under the fingernails and blood that did not match the suspects', where the victims had struggled to fight him off.

'So, what you're saying McCann is that we're back at square one, is that it?' asked the Poet. 'No suspects, no possible convictions for the murders?'

'We've a suspect sir,' said McCann. 'And he's sitting right in front of you.'

After the Poet threw them both out of his office, Deevery and McCann walked wordlessly, shoulder to shoulder past Deirdre's desk, their feet marching almost in unison on the bare boards. When they were out of earshot Deevery suddenly murmured to McCann: 'It gave us control McCann. Are you too thick to see that?' They stopped at the head of the stairs.

'There was a simple reason to do what was done at the Black Lodge. It made us stronger, more powerful. And the more powerful we became the less chance the paramilitaries would get control,' he said.

'So you're saying you done it?'

'Done what? Aye we put pressure on those abusing arse-holes to tell us what they knew about paramilitary operations. Bombs, punishment killings, robberies, all of it we could prevent. There's nothing wrong with that McCann. I was saving lives. How was I to know they'd get the girls killed once I put the screws on them? Jesus, McCann I regret that as much as you do, maybe even more.'

Chapter Nineteen

McCann signed for the sealed bag containing the evidence that had been recovered from the burned out van, took it back to the office and examined it again under the light. There wasn't much – the charred remains of a coca cola tin, a metal button from a man's shirt or overalls, the remains of a toothbrush and the bronze lapel pin. He turned the pin in its polythene bag so the light flashed on the detail; a crown, a King William, a red hand. Taking a magnifying glass from his desk, he peered at the pin. Underneath the crown was a flat piece of bronze, where normally one might have expected an inscription. McCann peered at it, turned the pin upside down, scraped away at the ash, revealing a hinge. He rootled in his desk drawer until he found a safety pin which he opened and prised up the hinged flap. Underneath was an inscription, like a sealed code:

'Necessarium est ad bonum.' He murmured the words, then scribbled them on a slip of paper which he handed to Thompson.

'Here, you were at college, weren't you?'

Thompson frowned, fearing a quip at her expense.

'Necessarium est ad bonum,' he repeated.

'It's been a while,' she said. Clarke grinned at her discomfiture.

'You any idea Clarke?' she said, passing the slip of paper over to him. He shook his head.

'It is good to do the necessary,' she translated. 'Or maybe better: it is noble to do the necessary thing.'

'I like that. Very nice,' said Clarke.

McCann folded the pin away carefully in its plastic pouch and slipped it into his jacket pocket.

The shop selling Orange regalia was on Sandy Row, in the heartlands of Protestant territory, with a modest double frontage, windows covered with iron grilles and bars on the door and a sign saying to ring for admission next to a bell push. McCann rang the bell and a face appeared, looked him up and down and pulled the bolts back so he could step inside. The shop seemed to open like a magic box, revealing an additional floor above reached by a wooden staircase, a corridor leading through to a rear atrium bedecked with banners, flags and other paraphernalia: flagpoles, drums, sashes, bowlers, stout boots and shoes, swords and sheaths, belts and buckles, as if from another century.

'I'm looking to replace this fellow,' said McCann, taking the pin carefully from his wallet, laying it on the glass display case. Underneath, a thousand types of pins and clips: jewelled tiepins showing the union flag, pinsticks proclaiming 'For God and Ulster.' The assistant bent over the pin, asked him where he'd come by it.

'It was my father's,' said McCann.

'Looks like it's seen some action,' said the assistant, turning it gingerly, then turning back to an array of wooden drawers running up the wall where the supplies were kept, his fingers counting up, opening one and taking out something wrapped in brown oiled paper.

'This might do it,' he said, spreading the pins out on the counter, placing a new one alongside the one that McCann had brought.

'Do you sell many of these?'

'A few.'

'When was the last time?'

'Couple of weeks ago. People lose them, or they're damaged like yours, sir. Had a fellow in a few weeks back wanted a replacement.'

'What kind of fellow? Did he have grey curling hair here, at the back?'

'That I couldn't tell you,' said the assistant, looking at McCann like he wasn't prepared to say another word.

Thompson and McCann left the July heat of Great Victoria Street behind and entered the cool air-conditioned atrium of Pyrie House. A fountain gurgled in the corner, water trickling soothingly over a granite plinth, the entrance to the building guarded by two security men who nodded them through to reception and the lift beyond. Once equipped with visitor badges it whisked them noiselessly to the sixth floor, where they stepped out into the offices of McElroy and Smith, forensic accountants and auditors.

'They said they could go over it in a day,' said Thompson. Compared to the cluttered chaos of Division, the open-plan office seemed a haven of peace and order. All the equipment and furniture seemed matching in its newness, even the people; slick, well dressed, attractive, professional. McCann felt a pang of envy, as he always did when he encountered the business world.

'Hi. Tom Courtenay. You'll be sergeant Thompson and Inspector McCann from the RUC?' The voice was a surprise, an English voice. McCann was more surprised to find its owner was much younger than himself, just a lad in fact, his age disguised by a well-cut suit and a silk tie over his crisp white shirt.

'Will you follow me?' He led them across the open plan towards a glass-fronted meeting room beyond, asked them did they want tea or coffee and flipped open a folder before him.

'Well this one's been pretty interesting actually,' he said, his face illuminated with boyish enthusiasm.

He laid the accounts of Alpha Motors across the smooth, polished tabletop, one by one.

'It looks like there's an income disparity which is covered by a pattern of discretionary payments which might indicate that it may be a shell company, a non-trading entity.'

'That's great, but what does it mean?' asked McCann.

'Its funds are not derived from trading. There's insufficient income from sales to cover its costs, or at least that's very poorly disguised. There's shadow transacting – large cash payments for work which is not evident in the order book or purchasing of the company. We've also found these,' he said, pulling four or five invoices from the file, tossing them across the table.

'DG Investments – £12000, £28000, £74000 in respect of van sales and repair work for which there is no sign of the vans ever having been brought in, or the work done.'

'DG investments?'

'Ah I thought you'd ask that,' said the accountant, with a satisfied little smile.

'I've looked into them and they are located at an address in Cullybackey. But we've checked and the address is a funeral parlour. We've the directors here.' He slipped over the company registration papers, the directors highlighted.

McCann ran his finger down the list. One name stood out.

'So where's Deevery now?' asked McCann. The office windows were open, but the room was still hot and airless, a single fan stirring the corners of the papers on Clarke's desk.

'He'll be walking today,' said Clarke. And with a shock McCann realised that of course it was the twelfth of July, the day when all loyal Protestants would be out on the streets and Deevery would be there. Even now he could hear them, like a low sulphurous thunder in the air, the tribal rattle and clatter of the Lambeg drums from the Shankill, the skirl and wail of the pipes.

'You'll not find him today,' said Thompson. 'There's a hundred thousand men walking and you'll never see him in that crowd.'

'You'd be surprised,' said McCann and pushed away out of the door, down the stairs and out onto the hot, crowded streets.

The July sun reflected back from the shopfronts, the paving slabs, the granite kerbstones. He struggled to see the marchers through the press of spectators, their great banners sailing along as if under their own secret propulsion overhead. He could see the bowler hats of the Orangemen bobbing along and pushed his way forwards to get a better view of the bands as they came up the Lisburn Road towards the field. Altnagelvin LOL, Killybrae Ancient, the banners and the marching men swept past, the drums hammering out laments and favourites accompanied by pipe bands, each a hundred strong, small boys in blue bandsmen's uniforms with their triangles, proud fathers strutting to the signature tune of the day:

'Sure it was worn and very beautiful and its colours they were fine,

And it's on the Twelfth Day of July that I'll wear the sash my father wore.'

McCann's eyes were keen, seeking out Collybrae number four. It would be a small band, it was a small village and Deevery would be in there marching with his lodge, like many loyal officers on that day.

'Excuse me mister you're in the way.' A small boy weaselled his way past McCann at knee height, his elbow digging him in the thigh.

'You watch yourself son,' said McCann.

'Away to fuck with you Mister.'

McCann smiled at that and his view cleared as the small boy shouldered his way through. Now he could see the roadway, the marching men straining to hold their banners high, their faces dripping red under their bowlers, smart with their swords. Then he caught sight of Collybrae number four, as he heard the thunder of their big drum, inexpertly rattling and battering, toted by a huge fellow stripped to the waist and tattooed, drenched in sweat and at the head of the band another fellow with his mace, twirling and chucking it high into the blue July sky.

McCann could not be sure, but on the far side of the marching ranks was a figure who seemed plausibly familiar, though it was hard to be sure at a distance if it was Deevery or not.

'Here, Oi!' he shouted, pushing forwards, barging a woman off her kerbside perch, out into the band, pushing through. But the fellow had seen him, turned and was now ducking away through the crowd. McCann could see the flash of his sword and sash, the commotion as he pushed through the spectators on the far side of the road and away.

'Oi!' he shouted again and lunged into the gap created by the fleeing man, pushing though bodies, arms, shoulders, then off down a side street, the man fifty feet away with his coat tails flapping behind him as he ran. McCann was not fast, but the man was unfit and his feet slapped on the paving stones as he rounded a corner and McCann ran after him, but when he turned the corner the man had gone. Desperately McCann looked up and down the street, then noticed a narrow alley leading down the back of the houses and on instinct, cut down it into an overgrown passageway reeking of dog's mess and summer vegetation, cluttered with bins and abandoned domestic appliances. The man stood there, panting. His sash was askew, his face red and sweating with exertion.

'Deevery,' said McCann. 'Deevery I knew you would be here.'

But Deevery grinned in his familiar way and fiddled with the strap that held the sword. McCann moved towards him and suddenly the blade flashed in the sunlight before him, two feet of honed steel, double edged and sharp.

'Always the smart boy who never knew when to stop,' said Deevery, and brought the blade down on him.

'I'm grateful to you Clarke, for following me. If you'd not done that I'd be in a far worse state,' said McCann. The hospital was rammed with Orangemen in various stages of inebriation or distress caused by the heat and the long walk. Blood dripped slowly from his bandage onto the floor. He found himself thinking that it could have been worse, but then, almost immediately, that it could not be better. They'd flushed Deevery out. He'd be in custody now and they could settle it once and for all. It was almost a relief to be able to sit and wait.

McCann dozed as the activity dwindled; a child who had fallen downstairs in the night came in with her mother, a noisy drunk with a gash needing stitches across his forehead, an old fellow with difficulty breathing, the sound of his rasping struggle for air filling the casualty area, each great inward suck followed by a longer silence. Finally, they stitched up McCann's arm, cleaned the abrasions on his chin and cheek, strapped him up and helped him dress and he walked out into the Belfast night, Clarke following with a few things in a plastic bag. It was a warm summer evening, beginning to cool with the first of the air off the mountain. He found a cab at Sandy Row and let the driver take them to Division.

'Been in the wars then?' asked the driver.

'Aye, bit of a ruck,' said McCann.

'Give as good as you got?'

'Not yet,' said McCann.

'That's the way,' chuckled the driver. 'Live to fight another day. '

'You said it,' said McCann, easing himself back in the seat, watching the shuttered shopfronts of Great Victoria Street sweeping past, the station, the Europa Hotel still lit up like a lighthouse of optimism in the night.

Chapter Twenty

Deevery faced McCann across a bare wooden table in the interview room. His fingers drummed with irritation. Clarke lounged beside McCann, seated slightly further back.

'When I saw you in the parade, what were you running from?'

'Running? Your head's cut McCann. I was desperate for a wazz, that's all, on account of the beers and there were people everywhere. I had to do it quick, otherwise I'd have lost touch with my people.'

'Why did you attack me then?'

'I was playing around McCann. You could never take a joke, could you? You just had to grab at the sword and then this eejit here has to do his *jujitsu* on me from behind.' Deevery gestured contemptuously at Clarke, daring them both to argue. The two men stared back at Deevery for a moment. McCann reached into his jacket pocket, extracted the lapel pin in its plastic wrapper and silently unwrapped it, shaking it out onto the table in front of Deevery.

Deevery peered at the pin, pushed it around the table cautiously with his finger, then shrugged and shoved it back towards McCann.

'We've a description of you, buying a replacement for this

that was found in the floor pan of the van that took Lizzie McCabe to her death.' McCann folded it away carefully in his inside pocket.

'If you're that sure, put me up in an identity parade McCann. You should be able to organise that. Though I doubt the Poet'll be pleased you're still at this malarkey, or if you'll get anyone that'll identify me.'

McCann took out the accounts, spread them on the table, showed Deevery his name highlighted.

'Very nice,' said Deevery. 'That'll be that Thompson won't it. Smart girl. Should go far.'

'Your name on the accounts of the firm that paid for the respray on the vans that were used in the killing of Lizzie McCabe,' said McCann.

'Is it indeed? You know how many Deeverys there are in Ulster, McCann?'

'William Deevery. Your address.'

'Aye anyone can use my name, McCann.'

'We've done the checks with Companies House. It's you.'

'Aye well, maybe I had a wee dabble in the transport business. Doesn't mean I'm involved.'

'You were behind it, Deevery.'

Deevery laughed then.

'If you weren't you won't mind us taking samples, just to eliminate you from enquiries.'

'Samples! McCann you're off your head. Look, wise up before it's too late for you. It's not me that's behind it, they all were. All the perverts that liked the girls. You'd be amazed. Did the Poet not tell you?' And here Deevery seemed to smirk.

'They were using the centre. Did you know that McCann? Why d'you think McGuigan was always out there, O'Reilly too? Do you think any of them boys give a damn for young people? Aye maybe to be seen to be working for peace while they bomb the fuck out of us all, like a little bit of image management, a bit of PR. To go out to Cushendun and talk to the girls, maybe to make the odd contribution, while picking up some underage girl. Seems normal to me once you've seen the darkness, McCann.'

McCann listened intently. The tape machine hissed gently on the table, the red light indicating the recording was continuing. The constable at the door coughed lightly, eased gently on his toes, his boots creaking.

'We all knew. You can't touch them McCann, no one can now,' he said.

'Why not?'

'The Poet knows they diddle the girls. He likes it when they do, because then he's got them.'

'Got them?'

'Speed up McCann for Christ's sake,' said Deevery.

'So you're saying it goes above you?'

'Boy, you took your time with that,' said Deevery.

'So why were the girls killed?'

'Likely they didn't want them knowing their game. Likely they knew they could pin that on O'Reilly and Sammy,' said Deevery, grinning again, a leering, red-eyed smile as he lay back in his chair and drew breath before continuing: 'You see McCann, without cruelty there's nothing, no civilisation, no permanence, nothing you can get your bearings on.'

'What do you mean?'

But Deevery's mind seemed to have wandered off.

'Ah,' he said and raised one hand limply as if exhausted and unable to make any further effort. 'Ah well there you are, if you've not the intelligence or imagination to see it my son.'

'I have.'

'So what do you think was going on then, eh? C'mon you tell me,' said Deevery and he gripped McCann's arm hard, his glazed blue eyes burning into his.

'You were doing something with the girls and it went wrong,' said McCann. 'It went terribly wrong and it needed to be cleaned up. Maybe you were warning them off, picked them up to give them a wee talking to, pretending to be investigating complaints to get them to come with you. Starting with Lizzie, then on to Mairead, using your uniform to get them into the vans maybe, but then something went wrong and you couldn't control it.'

Deevery's eyes glinted, almost laughing. 'It would be Lizzie wouldn't it, that would have worked it out first, why nothing had come of her complaints and you got wind of it didn't you? Went to warn her off and she argued. It all went wrong with her first, didn't it?'

'Not wrong, McCann, but right,' he said. 'Things went right with those girls' and he relaxed his grip on McCann's arm, let his hand fall away, a slow smile playing his lips at the memory.

'It was just one of the best things we've ever done.'

The tape machine hissed on, like an evil serpent.

'People have suffered enough. They need to see...' And here Deevery leaned forwards, banged his hand against his forehead as if trying to drive some idea or memory from it.

'To see the darkness McCann. At the moment they've seen

the sunset, dusk, the fading of the light; they've had children blown to bits, sons tortured, mothers murdered but they've not yet seen over into the real night that lies ahead if they don't change. They've to see their own children taken from them one after the other for no reason, over and over, on both sides, one Catholic, one Protestant, on and on and on. *Tick-tock, tick-tock*. Deevery moved his head from side to side, like the swinging of a pendulum. 'They've to see that and then maybe they'll start to think differently about the road they're taking. See how low we can sink if we let ourselves go, McCann? If all the priests and all of the vicars and pastors in all of their pulpits can't make them stop killing, if basic human decency can't make them stop, then this terror and darkness will do it, that's the irony McCann, the darkness is necessary for people to see! You can see the benefits already. There's talk of peace. There's talk that we've crossed a line. We're winning the battle for hearts and minds. I'm on your side McCann about that. We're all on the same side after all.'

Deevery leant low over the table, his red-rimmed eyes looked directly into McCann's and in them he saw mad certainty, but also torment and grief beyond release. It was as if every word was torn from him by an effort of will. McCann reached out his hand and touched Deevery's arm, but he looked down at the hand with a look of disgust on his face, as if some venomous insect had crept there upon the tunic of his uniform, so McCann withdrew it gently, tactfully, folded his hands over each other on the table top for a minute or so of silence, hoping that Deevery would reveal more. But Deevery's face was working, his lips forming noiseless words, at times he seemed about to speak but then another thought seemed to overtake him and extinguish the idea he had wished to express.

'I thought I could be better than all of them, McCann,' was all he said.

McCann nodded encouragingly.

'You could have been a good copper, once.'

Suddenly Deevery erupted, sending the steel chair flying, grabbed McCann by the collar across the table and hissed in his face: 'What do you know about good and bad McCann? You don't even know the meaning of the words. The reach and the scale of them. Why there are depths of bad you've never even conceived of. Places so dark that when you are in them you cannot tell which way is up and which way is down.'

He released his grip, shook his head, while McCann loosened his collar, motioned for the constable at the door to stand back, that he was OK.

'And the tip-off, the tape?'

'That was me,' said Deevery. 'Did you like that McCann. It took you a good while to catch on, but then it always did.'

'Why'd you do that, Deevery. Were you playing with us or what?'

'Someone'd got to stop the devil that'd got in me and I couldn't do it myself,' Deevery growled and looked about himself, as if finally seeing his surroundings clearly for the first time. A silence fell for a moment during which McCann heard the striking of the hour from the clock outside, the sounds of a laden tea trolley going down the corridor towards the custody sergeant's office.

'And Wilbur?' he said gently, prompting.

'Wilbur,' sighed Deevery. 'You know what they say about omelettes.'

Deevery smiled again, then suddenly snapped upright, business-like, clapped his hands.

'What do you think McCann? Now there's a puzzle with the fellow dead it's hard to tell now isn't it?'

'Did you tip off the IRA where to find him, Deevery?'

'That's another of your mad fantasies, McCann. Did you ever think maybe it's time you had some treatment for them?'

'You blackmailed O'Reilly so he was under your control. He was in Sinn Fein down in Newry, wasn't he? And the Newry Brigade took the boat Wilbur was butchered on.'

McCann watched Deevery closely. 'That would be really ingenious, wouldn't it, to set one group of dogs on another? To make it seem like Wilbur was the guilty party, that rough justice had been meted out. When in reality Wilbur had to go because he knew the truth about the Black Lodge and that the police wouldn't lift a finger.'

'It would be *genius*,' said Deevery, smiling a weird little smile.

He paused over the word, savouring it.

'You think you'll put a stop to it now, but you won't,' said Deevery, his foot tapping up and down with nervous pleasure, like he had some kind of further secret he was keeping from McCann. And then he began to laugh. The same great booming, cynical laugh that he had had at Achnakerrig all those years ago.

'Because they'll never let it get out that this happened, McCann. No one will believe you anyway. You'll see pal! Ha! Ha! Ha!'

McCann stood up, hitched his trousers and went to the door, banged on it for the custody sergeant to let him out, realised his shirt was heavy and black with sweat, that he wanted to be away. But as he heard the noise of the key turning in the lock behind him to close the cell door, he turned and shouted back:

'We're even now, Deevery. For Mary Channon.'

There was a moment's silence and then Deevery's voice bellowed through the steel door as if his face was pressed against it: 'You couldn't stop me then and you can't stop me now, McCann!'

And the old laughter, big and loud and echoing against the walls followed McCann down the corridor and outside into the fresh air.

McCann felt dizzy with exhaustion. The corridor ahead seemed to sway as he pushed his way along, his hand from time to time touching the distempered walls which dripped with condensation. He could see the custody sergeant at her desk through a blur of sweat that ran into his eyes. He had to have fresh air, he had to have sunlight. The custody sergeant unlocked the last steel door and Clarke pushed it wide open ahead of him. He could barely climb the stairs. As they reached ground level the natural light began to intrude, a golden glow of sunlight along the walls, as if he had escaped from some kind of hell, the hell of Deevery's mind.

'We'll go for a pint, shall we,' he said to Clarke, his own voice sounding far away. Ahead at the desk, he could see Thompson, chatting with the sergeant there, leaning forwards, her blonde hair falling over her face, sharing a joke.

'We're away for a pint,' said Clarke. 'You coming.'

'Something to celebrate boys?' she asked, then: 'What happened to your arm Inspector? Not another DIY accident?

Can you not get a man in?'

'Come on,' he said. 'We're away to the Strand bar.' It was code for a big one. She paused and he could see her wondering about her daughter, the pick up from school, all of that.

'C'mon and we'll tell you all about Deevery.'

'Aye alright Inspector,' she said and smiled at him.

Chapter Twenty-One

The light began to come up, seeping mysteriously through the misty hedgerows, making them distinct, dimming the beams from the headlights as McCann drove. In the fields beyond the road the shapes of ancient trees appeared, at first in dark monochrome, as shadows standing guard over the cows in the fields and later touched with a faint hue. The radio burbled just below the level where the songs could be identified. McCann liked it like this; the road empty, only bad men abroad at this time, his kind of people. He lit another cigarette, from time to time flicking the windscreen wipers on to take the morning dew from the windscreen, one window open ajar, a hint of grass and dung and rot and damp in the morning air, the smell of the country that was always so close here, even in the cities you could sometimes smell it, bringing its old primeval certainties. He sighed, opening the window wider, throwing the cigarette out, hearing the tyres sizzle on the wet tarmac. He yawned, the morning stretching strangely luxurious ahead.

At Drumbeg he turned off the road down a track and then pulled over in a narrow entrance set over with dripping rhododendrons, that drenched him as he stepped round to the car boot to get the tackle out. By now everything was silver light and the cold of the night was beginning to fade. It was raining very softly as McCann took out his equipment; the rod and line, the sinkers and flies, his chair, the hide.

On the river bank he found a spot where the trees would not drip, that would remain shady if the sun were to come out. In the distance he could hear the noise of the weir, an incessant murmur like spring water over stones. The river curved up towards where the weir lay, dark eddies at the turn indicating its hidden presence. McCann slowly unpacked, methodically placing everything as it should be, like some kind of sacrament. He pulled on his familiar waders. Then he took the box that contained the flies he'd had made, that he'd waited to use. He studied the lure carefully. It was almost too beautiful to use for this brutal purpose, too cunningly perfect in its blaze of orange and green feathers, that would jink and skip across the water, yet he was sure it would be the one if he could get it to the perfect spot.

The first light of morning was on the river as he cast out on the water, once, twice, three times until he found the precise place where the lure would worry and leap across the deep current, the hook at precisely that juncture where he instinctively knew the fish would be, beneath that dark glossy surface. McCann waded into the river knowing now there was time enough and that it did not matter if the fish were caught. The air seemed incredibly pure, as if somehow in itself comprising all of the river, the mountains that fed it and the fields around, as if scented with the dawn itself. He breathed in deeply, once, twice, then absorbed in the game he fished for an hour or so, pausing only to drink tea from a flask he'd filled and light himself another cigarette, blowing smoke rings, watching them in the still morning air drift out across the water. Yes, there was time, he thought. He was a patient man. Well, he would see if patience had its rewards. He stubbed out his cigarette in the leaf loam beneath his feet, so damp he could hear the cigarette hiss and resumed fishing, casting the line out with a smooth barely audible whirr from the reel, cutting it off so the lure skipped a yard or so further to the weir than before. He watched the water turning slowly in dark pools, its surface glazing in the occasional burst of sunlight, showing the reflection of the trees overhead, cursing the light because the fish would lie deeper along the bottom in such conditions, merging with the brown mud of the river bed, moving softly against the current with their mouths working, the glare of the sun on the surface distracting them from the lure he had set for them.

McCann spent a long while deep in thought, with his head shrugged far down into his jacket, almost as if asleep, from time to time flicking the line across into the dark swirling pool, making the lure dance on the water, until just before lunchtime there was a flash of silver and the lure was suddenly taken and disappeared as if swallowed whole by the river and started moving fast upstream as if carried by some powerful, purposeful force, the reel running out with a steady barely audible whirr. McCann jumped up, waded deeper into the water. His hat fell off. Something very heavy was pulling at his rod now, bending the end right down into the water. The fish was steadily swimming up towards the bend. He pulled back hard, hoping to turn it and reeled in as much as he could. Then the pulling started again, powerful frantic pulls, the line zig zagging and with every zig zag McCann brought the fish closer in. He could see the fish in the water now, resting impudently close to the surface, its dorsal fin still showing, the silver glitter of its back catching the sun, refracting light as if studded with diamonds. For a long while he watched it lying there. Then he took his knife from the box and cut the line clear. For a second or two the fish lay there, as if unable to believe its luck and then with one elegant swirl of its tail and a flash of gilded belly it dived down into the brown peaty water and away off into the deep.